INTENDED STRANGERS

BOOKS BY D. LIEBER

Minte and Magic

The Exiled Otherkin

The Assassin's Legacy

Intended Fates

Intended Bondmates

Intended Strangers

Intended Enemies

Council of Covens

Dancing with Shades

In Search of a Witch's Soul

Also by D. Lieber

Conjuring Zephyr

Once in a Black Moon

A Very Witchy Yuletide

The Treason of Robyn Hood

The Curse of Moonseed Manor

The Goblin King's Mischief

The Winter Sorcerer and the Summer Witch

Bitten by the North Wind

The Glass Moth

INTENDED STRANGERS

BOOK TWO OF INTENDED FATES

D. LIEBER

Ink & Magick, LLC
Kenosha, Wisconsin
contact@inkandmagick.com

Hardcover ISBN: 978-1-951239-22-0
Paperback ISBN: 978-1-951239-23-7
Ebook ISBN: 978-1-951239-24-4

✴ **HUMAN AUTHORED**

Reg #: 5002885, https://authorsguild.org/human

Cover by Maria Spada
Edited by Samantha Talarico and Vincent Czyz
Proofread by Julie Chyna Editing

SPECIAL THANKS

Thank you to my beta readers: John, Joyce, Aunt Debbie, and Laura. Thanks to Zech for help with research.

A special thank you to my sensitivity readers, Altaf and Ms. Sinha, as well as Andy and Emily for recommending them to me.

PROLOGUE

I did not love her at first sight. To me, she was the betrayer.

Runa had promised to bind with Konner, to protect him until his magic awakened and he could protect himself. But she'd abandoned him, left him vulnerable. And though it was my duty to protect his younger brother, Wilhelm, how could I not try to keep them both safe?

But I'd gotten it all wrong. Runa hadn't wanted to leave Konner undefended. She'd been young. She'd just seen her parents and her best friend, Isla, slaughtered by vampires. When pressured to bind with Isla's intended bondmate in that state of grief, she'd thought she was doing the right thing.

It was when I saw that she hadn't just taken the easy way out by binding with that upper-class fae instead of Konner. It was when I saw the wolf she truly was, saw her dedication, her drive to keep Konner safe. It was when she'd eyed me with that appreciation of a potential mate that I'd opened my heart to her.

It wasn't her fault. I told her as much. You can't control whom you love. She'd been so unfortunate as to love the one person she wasn't allowed to have: Konner. Even so, I wanted to help her. I loved her. So I asked her to be my promised. I knew that one day, when Konner and Wilhelm had awakened and we were full members of werewolf society, we could be happy together.

I ask myself every day whether it would have worked out if things hadn't gone so wrong. But the moment Konner was snatched by vampires, she was lost to me.

Don't get me wrong—I'm glad she saved Konner. We were practically brothers after all. But that didn't stop my heart from shattering, didn't stop my wolf from mourning his lost promised.

I've wondered many times since then what exactly this treaty has cost us, this treaty forged between the fae and werewolves for the mutual benefit of both peoples. Sure, werewolves haven't had to hide from humans ever since our territory was magicked into Faerie. And, granted, no fae children should fall prey to vampires because they don't have magic enough to protect themselves. But binding a pup to a faeling also has tremendous costs. Since coming to the human realm, or rather the realm of origin, I've seen that only too well. But before I can critique it too much, I think: Without the treaty, would Runa and I have ever met? Would I have ever known what it was to love someone?

Then again, the treaty is why so few werewolves

know love in the first place. The treaty is why we don't have the time or freedom to fall in love at our own pace.

1

Silvery moonlight streamed in through the windowless frames of the derelict factory. I caught a glimpse of the waning crescent in a cracked antique mirror beside me, but its light wasn't strong enough to bounce to the one facing it.

The eyes of my reflection glowed with eyeshine as the moonlight hit them just right. My black fur was raised along my spine, but I managed to silence the growl that tried to climb up my throat.

My nose twitched at the stench that hung in the air—damp and rich, like dark earth with the sickly sweet undertone of fresh decay. The disgusting scent of vampire likely wouldn't leave my nose for days to come.

The many mirrors, arranged like a twisted funhouse, confused my sight while I scanned the space. The effect made me dizzy as I searched for any motion that wasn't us.

My packmates were on either side of me, a few steps ahead. Grant's tail was stiff as he stalked slowly forward; Aryn stepped so quietly that her nails didn't make a sound on the concrete floor.

Our soft, mingled breaths were the only sound my strained ears picked up. If it wasn't for the strength of that awful smell, I might have thought Grant had gotten the location wrong.

Perhaps they're out hunting for the night. But I threw that thought away a moment after it came to my mind. Grant wouldn't have called me here if he suspected the hunt would be fruitless.

A gentle whiff of air brushed the tips of my ears. I looked up just in time to see my enemy descend from above. Its pale, bloodless skin appeared out of the darkness as it jumped down from the rusted rafters.

I sprang out of the way just in time, and Grant and Aryn whirled around to face the threat that had finally showed itself. It almost seemed to smile, its sharp teeth clicking as it gnashed them.

I let loose the growl I'd been holding in, my lips vibrating with the force of it. My packmates echoed my sentiment. But just as I was bunching my muscles to spring, two more vampires came up behind me. I twisted around, leaving the one in front of me to Grant and Aryn, but I wasn't quick enough. Something flashed in one of the new arrival's hands, and a searing pain erupted from my side as it slashed at me.

I didn't let it get away so easily. I grabbed its forearm, still outstretched from its attack, and sank my teeth in. Dead blood leaked into my mouth, and the thing hissed its pain. I yanked it down to the floor, my jaws closing on its jugular in less than a minute.

Once its strangled cries had ceased, I turned my attention back to my packmates. They had fared just as well, their quarries deader than they had been before we'd gotten there.

Grant shifted to human form and stood naked before us. "That should be all of them."

Aryn shifted as well. "It's a good thing they were so newly turned, or it might have been a real challenge."

Now that the fight was over, the fiery pain of my injury pulsed through me with every heartbeat. I shifted with difficulty; never had the action been painful before. "Speak for yourself," I wheezed.

Thanks to the many mirrors, I got a panoramic view of the damage. A nasty gash ran from just below my left pec over my ribs. The cut wasn't deep, but it was bleeding and the edges were turning blue. "That can't be good." My voice sounded far away as if it belonged to someone else.

My reflection looked the worse for wear. His black hair stuck up at odd angles, and his ice-blue eyes seemed unfocused. His broad shoulders were slick with sweat, and his solid legs trembled beneath him. His strong jaw and straight nose did nothing to hide what he was feeling as his face twisted in pain.

My head spun and the ground went out from under me before becoming a nice, cool compress against my backside.

I didn't know quite what was going on, but I got a sense of flurried activity. A few minutes later, I felt a sharp prick in my arm, and reality rushed back into focus.

"What the hell was that?" I groaned, cold sweat and the concrete floor making me shiver.

"The mirrors." Grant recapped the needle of a syringe. "I do *not* miss the days of silver-backed mirrors. That must've been what it cut you with."

"But don't worry." Aryn smiled as she sat cross-legged beside me. "We always pack an antidote in the van just in case. You'll be fine in a few minutes. The wound itself might take a day longer to heal, but you won't even have a scar."

They were right. In a few minutes, I felt normal again, despite the gash, which Aryn had cleaned and covered while I'd been down.

"Well, we better get this done before sunrise." Grant rose to a stand. "It'll be that much harder to take care of the bodies once the humans are up and about."

I stood, glad my legs weren't wobbly anymore.

Aryn frowned. "I think we can handle them ourselves. Don't you, Grant? Rowan doesn't need to stay any longer."

I opened my mouth to protest, but Grant cut me off.

"She's right. You have work on Monday, right? We appreciate your coming out to help us. A one-to-one ratio is so much easier."

"And safer," Aryn added.

"And safer," Grant agreed. "But take today and tomorrow to heal. We can clean up here."

I didn't like the idea of leaving my packmates to take care of the rest, but they were right. They were the experienced hunters in this realm. I was just an auxiliary when they needed an extra set of teeth, and that was hardly ever since they often teamed up with wolves from other packs. I wasn't nearly on the same level as they were, not yet anyway. But that's to be expected when they got to grow up in a pack their whole lives and I didn't.

Despite this little mishap, I was good at hunting though protecting had been the focus of most of my training, so I was much better at that. Even so, I had a lot to learn. And if my wound could heal before I went back to work on Monday, all the better—one less thing to have to lie to my boss about.

"All right." I wouldn't argue.

We headed back to the van we'd parked earlier in the night and dressed in the clothes we'd left in it. Grant gave me directions to where I could pick up a taxi to the airport. I said goodbye, wished them good luck, and headed back home to the ski resort.

2

The window in my room squeaked in its tracks as I slid it open. The fresh mountain air rushed in, cooling the small, stuffy space. The sun had been up for just over an hour, but it hadn't yet climbed above the mountains. It dyed the sky pink and yellow, but the sight did nothing to cheer me. In fact, I found it lacked sensitivity, clashing so heavily with my disposition. The view from my bedroom window was one of the best in the house. All I could see were trees and mountains. I got the morning light too. I didn't have to look at the guest cabins or the lift or any of the work sheds.

I closed my eyes and breathed deep the morning air, satisfied my wound had fully healed and breathing no longer stung. It was refreshing at this time of day, but I knew it would get hot later. It was still early June, and summer was well on its way.

I glanced over at my desk, where an unopened letter waited beside my laptop. My heart twinged as

I stared at my name written in Runa's neat handwriting.

I felt much older than my twenty-one years. I'd already lived a lifetime of sorrow. It had been nearly a year since I'd seen her last, nearly a year since Wilhelm had awakened. I'd even skipped his mating ceremony in an attempt to avoid her and Konner.

But now I was regretting that decision.

I'd thought that the memories of her—the memories of our time together, the memories of when we were promised—would haunt me forever. I'd thought that whenever I closed my eyes, I would see her gray eyes smiling up at me, that I would feel her soft, white hair slip through my fingers. The sharpness of those memories had been a blade in my heart, and I'd thought I would never know a deeper agony.

But now—when the memories were starting to fade, when I couldn't quite picture her smile in focus —now I knew real pain.

I was losing her all over again.

Sighing heavily, I went to my closet and put on a thin shirt and a pair of shorts. Then I left my quiet solitude behind for the day. As much as I appreciated a good distraction, like the hunt of a few days before, I still preferred being alone. I didn't have to pretend to be okay when I was alone.

At a quarter after six in the morning, the main house was just about to erupt into a flurry of activity. I sneaked through the common room to the kitchen.

My alpha, Lia, stood at the stove with her back to me, her sandy hair splayed across her slender shoulders.

"Good morning, Rowan," she said.

I huffed.

Lia chuckled and looked over her shoulder at me, her jade eyes glinting. "You're going to have to do better than that if you think you're going to surprise me."

I frowned.

"But hey, you got a lot closer this time. You're doing well."

"I suppose there's a reason you're the alpha."

"There is that."

On the counter beside her, a four-slot toaster popped.

"Could you butter those slices and put more in?"

"Sure."

By the time there was a stack of buttered toast piled onto a plate, the alarm on Lia's phone tinkled.

"Rowan, would you please go and drag Lune and Braylyn out of bed?" Lia turned off the alarm.

I abandoned my tower of toast and climbed the stairs to the second floor. When I reached their bedroom, I entered without bothering to knock.

The room was dark and smelled like it hadn't been aired out in weeks. I don't know how their sensitive wolf noses could stand the smell, but I did my best to breathe through my mouth.

I crossed the room to the window and thrust open the blackout curtains. Before I could turn around, Lune and Braylyn ambushed me from either side.

By the end of the wrestling match, I had them both in headlocks.

"All right. I give. I give!" Braylyn squealed as he tapped my arm.

I released the younger of the two brothers, and he rubbed his ear.

Lune fought for another minute before he called truce.

I smirked at the teenagers. "Maybe next time, guys."

Braylyn grinned, his freckled face pink from effort beneath his mess of reddish-brown hair. Lune squinted his determination, his freckles just a dusting over his nose and cheeks compared to his brother's. I reached out to rub Lune's recently buzzed, blond hair, but he swatted my hand away.

"Boys! Breakfast!" Lia called from downstairs.

"Now get dressed and come down to eat," I told them.

By the time I got back downstairs, two more pack members, Noire and Ashwin, had joined us. The siblings wished me good morning, Ashwin smiling warmly and Noire dipping her head. The Northern Pack was a patchwork group of wolves who had somehow found themselves under Lia's leadership. It wasn't a big pack, but it didn't need to be. There weren't many, if any, vampires around these parts, so the wolves who passed through and decided to stay did so because they liked Lia's loose leadership style. In the off-season, the pack was even smaller. But when winter came, those who spent their time traveling around—hunting like Grant and Aryn or looking for mates—returned to help run the ski resort.

"The lift is acting up again," Ashwin told his sister. "And I have two guided hikes today. Do you think you can fix it before then, or should I plan a different route?"

"I'll get to it right after breakfast," Noire promised. "It should be done in time."

"Cabin five is checking out this morning, but we have a few days before the next guest comes. You boys will be helping me clean the room after school today," Lia told her sons.

The boys sighed but didn't argue.

"I have the afternoon shift today," I said. "But could I catch a ride to the university when you drop Lune and Braylyn off at school?"

Lia nodded.

When we were all finally seated at the table, we looked over at Lia. She picked up her fork and took a bite of egg, then signaled that we could begin eating.

3

Lune and Braylyn said their goodbyes and shut the car doors before heading toward the brick school building. Lia paused a moment and met my gaze in the passenger's seat. Then she pulled out.

"Do you want to talk about it?" she asked.

Wind from an open window fluttered my hair into my eyes as I looked down at my hands in my lap.

"After your mate…after he died… Is it normal for memories to fade?" I glanced over at Lia, her gaze fixed on the road ahead of us. Her expression gave nothing away. Her gracefully arched eyebrows and wide forehead were relaxed, her small mouth unmoving.

"Yes," she answered softly. "It's normal."

I followed her eyes to the sun-speckled street. The sun was bright in the clear, blue sky, and I squinted against the too-vibrant colors it seemed to paint everything. The shadows from the trees were textured as if they'd been dabbed onto the landscape with a sponge.

Stopping at an intersection near the university, Lia let another car go ahead of her. She brushed a sandy lock of hair from her face and tucked it behind her ear. "So far, everything you've gone through is just like you've lost a mate. You must have loved her very much to react this way to a broken promised bond."

I flinched. *I still do.*

She glanced over at me before turning onto the main street that cut through the campus. Her voice was steady and clear, with a wistfulness that reflected an old pain, accepted but never fully healed. "When Charlie died, I was crushed. But, like you with Wilhelm, I still had a job to do. I had my pups to take care of and a whole pack to lead. There are times, even now, I can see his face in my mind so clearly. I can hear his laugh, and I think I'm going to round a corner and he'll be there smiling at me. And then there are times when I can't picture him at all, and that's a different kind of sorrow."

She pulled into a parking spot near the Student Union and shut off the engine. "For me, my consolation is my boys. What about you, Rowan? How are you dealing with this pain now?"

I let my breath ease out of me and looked out the window at the quiet campus. "I'm...not. I'm just sort of letting my instincts take over. I do the things I need to do: I work, I train, I hunt, I run. But...it's almost like I'm afraid to do anything else. If I fill my life up with other things, will there be room left for her? Thinking about her hurts, but *not* thinking about her hurts more. What am I supposed to do?"

"I guess that depends on when and how ready you are to move on. Why not start simple? Maybe do something that isn't strictly needed."

I frowned, her words seeping into me. Then I felt Lia's hand touch my shoulder, and I turned to meet her gaze.

"You'll heal in your own time, in your own way."

I bowed my head in acknowledgment.

She gave my shoulder a squeeze. "I'll send someone to pick you up after your shift, okay?"

"Thanks, Lia."

I got out of the car and lifted my hand in farewell as Lia drove away. Then I started walking toward the quad. The university wasn't nearly as busy as it normally was since most of the students were away for the summer. But there were enough people during summer semester that I could still practice.

Settling on the lush, green grass of the deserted quad, I leaned my back against a thick-trunked maple. Its sprawling branches and huge leaves would provide shade once the sun started beating down.

Taking out my cellphone, I stared at the blank screen for cover. Then I took a steadying breath and started to concentrate.

The wind was lazy in the trees, brushing the leaves together in a soft rustle that sounded like distant ocean waves. I sniffed the air. *There. A human male. No, two human males.*

I stared at the building across the quad and smiled to myself when two men rounded the corner and came into view.

I pricked my ears, listening hard to see whether I could pick up their conversation from so far away.

"So what did she say?" the shorter of the two asked.

"She never answered my texts," his companion said.

"You've been after her for months, and she isn't giving you the time of day. Maybe you should move on."

"That sounds like something a quitter would say."

Even from this distance, I could see the shorter male frown as he opened the door to the library. "Man, she obviously isn't interested in you."

"That's not a thing."

"Serio—"

The door shut behind them, cutting off the rest of their conversation.

I may not have been up to the level of surprising Lia, but I had gotten much better since I'd joined the Northern Pack. Every day I tested my skills as a wolf—more by passive observation than by an active hunt like the one I'd joined Grant and Aryn for. I smelled a bit keener, saw a bit farther, heard a bit clearer. I could smell things now that I could never smell in Faerie, such as certain emotions. And not only was the university the perfect place to practice in human form—a form not to neglect when I wanted to be a better werewolf overall—it was also the perfect place to watch humans and learn how to act in the realm of origin.

Everything I'd been taught my entire life about werewolf and fae societies was useless when it came to living here. But I couldn't live in Faerie after Wilhelm had awakened.

Runa's friend, Isla, had told us that the werewolves in the realm of origin lived differently, and I wanted to learn what they could teach me about being a werewolf. I also didn't want to choose a mate and start a family, which is exactly what my birth pack and my parents expected of me.

And, if I was being truly honest, Runa was here. Even if we weren't in the same pack, it was easier to stay in touch with her if I was here too. I was that much closer to her on this side of the veil.

Perhaps that wasn't the healthiest choice I could have made, but that didn't stop me from making it.

After a few hours of practicing in human form, I got up, brushed the dirt from my shorts, and started walking toward work.

The Rapids Café was close to campus, so the bulk of its customers were students, professors, and other university employees. It was near a walking bridge over the river that ran through town. I wouldn't say that the river was so rough that it had rapids, but it did have bubbles and foam enough to make a pleasant babbling sound.

We had the usual morning and lunch rushes as well as the class-break crowd. But since it was summer semester, that particular problem wasn't nearly as bad.

I arrived for my afternoon shift fifteen minutes early. The lunch push was over, and there was only one customer left. Staring at the computer in his lap, he was tucked into an overstuffed armchair in the corner. Scottie was there every day. He didn't look up when I came in, but Max and Camille did.

Camille was the owner and manager of The Rapids, a curvy woman with short, blond hair that was dark at the roots and was combed over in an artfully messy sort of way. She had a penchant for low-cut tops and hexagonal sunglasses, of which she owned a wide range of colors. Today her lenses were yellow.

Max was my coworker. He was large and soft and eager to please. He reminded me of a giant teddy bear someone would spend tons of tokens trying to win at a carnival. At work, he wore his long hair up in a bun, and his beard, while bushy, was always kempt. We were the only full-time employees. During the fall and spring semesters, we had any number of part-time student counterparts. But during summer and winter breaks, it was just the three of us on weekdays, and Camille and Carl, the forever part-timer, on the weekends.

"Hey, guys," I greeted them.

Max's head snapped in Camille's direction, and he raised his eyebrows. She waved her hand, telling him he could leave now that I'd arrived.

"Thank you!" he called as he rushed out the door.

"What was that?" I took my place beside Camille behind the counter.

"Oh, Max has a date and wanted to know if he could get off as soon as you arrived."

"He should've told me. I would've come in earlier."

"Nah, it's a dinner date. He has more than enough time."

I smiled at Max's enthusiasm. "Ah, I see."

"Can you watch the counter for a sec? I have to hit the washroom."

"No problem."

There really wasn't anything to watch, so I grabbed a spray bottle and towel and started to wipe down surfaces. But just as I was rubbing at a particularly stubborn coffee stain, the bell above the door tinkled. Even before I could turn around, a familiar voice made my shoulders tense.

"Hey, Jaaneman! You going to take my order or what?"

4

I sighed out the tension in my jaw before turning around.

Yutika raised one eyebrow, her large, almond-shaped eyes fixed on me. I didn't know what she'd done to them, but somehow they looked even bigger and darker than normal, fringed with thick lashes. Not that it much mattered since they still held that glint of mischief. Today she wore an ice-blue nose-stud, bright against her dusky-wheat skin.

Her mouth twitched into that irritating half-smirk as I approached the counter to take her order.

"You aren't going to greet me, Jaaneman?" she asked. "I'm a loyal customer after all."

"You haven't bothered to learn my name. Why should I use yours?" I muttered.

"You're feisty today."

She grinned, and I scolded myself for engaging her.

"What can I get you, loyal customer?" I kept my voice as deadpan as I could.

She tilted her head, staring up at the chalkboard behind me. "What takes more effort on your part? A mango smoothie or a blended chai latte?"

"A mango smoothie has more ingredients."

"I'll have that then," she said with a smile that was both too innocent and fully aware of what she was doing.

I stifled a sigh but couldn't help glaring at the cash register while I rang up her order. There was no use getting irritated with her. She was like this every day, every single day. I'd hoped that I would at least get a reprieve during university breaks, but no. She hadn't gone home for winter break, and she'd obviously decided to stay for summer break as well. She always managed to come when I was working too. I'd tried taking a morning shift. I'd tried evening. I'd even tried split shifts. But any time I was working, she was there.

Maybe that was an unfair depiction. It's not as if she even talked to me most of the time she was there. She let me work. And it's not like she didn't come to the café when I wasn't working. She did. Still, I couldn't help but feel she had it in for me, and I could never quite figure out what I'd done to make myself her target.

After taking her payment and punching her loyalty card, I went about making her order. Camille returned as I was scooping frozen mango chunks into the blender.

"Hey, Yuti." Camille greeted her with a smile. "Ooh, looking gorgeous today. Isn't she, Rowan?"

I frowned but glanced over at Yutika again. She wore a jean jacket over a yellow sundress with white flowers on it, which accentuated her full bust and narrow waist. Her chin-length hair was topped with a broad-brimmed, felt hat.

I turned back to making her smoothie.

"Hoping to catch someone's eye?" Camille asked her.

I snorted. *As if it would matter. She'd only ruin it by annoying them.*

Yutika smiled, bright and happy. "Maybe, maybe not. We'll see what the day brings."

I delivered the mango smoothie to Yutika, who'd taken a seat at the counter.

"Looks like you got your barista back," Yutika addressed Camille. "It was too quiet while he was gone last week."

I turned away and began cleaning the dishes I'd used to make her smoothie. The sound of the faucet drowned out my sigh.

After finishing her smoothie, Yutika moved over to where Scottie sat, still hammering at his keyboard. She pulled out her sketchbook and pencils and started to draw. I'd overheard a while back that she was an art student. I'd never asked for clarification, and I'd never seen any of her art, but she always seemed to have her sketchbook with her.

I liked it when she pulled out her sketchbook; she was always quiet when she was drawing. Her expression took on an open, free sort of quality. She didn't smirk. She didn't snark. And most importantly, she left me alone.

Even though she sat quietly until closing, I could never quite relax when Yutika was there—she could strike at any moment.

Lia sent Noire to pick me up after work that night. Noire was the silent sort. Out of everyone in the pack, I felt the most comfortable around her. She never forced conversation, and she didn't pry into how I was feeling. She just let me be, and I did the same for her.

The tips of Noire's short, black hair curled gently around her forehead and the lobes of her ears. She had bright yellow eyes, and, in human form, she always wore blue contacts so her eyes looked a more human-green color. She looked to be in her late thirties or early forties. I'd never asked. But she had straight eyebrows, and more lines on her forehead than around her mouth. She was a serious sort of person, a woman of few smiles. But when she did smile, it was always genuine.

She and her brother had grown up in Faerie as I had. I didn't know how they came to be in Lia's pack. I just knew they'd been there the longest.

"New moon tonight." Noire's soft, unobtrusive voice finally broke the silence as we drove home. "Do you want to go for a run?"

"Yeah, we'll be able to go a little farther out with it being darker."

We didn't speak again until we pulled up to the main house. I told her I'd meet her out back in five minutes.

5

Leaving my door open a crack, I took off my clothes. While the other werewolves didn't care whether I ran around naked, the humans certainly did. And avoiding shifting where a human could see you was one of the rules of living in the realm of origin. There weren't a lot of humans at the lodge in the off-season, but it was always better to be cautious. In any case, I'd spent my whole time bound with Wilhelm changing in private, so it wasn't a big deal for me.

Closing my eyes, I breathed deeply through my human nose. Then I sighed out of my wolf snout. I shook out my fur and nudged the bedroom door open. I trotted through the house, my nails clicking on the wood and tile floors, and out the already-opened sliding glass door.

The back of the main house butted up against an evergreen forest, which sloped and climbed in hills not at all comparable to the mountain our visitors skied on.

The air had cooled significantly since the sun had gone down, and the wind felt pleasant in my fur. Even in the moonless night, it wasn't difficult for me to find my packmates though Noire's black fur was a little harder to see among the trees than her brother's grizzled gray.

Once I'd joined them, Ashwin met my eyes, then Noire's. Bowing his head at us, he turned around and started to run farther into the forest. We followed him not a heartbeat later.

Ashwin was younger than Noire, but he had a higher status in the pack. He was stronger than either of us and had a keen instinct to protect. This made him the perfect beta for Lia though the relaxed nature of the Northern Pack meant that the status of pack members didn't come into play all that often.

My paws pounded on the forest floor, the dirt beneath their pads already cool. Above the sound of the wind in the trees, I could hear the nighttime creatures skittering all around us. My heart raced, pumping adrenaline through my veins. I breathed deep the night air. I could smell a rabbit not far away. But tonight I didn't want to hunt. I just wanted to run.

Filling my lungs, I let out a long, soulful howl. Noire and Ashwin joined me, their voices harmonizing with mine in a chorus of nature at its most pure, its most powerful.

It was moments like this that I forgot all of my troubles. There was no Runa. No heartbreak. No loss. There was no Rowan. There was the dirt under my paws, the wind in my fur, and the song in my throat. And I was at peace.

But, as all things do, it always came to an end. The run, the hunt, the momentary distraction—however long, however fulfilling—would be over. And the pack would return home.

Normally, I would run myself to exhaustion. But for whatever reason, when I returned to the main house that night, I was energized. It didn't really matter since I had the late shift again the next day, so I hopped onto my laptop and pulled up the Internet list: "100 Movies to See Before You Die."

I'd made good progress on the list since I'd come to the realm of origin. I found movies most helpful in understanding humans and how to live among them. At the very least, understanding cultural references was a must. I tried to watch a movie at least every other day. I alternated between going to the theater in town, borrowing from the library, and streaming online. The theater was great because they showed older movies every Wednesday.

I skimmed the list. I wanted to watch *Jurassic Park*, but I knew it would be showing at the theater that week, and I wanted to see it on the big screen if I could. I settled on *Back to the Future*.

Two hours later, as the credits rolled, I looked at the clock on my cellphone. It was too late to start the second movie, no matter how much I wanted to know what happened. I shut my computer down and closed the screen. But as I stood, I knocked something onto the floor.

I bent down and retrieved a white envelope. Standing in the center of my room, the only light the dim lamp above my desk, my heart squeezed. I didn't allow myself to think as I tore open the envelope, the rip of paper loud in the still night.

I pulled out the single sheet of thick paper, stiff and rough in my fingertips. And in my quiet, lonely space, I began to read.

Dear Rowan,

How are you? Did you get my other letters? You haven't written back in a while. This is the third letter I've written since I heard from you last. I don't want to bother you if you need space, so I'll wait to hear from you before I write again.

I tried to get a cellphone so we could use email, but Konner just can't help himself. He shorted it out not a day after I got it. In any case, I don't think I'm going to be able to use electronics until after the baby is born. The little one must have some magic because even I've been killing circuits recently.

The doctor from the Mesa Pack came to visit the other day to check on us. She said she'd never delivered a half-fae, half-werewolf baby before and told me not to shift until I give birth, just to be safe.

When I was bound to Mikhail, I would go months without shifting. But this is different. I wasn't told I physically couldn't. I never had to worry that shifting could be harmful. Now I feel sort of itchy in this skin.

Have you kept in touch with Wilhelm? He and Arete are doing well, I hear. They're still on the farm if you'd like to write to them.

Have you gone to visit your parents at all? I know last time you said they kept asking you to visit.

How about your GED test? Did you take it yet? I'm not worried about you passing. I'm sure you did just fine. What will you do once you have it? Will you keep working at the café?

Well, I don't want to take up too much of your time. I just hope you're doing well. Even if you don't write a long letter, could you write me back to tell me you're all right? If you don't want to exchange letters after that, just say so. I get worried when I don't hear from you for so long.

Your friend,
Runa

I swallowed around the lump in my throat as tears blurred the ink on the page. I couldn't hear her voice anymore, the voice that used to be so clear when I read her words.

I'd told her I wanted to be friends, and I did. But it was truer to say that I just wanted her in my life. The time I spent falling in love with her, the time when we were promised and I could feel the mate bond growing stronger, that was the best time of my life. And even though she never loved me, and even though I'd lost her in the end, I had *believed* for a while. And belief, even in something false, is a beautiful feeling.

But with every moment that passed, that time — Runa herself — became more distant, more removed. As the pain of loss and rejection faded, so did the good things. I started asking myself if I'd ever really loved her at all. How could I keep forgetting if I really loved her?

I knew that memories faded; even Lia had assured me it was normal. But that didn't stop the thoughts swirling in my mind, haunting me, mocking me. *Is it better for me to just let her go entirely? If I don't respond to this letter, will she really stop writing?*

Maybe being friends was too much for me to expect from myself.

Putting the letter back in its envelope, I crossed to my bed and pulled a shoebox out from under it. I tucked the letter among its predecessors, closed the lid, and went to shower before bed.

6

The sound of ravens croaking at each other woke me the next morning. Turning my head, I squinted against the bright sunlight coming in the window. Then I squeezed my eyes shut and thought about rolling back over. Instead, I sighed and sat up.

It was a miracle I'd been able to sleep so late. Even when I stayed awake well into the night, I was usually up near dawn. And even when I wasn't, the boys' morning rambunctiousness didn't much allow anyone to sleep in.

I listened intently. I could hear someone puttering around in the kitchen, but the rest of the house was still. After getting dressed, I shuffled toward the noise.

Lia was assembling baskets of food on the kitchen table. Each one had an assortment of muffins, tea and coffee packets, fruit, and cups of yogurt.

"Thanks for letting me sleep in," I said as I

entered.

"You seemed like you needed it. It's almost lunchtime. Just let me get these to the cabins while Ashwin is still leading the hike, and I'll make you something to eat."

"I'll give you a hand."

The ski resort that the Northern Pack ran billed itself as a private getaway. It was for travelers who wanted to keep mostly to themselves. It had seven cabins of varying capacities, and it provided light victuals for breakfast only. In winter, some of the pack members offered ski instruction. In summer, Ashwin led guided hikes up the mountain. Other than that, check-in and checkout were the most interaction any of us got with the patrons. And Lia handled much of that herself.

It didn't take us long to deliver the baskets to the cabins. I made sure to put the yogurts in the refrigerators; I'd learned to do that in my first week after the key-lime-yogurt incident.

Everyone was out for the day, except for cabin seven, who seemed unnecessarily embarrassed that we'd interrupted their honeymoon.

Back at the main house, I sliced tomatoes while Lia fried bacon so we could all have BLTs for lunch. Ashwin and Noire turned up exactly at noon just as Lia and I were setting plates on the table.

"I've got to pick up some paint at the hardware store this afternoon, so I can drop you off at work today, Rowan," Noire said after swallowing a notably large bite of sandwich.

I thanked her.

"It has been a while since…that time," Lia's eyes flicked toward me. "Do you think you're ready to try to learn how to drive again? I promised to start teaching Lune this weekend. I could teach you both at the same time."

Driving had been quite overwhelming for me when I'd first tried to learn. I'd been new to the realm of origin at the time, and many things had been completely foreign to me. But how I'd managed to hit a light pole in the middle of an empty parking lot I never did figure out. On the other hand, I didn't like being a burden to the pack every time I had to go somewhere.

"Sure…I can sit in the backseat while you're teaching Lune."

Lia's eyes sparkled with laughter, but she managed to keep a straight face. "You don't have to get behind the wheel until you're ready."

I stared at the glass of milk beside my plate.

"Don't be so hard on yourself." Ashwin clapped me on the shoulder. "The first time Noire tried to drive —"

Noire glared at her brother, her eyes looking a little more yellow through her contact lenses. "We don't need to talk about that. Ever."

Ashwin grinned, showing his dimples even through his close-cropped facial hair. He winked one gray eye at me in a playful gesture, but he didn't continue.

The weather was perfect as Noire and I headed into town—not too hot or too cold. The breeze through the open window was pleasant as the sun heated my skin. Noire dropped me off in front of the café half an hour before my shift started. And with the weather being as nice as it was, I decided to sit at one of the picnic tables outside before heading in.

Closing my eyes, I relished the feeling of the air brushing the hair from my face. It carried the fresh scent of pine and clean water from the nearby river.

"Was that your mom?"

My contentment faltered, and I looked over my shoulder as Yutika approached the table.

Her dark eyes stared down at me under the brim of her bucket hat.

"No."

She tilted her head. "Your sister?"

"No."

Her mouth twitched into a sarcastic smirk. "Don't tell me she's your girlfriend?"

"She isn't my girlfriend, not that it's any of your business."

"I should've known that anyway. Who'd date you?"

My heart panged as my face heated. I clenched my jaw while shame and anger twisted in my gut. But before I could snap at her, the wind changed direction.

I could smell the familiar sweet and spicy scent of cinnamon and citrus unique to Yutika, the stale whiff of chalk and the faint note of wax. But underneath her usual aroma, something else clung to her.

I scrunched my eyebrows and stood from the picnic table, my pulse racing. As I took a step closer, her eyes widened ever so slightly. She turned her head, eyeing me suspiciously while I tried to get a good sniff without being too noticeable.

And there it was: that dark, heavy scent of damp earth. The smell of moist clay, of fresh graveyard rain.

I stared at her hard. Her skin was the same rich

tone it always was — no loss of color. I tilted my head from side to side, but I couldn't see any indication of eyeshine. Most importantly, her teeth didn't look elongated although I couldn't be certain with her mouth closed.

"Where have you been?" I interrogated. "What have you been doing since last night?"

She squinted up at me and snorted. "Now who isn't minding his own business?" Without another word, she turned and headed into the café.

7

I fumbled in my pocket for my phone, the hair on the back of my neck standing on end. I called Lia as I watched Yutika through the window.

"Rowan? What's up? I thought you'd be at work right now."

"I am. Listen. Something…weird happened." I glanced around me to make sure no one was nearby. "You know that girl who always comes into the café?"

"The one who teases you?"

"Yeah. I…" I dropped my voice even lower. "I smelled something on her."

"What do you mean?"

"I mean, her scent has changed. It reminds me of vampire smell, but it's different."

Lia's voice was serious but steady, unalarmed. "How is it different?"

"It has those sort of musty earth tones but not the sickly sweet notes of decay."

The line went quiet.

"Are you there?" I asked.

"I'm going to call Noire and send her to the café. She should still be in town. Is the girl still there?"

I watched Yutika settle onto a stool at the counter. She dug into her bag and pulled out her computer.

"Yeah, she could be here for a while."

"All right. Call me back on your break, and I'll let you know more."

"Okay. Thanks."

The phone beeped as Lia hung up.

I inhaled fresh air before entering the café. My eyes analyzed Yutika with every step I took toward the counter.

"Hey, Rowan." Max smiled brightly while Camille made whatever Yutika had ordered.

His words were like the buzzing of a fly near my ear as I studied my quarry from the tall grasses.

"Hey, Max," I murmured, not taking my eyes off Yutika. "How was your date?"

"Great," he answered. "I texted her today, and we made plans to meet up again this weekend."

The sound of his voice, the sounds of the café — the blender, Scottie's keyboard, the soft whir of the fans — were distant, ambient, barely a distraction as all my senses keyed into Yutika.

"That's good." I pried my gaze off her only long enough to put on my apron.

"Here you go." Camille placed Yutika's order beside her computer.

Yutika looked up to thank her and met my eyes. The dim lights of the café shined at just the right angle for me to be fairly certain she didn't have eyeshine.

"Thanks." She tugged slightly on the brim of her hat as she lowered her face.

Max said his goodbyes and headed out for the day. I hardly registered the change.

Sniffing deeply through my nose, I stretched my back as cover. The scent that had been ever so slight outside was stronger in the enclosed space. But it definitely wasn't as strong as the scent of an actual vampire.

"Did you stay up late watching movies again?" Camille asked, marking my stretch.

"Yeah."

"What did you watch?"

"*Back to the Future*."

"Did you like it?"

I nodded, stifling my irritation at Camille's small talk. She didn't know that there was a potential threat sitting at her counter, and I didn't want to alarm her, especially when it could be nothing. "Yes."

"Are you going to watch the sequels?"

The bell above the door chimed, and I glanced over to see Noire enter.

"I'm not sure," I said, distracted.

Noire's eyes swept the room, marking the two customers besides Yutika. When she met my gaze, I flicked my eyes to Yutika, then back to Noire. She lowered her chin and approached the counter.

"Ah." Camille pointed to Noire. "I've seen you take Rowan to and from work." She smiled. "You finally got curious and decided to come inside, eh?"

Noire inclined her head. "Yes, I've been meaning

to, but I never seemed to have the time." She glanced up at the chalkboard menu, using it as an excuse to move closer to Yutika. "Is there anything you suggest for my first time?"

Camille looked over her shoulder at the menu. "Our smurfberry smoothie is seasonal if you'd like to try that."

Noire turned toward Yutika. "Have you tried it?" she asked.

Yutika's eyes widened, but she nodded. "Yeah, it's good if you like blueberries and bananas."

"All right," Noire said. "I'll try that then. Thanks."

"No problem," Yutika answered, watching Noire as Camille took her payment.

While I went about making the order, Noire sat beside Yutika to wait. I listened intently to their conversation, my werewolf hearing easily picking up every word even above the sound of the blender.

"You're a student?" Noire asked.

"Yeah. I'm a fine arts major."

"Very nice. I was just on my way to the hardware store to buy paint though I wouldn't say I'm doing anything artistic with it."

"Are you repainting your house?" Yutika asked.

"Some of the cabins need to be repainted."

"Oh, do you work up at the ski resort, too? Is that why you often give Jaa — R-Rowan a ride?"

My hands stilled in their work. *I never told her I lived at the resort. Maybe she overheard me talking about it with Camille?*

I glanced over my shoulder at them. We'd never had any real conversations, Yutika and I. And I was certain that was the first time I'd ever heard her actually say my name even if she'd stumbled over it. I scrunched my eyebrows and returned to my task.

"Yes, I'm head of maintenance up at Beyahish Mountain Retreat."

"Cool. It must be nice out there. I've never been."

"It is."

I placed the smoothie before Noire.

"Thank you." After sticking the paper straw in, Noire took a sip and nodded. "Very good." She lifted her cup to Yutika. "It was nice talking with you. Good luck with your art."

Yutika gave her a friendly smile. "Thanks. Good luck with your cabin painting."

Noire met my eyes briefly before leaving the café. My skin prickled with anticipation. Noire hadn't given any indication that I should be concerned, but with her being as straight-faced as always, it was difficult to tell.

Camille beamed as she watched Noire go. "Oof, there's something about her… She's just my type. I don't suppose she's single?" She raised an eyebrow at me.

"I think she is."

Camille sighed. "I bet she's straight though, eh?"

I shrugged. "I never asked."

Camille pursed her lips. "With my luck, she's straight. But damn, she's pretty." She tilted her head thoughtfully. "She's sort of like a female you, actually. She's got a similar…feel about her. And she's got that same black hair."

"Is that supposed to be a compliment?" I asked dryly.

"I said she was pretty, didn't I?"

8

I was a complete goof while waiting for my break, so preoccupied with thinking about what Noire had gleaned. I messed up orders—I even broke the mug Scottie was using when he came to the counter for a refill.

"What is *with* you today? You aren't normally so clumsy," Camille said while I threw the pieces of the cup away.

I glanced at the clock. "Can I take my break now?"

She waved her hand. "Yeah, go. Get your head on straight."

Instead of going to the small break room in the back, I went out the front door so I could keep an eye on Yutika through the window.

The evening air was heavy, and a single moth fluttered near the light outside the café. It had just flickered on as the sun dipped behind the mountains.

I bounced on my toes while my phone rang

loudly in my ear; the pause between each ring seemed minutes. As soon as the line connected, I started to talk. "Anything?" I asked.

"Yes, there is something…" Lia confirmed. "Noire agrees with you. The scent is similar to vampire, but it's off somehow. We need to know more. Let's all have a meeting when you get home, and we can discuss what to do."

"Or…I could just find out what's going on with her," I suggested.

There was a short pause, long enough for me to wonder what Lia was going to say.

"I thought you didn't get along with this woman."

I pursed my lips. "I don't. But everyone else is busy with stuff. You're coordinating with the other alphas for hunts and running the resort. Ashwin and Noire have their duties. And, even though I don't much like her, I'm in the best position to get close to her and find out what's going on. She at least knows me better than she knows any of you."

"All right. If you're up for it. But we're here to back you up with whatever you need. Just ask."

"I will."

"And keep a lookout. It's possible the scent is coming from a different source. Or she could have only gone through half of her transformation, been fed blood but not bitten yet or vice versa. Or something entirely different that we can't conceive."

"Okay. I'll call for a ride when I'm ready to be picked up tonight."

Then we said goodbye.

Squinting past my own reflection in the window of the café, I stared at Yutika's back. I took a deep breath, easing my nerves as my mind raced. Despite my confidence in how to deal with a vampire, I wasn't so sure how to handle this woman. *How can I get close to someone who so clearly dislikes me? What can I possibly say?*

When I returned to work, I was just as distracted as before. My gaze was constantly drawn toward Yutika, and she was beginning to notice. The third time she met my eyes, she squinted at me.

"What?" she demanded. "What's with you today? Do I have something on my face?"

I swallowed my apprehension and softened my voice, hoping to defuse her defensiveness. "No, I just...wanted to talk to you about something, but I'm not sure how to say it."

"Y-you want to talk to *me*? About *what*?" she asked, her tone not as sharp as I was used to.

I glanced around the café. There were a handful of people amongst the armchairs and tables. None of the customers were paying us much mind, but Camille stood very still all of a sudden as if she was listening closely to what I was about to say next.

"I'd rather not talk about it here. Could you wait for me after we close? I could walk you home, and we can talk on the way."

Her dark eyes clung to mine for a long moment, then she nodded once.

"You know, Rowan," Camille said in a tone that would've been offhanded if it wasn't for its precise timing. "You're pretty useless today. Why don't you head out early? I can close by myself."

I glanced at my boss.

She gave me a conspiratorial smile, her wink

implied. "There's less than an hour left anyway. These guys should be clearing out soon."

I wasted no time returning my apron to its hook and approached Yutika on her side of the counter. "Are you ready to go, or do you still have more work to do?"

"Nope. I'm ready." She closed her laptop and shoved it into her bag. Then she slipped the strap over her head and onto her shoulder.

The atmosphere between us was strained and awkward as we stepped into the night. She gestured toward the bridge, and we slowly started walking. The air was so thick, I thought I'd choke on it. We'd never said much to each other except to exchange barbs, and I had no plan at all for getting closer to her. I couldn't seem to ease my awareness of Yutika's every move, every breath. Yes, she could become a threat later, but at this moment, she was the one potentially in danger. We were already over the bridge before she broke the silence.

"So what did you want to talk about?" Her voice was gentle and hesitant. But as I listened closely, I could hear her shallow breathing while she awaited my answer.

"I...uh...I'm a little embarrassed." I was still trying to land on an excuse to get closer to her.

But when the university clock tower tolled ten, inspiration struck.

"I don't know if you know this, but I just got my GED. And I've been thinking about the future. I want to apply to the university, but I don't know how to go about it. You're really one of the only students I know well enough to talk to, which, given how little we know each other, is saying something.

So I was wondering if you could help me with the application process."

I glanced over at her. The bright campus lights plastered our shadows onto the brick path. Her eyes and face were dark, obscured by her hat.

She was staring at the ground ahead of us as we walked, her hands shoved into her jeans pockets. She breathed out slowly. "So that's what it was," she murmured. "Why are you embarrassed about that?" she asked at a normal volume.

I shrugged. "I don't know... You don't seem to like me very much. I guess I didn't want to look stupid in front of you."

We went another ten steps, our sneakers hardly making a sound except to occasionally kick a stray pebble.

"That's not true. I don't dislike you."

I blinked. "Then—"

"I'll help you," she interrupted before I could ask her why she always tried to goad me.

"You will?" My voice carried my surprise. I hadn't thought it would be so easy.

She nodded.

"When? Now?"

Her answering chuckle was indulgent and comfortable. It was the sort of laugh shared between friends, and for once it didn't feel like it was aimed directly at me. "It's late. I have an early class tomorrow. And besides, I have to do some research about what someone in your situation needs to do to apply."

"Okay." My mind swirled with what I could do next.

"It shouldn't take me long to find out. I can look

it up after class. You work the morning shift tomorrow, right?"

My eyebrows scrunched. *How does she know?*
"Yes…"

"Then we can do it after that. Do you have a
laptop?"

I nodded.

"Okay. Bring it to work. We can go to the
library when you get off."

"Thanks." *What else can I say? What can I do? Will
tomorrow be too late?*

We turned onto a quiet residential street. Among the slightly cracked sidewalks and lawns that were a day overgrown, the streetlamps cast yellow pools of light. They dwindled along the street to pinpricks surrounded by deep shadows. These weren't the bright lights of campus anymore.

A tingle ran over my skin. "*This* is where you live?"

She glanced up at me. "Yeah, just over there." She pointed at a large house. "The owner converted the rooms into efficiency apartments and rents them out to students."

"And you walk home after dark? *Alone?*" *How could this human not see the danger? There are so many shadows, so many places to lurk.*

She lifted her chin. "I'm a big girl. I can take care of myself."

Not against a vampire you can't. "Don't you have anyone who can walk with you?"

She squinted up at me, indignation clear in her eyes. "Are you suggesting — "

"I'll do it."

Her breath hitched, and her anger dissipated. "You will?"

"Yeah, if you need to walk home after dark, then call me."

"I don't...have your number."

I snorted. "Then I'll give it to you."

She pulled her phone from her pocket. "Okay. What is it?"

"Here. I'll type it in for you."

I reached out to take the phone from her, but she snatched it away. "No, I'll put it in."

"O-okay." I told her the number, and she shoved the phone back into her pocket.

A few minutes later, we stopped as we reached the walk leading up to her building. She turned back to me, and it was clear that she was not going to invite me inside. I looked over her shoulder at the historic house. One of the windows on the upper floor had a little balcony, which displayed a variety of flowerpots.

"Is that one yours?" I asked, with no better way of discerning where in the house her apartment was located.

She looked up at where I was pointing. "No, that's where Kyo lives. He's great with plants. I've asked him to teach me, but everything he gives me dies." She indicated a window on the ground floor to the left of the door. "I live in the apartment behind that one. I have a great view of the trees that surround the backyard."

Possibly the worst position should a vampire want her.

"Well." She clutched the strap of her bag, bunching the fabric in her fists. "I guess I'll see you tomorrow then."

I bowed my head. "Right. Goodnight."

"'Night."

I didn't make a move to leave, and she hesitated.

"Go on in. I'll just wait for you to get inside."

"Oh, okay. Thanks. Goodnight." She headed up the walk and into the house without looking back.

I needed to take a good sniff around, but I had to be careful too. I couldn't be seen lurking around in my human form, especially when she knew I was there. And I certainly couldn't be seen in town in my wolf form.

I sniffed deeply, putting everything I'd learned about honing my skills over the last year into practice. But I couldn't smell anything out of the ordinary. I couldn't even pick up the faint scent Yutika had on her.

Frowning, I started to walk back to campus. The nighttime creatures bustled all around me. Birds, bugs, and furry little rodents went about their nocturnal activities. The sounds relaxed me in a way that only the night could—reminders that I belonged there, that no vampires were lurking about. Once I'd reached the clock tower, I called Lia for a ride.

My thoughts ran away as I waited, my mind able to think more clearly as my body's tension eased. Hunting vampires in the realm of origin was completely different than in Faerie. In Faerie it was a werewolf's duty—when you came across a vampire, you killed it. But here werewolves had to be careful. We had to plan everything ahead as best we could. We couldn't risk exposing our existence. And we couldn't risk the humans finding any dead vampires either. Of course that meant we couldn't always save the humans. It meant that sometimes the vampires got away.

But as I sat in the shadows, the light from the streetlamps not quite reaching me, I vowed that I would figure out whatever was going on with Yutika.

I didn't have to wait too long for Lia. On the drive back, I told her everything that had happened since I'd called her on my break.

The tense frown she had while I was relating my story eased as I finished. She nodded slowly, her eyes concentrating on the winding road.

"It's promising that you didn't smell anything at her apartment though that doesn't explain the scent you and Noire smelled on her."

"Any ideas?" I asked.

She glanced over at me. "No more than I had before. It was good thinking telling her you'd walk her home at night. But your university application ruse isn't going to buy you a lot of time. You'll have to come up with something else after tomorrow."

"I thought that too."

Silence settled comfortably in before Lia broke it. "So you decided to apply then?"

I shrugged, gazing out the window at the dark trees, their shadows merging as we drove past. "I needed an excuse, and that's the one I landed on. Even if I get accepted, I don't have to go."

"Or...you could go."

I thought about how much money that would

cost the pack. I thought about how Lune wanted to become a doctor. "Maybe."

When we arrived at home, I ate a snack while Lia told the rest of the pack what we knew about Yutika.

It was late by the time I crawled into bed, and my mind spun with everything that had happened. In my dark bedroom, I glanced over at my desk. I had planned to reply to Runa's letter that night. Instead, I faced the wall and willed myself to sleep.

10

The early morning sun had yet to deactivate the streetlights outside the café as Camille and I prepared to open the next morning. I loved that hushed moment of in-between time, that moment pleasant and still but ripe with potential energy.

The rich, earthy scent of brewing coffee filled the space. One of the perks of working at a coffee shop was that smell, a strong smell that cleansed the other scents in the air. In a way, it helped focus my nose; I could tune in to only the scents I wanted to pay attention to.

"So how did it go?" Camille fluffed armchair pillows while I put pastries and sandwiches into the glass display case.

I pretended I didn't know what she was talking about. "How did what go?"

While good-natured, Camille was the nosy sort. I didn't really have a reason to keep anything besides our werewolf stuff from her. But I found myself doing it anyway. She was fun to tease.

She snorted, giving the pillow in her hands a hard whack. "Are you kidding me?"

I smirked but knelt behind the case so she wouldn't see. This was the feeling I remembered, a familiar feeling where I teased my friend just to get a rise. It used to be so much a part of my life, my personality, but I'd grown serious over the last three years. Dealing with a broken heart will do that.

"Stop joking. What happened with Yuti?"

"What *should* have happened with her?" I asked blandly.

I watched Camille through the glass as she pursed her lips and threw the pillow into place. Then I slid the door to the case closed.

"You're doing this on purpose, right? You guys flirt every day for a year. Then you suddenly want to 'talk' to her about something. And now you want to pretend like *nothing* happened?"

I stood and turned toward the espresso machine. "First of all, we have never once flirted," I said with confidence as I took the lid off the machine to fill it with beans. "Secondly, nothing *did* happen. I asked her for some help with something, and she agreed."

Camille threw her head back and sighed loudly. "I can't even listen to this nonsense anymore."

"You're the one who asked," I muttered.

She shushed me while letting her limbs go limp in a sort of wiggly sulk. "I can't believe you're ruining this for me."

"What—"

"Nuh-uh." She waved her hand in front of her.

"I don't want to hear any more from you. Ugh, I'm so disappointed!"

I huffed out a laugh at the display. She never failed to entertain me with her over-the-top antics.

But I didn't get to enjoy Camille's reaction for long: as soon as we opened the doors, the morning rush began. And there wasn't much of a lull between the morning and lunch rushes that day.

Every free moment I had, I watched the door. Yutika always came in while I was working. Always. *Did she make it through the night? Was the scent a fluke, and she'll be back to normal?*

I needn't have watched so closely. I knew the moment she came in. The rich, wet scent of earth reached me from across the room. It had gotten stronger, drowning out even the smell of the coffee beans.

My gaze snapped to Yutika as she walked toward the counter. Did she seem pale? Or was it just because she wore her baseball cap backwards and the bill didn't shadow her face? She smiled softly but didn't show her teeth.

"Yuti, you're here!" Camille called. She grinned when she saw how I watched Yutika. "I thought you'd never come."

Yutika tilted her head. "Yeah, I've had a busy morning. I had class, then I needed to do some research. Plus, I promised to help a friend move some stuff. Why? Am I late for something?"

"No," Camille said lightly. "Not at all. I just... expected you to be here before the afternoon shift started."

Yutika lowered her face, not quite hiding her self-conscious smile.

"What can I get for you?" Camille asked with a smirk.

This question forced Yutika to look up, and her expression smoothed as she read from the overhead chalkboard. "I'll have a blended chai latte, please."

As Camille took her payment, I moved to make her order.

Camille glanced over her shoulder at me. "I'll take care of it. You're almost off the clock anyway."

I stared at my boss, at the little twinkle in her dark eyes.

"Okay." I abandoned my task and approached Yutika at the counter. "Are you too busy to meet up today?" I asked her as quietly as I could.

"No, no," she said, her voice urgent as she rushed to answer. "I took care of everything early so I could help y—" Her words came to a sudden halt, and she continued in an easier, more measured tone. "I mean… No, it's fine. I have time."

What's going on with her? Is she all right? I have to find out why the scent is getting stronger. What happened between last night and now? "Okay. Thanks. I'm off in fifteen minutes if you don't mind waiting."

She took a seat on a stool.

But fifteen minutes turned into twenty-five as a stream of customers decided it was a good time to visit The Rapids, and just when Max was running late too.

"Sorry about that," I said to Yutika as we finally escaped the café and stepped out into the afternoon air.

The clouds overhead were thick and fluffy, but they dotted the blue expanse of sky sparsely, not providing any shade from the sun. The temperature was still climbing but had yet to hit the full heat of the day. It was pleasant in that late spring sort of way.

"No worries," Yutika murmured, shifting her weight from one foot to the other.

The strange atmosphere from the previous night returned, that awkward spot between what we had always been and what we would—or could—be. I'd reached out to her, however clumsily, and she'd said she didn't dislike me. We had changed the beat. And now we were two dancers listening to the new song and trying to match the new rhythm.

"Are you ready to go to the library?" she asked.

I nodded. "Yeah, I brought my laptop, too."

"Great," she breathed. "Let's go."

As we walked, I searched for a way to determine how her scent had changed. My eyes were fixed on the path ahead of us, watching our shadows on the pavement shift and flow beside one another.

"It sounds like you had a busy morning…" I stumbled over my words, the sound of my voice odd in my own ears.

"Hmm? Yeah."

Yutika's soft response left no room to continue. All I needed was an opening, some way to make the atmosphere more comfortable. But my own awkwardness kept getting in the way. I'd never had to be so devious before, and I didn't know Yutika well enough to know the right way to approach her. Swallowing my discomfort, I tried again. "Did you sleep well last night?"

"Y-yeah, it was all right."

Her tone was hesitant and uneasy. I looked up

from our shadows to her face. *Was she visited after I left her?*

Seeing no other way, I fell back into what had always worked for me. I smirked. "You don't sound too confident about that." I made sure my tone was light and teasing, nothing accusatory, nothing suspicious.

She glanced over at me, a glint of mischief in her eyes. "What can I say? I was up all night thinking of you."

A shiver ran over my skin, and I halted to a stop. But before I could even think of what to say, she burst into laughter.

"Is that what you were hoping for me to say? Pff, keep dreaming, Jaaneman."

My face heated. "That's not funny."

But her smile widened. "It is to me."

Despite my embarrassment, the uncomfortable atmosphere between us had shifted. Banter we could work with; banter was familiar. And the knot in my stomach—the knot that had formed when she'd arrived with an even stronger scent—eased as she flashed her teeth, loosened by the distinct lack of fangs.

"Are you really not going to call me by my name?" I asked, slipping into my old self, my pre-Runa self, like an old shoe that I wasn't sure still fit.

She raised an eyebrow. "What about you?"

"I will if you will."

She eyed me suspiciously as if this were some sort of trap. But after a tense moment, she took a deep breath through her nose. "All right then, *Rowan.* I slept fine last night. How about you?"

I stifled my smile, mimicking her dignified

expression and tone while internally celebrating my ever-so-small success. "I also slept fine. Thank you for asking, *Yutika*."

"My friends call me Yuti."

"Then what should I call you?"

She smirked, and for once I didn't find it irritating. "Well, I suppose that depends on how friendly you're planning on being."

The friendlier I am, the easier it will be to know what's going on with her.

When we reached the library, I opened the door and waved my hand ahead of me. "After you, Yuti."

11

The group study area of the university's library was on the top floor. It was a bright room lit primarily by a wall of windows that provided a gorgeous view of the distant mountains. The blues and whites of winter had given way to the warm browns and cool greens of summer.

We sat at one of the tables near the windows. I glanced over at Yuti while my laptop booted up. The picturesque scenery seemed to pull her into it like a vacation photo hung on a wall. I couldn't imagine how anyone got any studying done.

How can anyone stay inside when the wilderness beckons?

"Are you going to log in?" Yuti gestured to the screen.

"Right." I logged into my computer and pushed it toward her.

With a few keystrokes and a click of the mouse, she navigated to the university's admissions page. "You're going to have to create a username and password first." She slid the computer in front of me.

She continued her explanations while I created my login credentials.

"The first part is pretty much just your personal information: your address, your birthday, stuff like that. You shouldn't need much help with that. But when you get to a question you don't understand, just ask. Okay? And if you don't want to write the essay right now, you can do it at home later. Just log back in, and it should've saved your progress."

I began typing my personal details into the form. But as I clicked the *next* button, I was confronted with a question I didn't have an answer for. And the little red asterisk wouldn't let me proceed.

I looked over at Yuti, who sat close beside me, resting her head in her hands.

"It says I have to pick a major."

"Yeah, but if you find something you like better once you're in, you can always change."

"Why do I have to choose one at all?"

She sat up straighter in her chair as if answering my question required proper thought. "Well, each major, each school within the university, has different requirements for graduation. They're designed to make sure you have everything you need to enter the workforce in that field."

I frowned, and my thoughts slipped out unfil-tered. "So everything is set up for you to get a specific job? What if you want to learn just to learn? Is knowledge for the sake of knowledge not a thing?"

She stared at me a moment. "Do you not have a

particularly strong interest in one area? Is there no subject you like to learn about more than others?"

I shrugged. "I like to learn about whatever interests me at the moment. One minute I could be taking clocks apart, the next I could be reading about extinct species or how crystals form. I can't imagine confining my interests to one area."

"Is there a certain job you want to do once you graduate? A lot of people choose a major that way."

"I've never had any particular job I've wanted. I…" I pursed my lips, trying to find the right words. "I grew up in a sort of…communal-type situation, like a tight-knit group of families who all do their part for the larger group. Some members wanted certain jobs, and they were more than welcome to do them. But then there were others who just did whatever needed to be done, whatever they could to contribute. To me, it doesn't matter so much what I'm doing. It matters more who I'm doing it with, who I'm doing it for. I know money is necessary. I just don't think it's as important as other things."

I glanced up at her, searching her dark eyes for understanding. "Does that make sense?"

She smiled softly, a gentle smile that was warm and kind. "I understand. I mean, no one majors in fine arts if they want a sure way to make tons of money. I do it for the love of it. 'Starving artist' isn't just a trite phrase. It's a real struggle to make a living this way. I find my passion here. It sounds to me like you find your passion in helping those you care about. I can appreciate that."

My chest warmed at her words and the tenderness in her eyes. I'd never thought to have this sort of conversation with Yuti.

"If you want to take classes just to learn, and you aren't seeking a specific degree, you can still do that."

I pointed to the red asterisk. "But this question has to be answered."

"Right. But only if you're doing a normal application. If you just want to take classes, you can do that as a nondegree student. You have to look at the course catalog for classes you want to take, then fill out a registration form with Admissions. But, just so you know, you can't use financial aid if you do it that way. And you have to pay for each credit hour separately."

I nodded slowly. "I'll look at the catalog for fall semester and see."

Our shared moment of understanding slipped, and a heavy pause settled in when we realized there was no other reason for us to be there. *What else can I say?*

"I—"

"You—"

We both stumbled and stopped as we started to talk at the same time.

I gestured toward her with my hand, palm up. "You can go first. What were you going to say?"

She cleared her throat. "No, it's fine. You go."

"Okay." Though I'd agreed, I hesitated, second-guessing my earlier confidence. I'd spoken without thinking. I needed some way of spending more time with her. I needed to find out more about her and what she'd been up to. *But what if she doesn't want that? What will I do then?*

My knee bounced under the table. "I was going to say that I usually go to the movies on Wednesday nights. The theater in town plays older movies at a discounted price. It's still a few hours before it starts. But we could go get some food and then go to the movies if you want. They're showing *Jurassic Park* tonight."

Her dark eyes met mine, but I couldn't read them. One breath turned into two, turned into three.

"A-as a way of thanking you for your help—" I continued, more softly than before.

"Yes," she said, her voice clipped as she rushed to answer. Then she looked out the window. "I mean, sure. That sounds like fun. It's a great movie and seeing it on the big screen would be cool."

I stilled my leg, the nervous energy easing.

"But it's still early for dinner. What time does the movie start?" she asked.

I dropped my gaze to the table. "Yeah, I guess it is a little early, isn't it? The movie is at seven."

Gone was the easy banter and the comfortable atmosphere it had provided. Silence wedged its way back into the conversation, and I searched for something—anything—to say that would keep her in my sight.

"We could…go to the Student Union," she suggested. "They have games and stuff there. There's a ping-pong table, a few pool tables; there are even some arcade games. You know…if you want."

I gave her my most encouraging smile. "Sounds fun—if you don't mind losing, that is."

The smirk returned to her face, and I was relieved to see it. "Pff. You don't know who you're up against."

12

The rec room at the Student Union was far more expansive than Yuti had led me to believe. Not only were there pool tables and a ping-pong table, there was also a rock-climbing wall and a big, white room with a wood floor and a glass wall on one side. There were various arcade games, from *Street Fighter* to *Pac-Man*. There was even a pinball machine.

It wasn't what I would've called crowded, but I was disappointed to see the ping-pong table in use. I'd seen ping-pong played in *Forrest Gump*, and I wanted to try it. In fact, besides *Pac-Man*, I'd never played any of these games. Some of them I couldn't even identify. I had no idea what the white room was for.

As I stared at a table with a white top, Yuti asked, "Is that what you want to play?"

"What?"

"Air hockey." She pointed to the white table beside us.

"Sure. But, uh, I've never played it before."

She reached for the toggle switch on the side of the table and pressed it. "You'll pick it up," she assured above the sudden sound of a gentle but constant breeze.

Then she gave me a quick rundown of the rules.

"That sounds easy enough," I said.

"Right. So what do you say we make things interesting?" Her smirk was back, challenging me, daring me.

But what she didn't know was that I'd never lost a bet in my life. I smiled. "All right. How's this: for every point, the winner gets to ask the loser a question. And the loser *has* to answer honestly."

"Agreed."

With the terms of the wager sealed, she placed the plastic puck on the table. With one loud *plink*, the puck floated across the table and right into my goal.

I blinked. *All right. That's okay. Now I see how it works.*

"One question then?" She grinned.

I hoped she wouldn't ask anything I'd have to lie about.

"How old are you?"

My stomach eased. "Twenty-one," I answered truthfully.

She made a little sound of acknowledgment, and I wondered whether I was older or younger than she'd expected.

Taking up the puck, I placed it back on the table. And with a *plink* from my striker, it was back in play. It flew across the table, knocked against the sides, and was sent back by Yuti. I defended my goal. But as it came back again, I misjudged. Yuti claimed another point.

Are you serious? My eyebrows scrunched.

"What's your favorite thing to do?" she asked as I squinted at my useless striker.

I paused for only a second, only long enough to find the word that would tell her honestly without telling her too much. "I like to run," I answered.

She tilted her head, her mouth not quite a frown but a thoughtful line.

As I bent to retrieve the puck again, I swore to myself that this time I would get a point for sure. I needed to ask her about the scent, about what she'd been doing the last few days that had changed. But while I gave it a valiant effort, I didn't succeed.

I can run down a rabbit. I can catch a Frisbee in midair. But I can't track this stupid little puck across this stupid table?

I didn't stifle my exasperated sigh as I looked up at Yuti. This seemed a very one-sided conversation, and I wasn't getting any closer to the answers I needed.

She was unexpectedly serious, her lips turned slightly down as her eyes fixed on the center of the table.

My chest squeezed at her expression. *What is she going to ask me?*

But then her face eased, and she looked sort of bland as if she didn't even really care what my answer would be. "Have you ever...had a girlfriend?"

I froze, the wind knocked out of me when her words kicked me in the chest. My heart ached as though no time had passed, as though I were standing in Runa's room begging her to run away with me. How long had it been since I'd thought about it? A day? A few hours? Whatever respite I'd had while busying myself with this scent business, it was over now.

I swallowed around the lump in my throat and took a shallow breath. *I can answer honestly. There's no reason to keep this a secret.*

But just as I opened my mouth to speak, a pair of men approached.

"Yuti," the taller of the two called out.

Yuti turned toward the sound of her name. And as she did, a new scent surfaced from her. Beneath the new must of damp earth, mixed with her natural cinnamon and citrus, there was a tangy undertone like vinegar. I froze as Yuti frowned at the men. That tang meant only one thing: Yuti was afraid.

My eyes snapped to the newcomers' faces. The taller one smiled in an easy, nonthreatening manner, his predatory gaze trained on Yuti. His friend stood slightly behind, his attention on the floor as if he'd rather be anywhere else. *Have I seen them somewhere? At the café? On campus?* I couldn't place them.

"Did you get a new phone?" the smiling man asked. "I texted you over the weekend."

"I don't recall ever giving you my number, Warren," Yuti answered. She stood stiffly, her back straight with her arms crossed over her chest. There was a bite in her tone, far more hostile than the sharp words she'd directed at me over the last year.

She doesn't want him to know she's afraid.

Warren just kept smiling. "Are you free later? Dustin and I are going for a drive up to the canyon. He's got a new telescope or something."

Dustin's head snapped toward Warren. "But you said you didn't—"

"What do you say?" Warren pressed, cutting his friend off.

"No, thank you," Yuti answered flatly.

"Come on, Yuti—"

"She already said no," I growled, a little too much wolf coming through in my tone.

Warren turned his hard eyes on me, acknowledging my presence for the first time while I moved closer to Yuti's side of the table. "And who are you to answer for her?" His lips curled as if his teeth were any kind of threat.

I stepped between Yuti and the men. "I didn't answer for her. She gave you her answer, and you didn't accept it. And who am I? I'm the man she has plans with this evening. And I didn't even have to coerce her. Imagine that."

His hard eyes, glinting with hatred, met my glare. He inhaled deeply, puffing his chest out.

His instincts aren't very good. Anticipation zipped through me, and my nerves tingled. *Do it. Accept the challenge. I'd love to teach you what fear really is since you're so keen on giving it to her.*

But Dustin's instincts were more astute. "Come on, dude. It'll be easier to set everything up if we get there before dark."

Warren pursed his lips but took his friend's opening to back down. He smiled at Yuti, who stood half behind me. "Next time, eh? When you aren't so busy."

She didn't respond, but the tang in her scent faded as they retreated.

13

I turned around, looking down at Yuti as she took a deep breath.

"Are you okay?" I asked.

She frowned, shaking her head. But the gesture seemed more an indecisive motion than an answer. Her scent shifted, turning sharp with the aroma of salt. "I don't know how to feel right now except angry. I've done everything I could to tell Warren I'm not interested. But he won't take no for an answer. I'm glad you stepped in, I am."

As she continued, her voice rose in volume, letting her anger blaze. "But I'm pissed off that you even needed to. Why should my answer not be good enough? Why should Warren need another man to tell him to back off?" she growled.

My inner wolf's ears pricked up, impressed by the sound. I felt as though I was getting my first real glimpse of Yuti. In this moment, she was real; these feelings were true. There was nothing sarcastic or snarky about them.

But I could only sympathize. I'd never experienced what she was going through. And I likely never would. Though female werewolves could be just as persistent as their male counterparts when they had their mind set on a certain mate, and they could definitely be as territorial, I'd never had to worry about that particular problem. Nothing I said right now would comfort her. Still, I had to say something. "I'm sorry some men are pricks."

She huffed a sardonic laugh, but she uncrossed her arms, letting them fall to her sides, and the scent of salt faded.

"It's not an ideal answer, but you can call me anytime he bothers you," I offered.

Yuti sighed through her nose, and the corner of her mouth quirked in a sad little smile as she looked up at me. "Thanks, Rowan. I appreciate that."

As her eyes met mine, the awkwardness that kept popping up between Yuti and me disappeared. I don't know whether it was her little smile, the warmth in her eyes, or her sincere words of thanks, but it didn't really matter. In that instant something changed, slid into place like two gears finally threading in perfect time. We still had a long way to go — I wouldn't have even called us friends — but I knew I could at least talk to her as I would anyone else, any human that is.

I returned her smile. "I don't know about you, but all that testosterone made me hungry. I know it's still a little early, but what say we go get some burgers?"

She lifted her chin, the gesture seeming to dismiss her earlier frustration. "I say, okay. But only if we go to Abby's."

"I've never been. Do they have good burgers?"

She shrugged. "I don't know. I've heard they're pretty good. But more importantly..." She pointed at me for emphasis. "They have veggie burgers."

"What the heck is that?" I scrunched my nose.

Yuti laughed. I'd heard the sound many times before, but it had never seemed so bright and happy in my ears.

"It's a burger made from vegetables, obviously."

"But why?"

"Because I don't eat meat. I'm a vegetarian."

My jaw dropped in horror, and I shook my head. "Nope. I'm sorry. Everything I said about us being friends, I'm going to have to take it all back."

She laughed louder, and I couldn't help but smile.

"Oh, shut up. Are you hungry or not?"

"I am. For *real* food."

"Do you want to walk the whole way there? Because that can be arranged."

I held up my hands in defeat. "Fine. Fine."

"All right then. My car is parked at my place."

Walking alongside her as we headed out, I asked, "You really don't eat meat?"

"I really don't eat meat," she confirmed.

"Huh."

Abby's was a sleek retro diner on the other side of town. It was bright and clean and had everything from burgers and fries to milkshakes and ice cream floats.

I ordered the big, beefy hamburger I was craving. Yuti ordered her veggie cheeseburger and a strawberry milkshake.

"So," she began once we'd placed our orders, "when was the last time you watched *Jurassic Park*?"

"I've never seen it," I told her, playing with the knobs on the little tabletop jukebox.

"What?" Her wide eyes stared at me for a second, blinked a little too long, then reopened to stare yet again. "How is that even possible? That movie is a classic. It's been out forever."

I frowned. It had been a while since I'd talked to anyone new, since I'd had to explain how I didn't know many pop culture references. "I didn't really get to watch movies while I was growing up," I said. "I only just started when I moved here. A year isn't a lot of time to catch up on everything I missed."

"I guess not," she relented. "But why didn't you watch movies? Were your parents strict or something?" Her initial shock gave way to simple curiosity, and my inner tension eased.

"No, nothing like that. We just didn't have a TV. And for a lot of my childhood, I lived on a farm. There was always something that needed doing."

She nodded.

"But I really like movies now that I have the time to watch them. I try to go to the theater every week, and I watch them on my computer at home."

"Have you seen any foreign films?"

I leaned forward. "Like from where?"

"My family is huge into Bollywood movies. My parents came from India, so I grew up with all those."

"I don't think I've seen any Indian movies," I admitted.

"Well, Indian movies and Bollywood movies aren't interchangeable. All Bollywood movies are

Indian, but not all Indian movies are Bollywood." She waved her hand. "There's a lot going on."

I nodded. "Are they in English? I've only seen English-language movies so far."

She shook her head. "There are some English words peppered here and there, but most of them aren't entirely in English. There are English subtitles though. I have some if you're interested in giving it a try sometime."

It's another one-off meeting, but at least it's a start. I smiled. "Yeah, sounds good."

Yuti had been right about *Jurassic Park*. It was a great movie. She sipped at the remains of her drink while I went on about the film in the parking lot.

"Oh man, and the raptors! I was so nervous."

I could feel the other patrons' eyes on me as we walked toward her car, but Yuti just smiled at my enthusiasm.

"You know there are more movies, right? It's a whole series. And that's not even including the *Jurassic World* movies," she informed me.

"Really?"

"Yep."

"I know what I'm going to be doing this weekend."

She chuckled as she unlocked her car door. "I'm sure you'll enjoy them."

After we'd climbed into her car, she asked, "Do you want me to give you a ride home? It seems silly for you to call for a ride."

I wanted to sniff around her apartment again. And as I thought about the deep shadows on her street, I couldn't help but remember the fear in her scent when Warren had approached her. I hadn't considered any other threats at the time, but vampires weren't the only things that could hurt her.

"I'd feel better if I could see you safely home," I admitted.

She watched me for a long moment, the only source of light the parking lot streetlamps. "It's not like the other night, you know. I'm driving, not walking. And it's a short path from the street to my building."

I frowned.

"Let me just take you home." She started the engine as though the discussion was over.

I wasn't pleased, but I didn't argue either. Fighting with her would only make it more difficult to find out what was going on with her overall. And I could always come back and take a sniff around after she dropped me off. She never had to know.

14

uti's scent was strong in the enclosed space of her car. Strangely, the damp earth smell seemed less pronounced than it had earlier in the day, despite the close quarters. Her cinnamon and citrus essence had taken over again. And as I analyzed the scent with every breath, I memorized its unique hints. Cinnamon, citrus, and something I'd never noticed before: the warm sweetness of sandalwood.

"Out of curiosity," Yuti asked, "why are you always dropped off at the café?"

"I don't have a driver's license." My face heated as I thought of the lamppost that hadn't deserved my assault.

Yuti nodded but didn't ask why.

"I should be getting one soon though, I hope. Lia, the owner and manager at the resort, said she would teach me."

Yuti's eyes flicked toward me for only a second before they returned to the road. "I could teach you…if you want. I mean, she must be busy, right? Running a whole resort and everything."

I imagined crashing Yuti's little, yellow car into another unsuspecting pole. "Oh, no. You wouldn't want to do that. I'm really bad at it."

She smirked. "How bad could you be?"

"Bad."

"All right. I mean, it was just a suggestion." Her tone was light, but she frowned in the dim light of the dashboard.

I scolded myself silently. *That would've been the perfect excuse to spend more time with her on a recurring basis.* "A-actually, I'd really appreciate the help…if you don't mind. Lia has to teach her son, too."

"I don't mind at all," she said brightly, her frown disappearing. "When would you like to start?"

The apprehension I'd felt since I'd first decided to get close to Yuti eased a bit. I'd finally landed on a reason for us to meet, a way into her life. "Tomorrow? I have the early shift again. Are you busy after class?"

"Not with anything that can't be moved around."

My chest warmed at my success, and I smiled as I stared out the passenger window. "Thank you."

If Yuti had heard the relief in my voice, she didn't acknowledge it. "No problem," she answered.

When we got closer, I gave her directions. The resort's drive was unlit, and she drove slowly, her headlights bright as they pierced the darkness.

"It must be nice to live way out here." Her voice was hushed as if she didn't want to disturb the trees. "Peaceful. I bet you can really see the stars."

"Yeah, it's beautiful."

Yuti parked near the main house. "Well…" She

turned to me while I unbuckled my seatbelt. "I guess I'll see you tomorrow then."

The awkward tension between us resurfaced as if, after so many hours together, we didn't know how to say goodbye. I smiled through it, wondering why it was back. *Should I stay and talk more? Should I get out quickly? Will she be all right getting home? Will she make it through the night?* I tried to ease the pressure by talking, but my voice was laced with hesitation. "Thanks again for helping me out with my application and for telling me about the nondegree option."

Her tone reflected mine. "No problem. Thanks for the veggie burger and the movie."

Silence pressed in on us, heavier with every moment that passed without a remark.

"All right." I huffed a self-conscious laugh and reached for the door handle. "Goodnight then."

"Wait!" Yuti's voice was high and desperate, and I caught the pungent scent of vinegar. She grabbed my shirt, her fists clenching the fabric as if my life depended on it.

"What? What happened?" My senses spiked to full alertness.

She stumbled over her words as she tried to communicate her distress. "I—I just saw something run across the front of the car. I-it looked like a... *wolf.*"

I peered into the dark just beyond the headlights. And sure enough, I could see the lean lines of Braylyn as he ran around to the back of the house.

I looked over at Yuti, her dark eyes wide and glittering with fright. Resting my hand on hers, I urged her to meet my gaze. "It's all right," I gently assured her. "There's nothing to worry about. There are tons of wolves around here. We're a...sort of refuge for them."

Her grip on my shirt eased though she didn't let go. "They don't hurt anything?"

I shook my head. "Not at all. We welcome them here."

Yuti took a deep breath and sighed. The tickle of air brushed over the skin of my neck and collarbone where my shirt was pulled aside. The tang of her fear decreased though it hung in the air. "Okay. But shouldn't you wait until it's gone before you get out?"

"I'm sure he'll run away as soon as he sees me."

"Still..."

I smiled softly at her. "All right, I'll give him a minute."

The rest of her anxiety faded, and she released my shirt, pulling her hand from mine.

She laughed, hesitant, embarrassed. "Jeez, that scared me."

"It was a bit of a surprise," I agreed.

"You said wolves come here a lot?"

I inclined my head. "There's pretty much always one around."

"Really?" Now that she was no longer afraid, her tone lit with excitement. "Do you think I could come up here sometime to draw? I'd love to have a live subject."

I shifted my weight in my seat, wondering whether I'd gone too far in trying to comfort her. "I thought you were afraid of them?"

Her lips pursed ever so slightly in a pout. "Well...I mean, you were about to get out of the car, and I didn't know what to expect. And anyway, I'm not saying I want to reach out and pet them or anything. But I wouldn't mind drawing one from a safe distance. They are beautiful creatures."

I didn't know what to feel. On one hand, she'd been terrified only a moment before. But on the other, she thought we were beautiful—so much so that she wanted to create art of us. Still, I couldn't imagine it was a good idea for a human to be sniffing around so closely. I'd had to tell her something to calm her down, but I didn't know my explanation would have this effect.

"I'll…ask Lia about it," I hedged.

"I appreciate it. Thanks."

I nodded, our clumsy goodbyes from only minutes before gone and forgotten. "All right. Are you okay now? Do you think I've given him enough of a head start?"

"Yeah, I'm fine, and I think you're good."

I opened the car door and stepped out. Then I bent to meet her eyes. "Goodnight."

"'Night," she called, waving her hand.

After closing the door, I watched her turn around and drive up the private road. Then I turned on my heel and stomped toward the back of the house. "Braylyn!" I barked.

15

found Braylyn cowering in the shadows behind the house, his tail between his legs. My anger dissipated at seeing him so downcast, but I couldn't let him know that.

I crossed my arms over my chest. "Explain yourself."

He lowered his head.

"Go on. She's gone now."

A moment later, the naked boy stood before me, his head still bowed. "I-I didn't know," he whined. "T-there was a raccoon, and I wasn't paying attention, and—"

I sighed heavily. "You're lucky I was able to calm her down, but now we have a different problem on our hands." I eased my stern look a bit. "All right. Go on inside. I'll explain everything to your mom."

The boy at least had the decency to look scolded as he did what he was told.

I followed shortly after. I found Lia and Noire in

the study. Lia was on her computer at the desk, and Noire was lying on the couch with a book.

"We…may have a problem," I said, stopping to stand before Lia's desk. Then I related what had happened with Yuti and Braylyn.

Lia listened carefully, her expression smooth and unconcerned. "Werewolf is not the first explanation most humans land on," she said when I told her Yuti didn't seem suspicious.

"But I don't know how long it will stay that way, especially if she comes up here to draw us," I countered.

Lia laced her fingers together as she rested her elbows on the desk. "I'll table that decision for now. It's never a good idea to let humans who aren't joining the pack get too close. But I also don't see how it could hurt. Your explanation left something to be desired though. You couldn't have come up with something better?" She waved away any excuse I had. "Never mind. Did you find out more about her change in scent?"

I shook my head. "No, but it was stronger when we first met up this afternoon, then it sort of faded as the night went on."

Lia frowned but didn't share her thoughts. "Did you come up with a better solution for getting closer to her?"

"She offered to teach me to drive. I'm supposed to meet her again after work tomorrow."

"Good idea." She turned back to her computer, and it was clear I was dismissed.

I shifted my weight from one foot to the other. "Uh, Lia?"

She raised an eyebrow at me.

"Given that the scent was stronger today than yesterday, I'd like to take another sniff around her apartment tonight. Do you mind if I go back into town? Just to check that she's safe at home."

Lia stared at me a moment, and I froze, trying not to squirm under her steady gaze. "All right," she said finally. "Have Ashwin take you. He's our best tracker. He may pick up something that you can't."

I bobbed my head and left the study.

Ashwin and Lune were in the living room, playing some racing game on the television. Ashwin cheered and held up his arms just as I entered.

"Victory!"

Lune shook his head dramatically. "This is literally the first time you've ever beaten me."

"First of many, pup," Ashwin corrected.

Lune rolled his eyes. "Whatever."

"Rowan, did you see that?" Ashwin stood and gestured at the screen. "Did you see me decimate this little punk?"

"Decimate?" Lune protested. "I was only a second behind."

"Someone is being a sore loser," Ashwin teased.

Lune sucked air in through his nose, his face reddening in preparation for an outburst.

"Ashwin, Lia wants you to take me into town." I hoped that changing the subject would prevent Lune's rage from taking hold. "I need your nose."

Ashwin raised his eyebrows.

"I'll tell you on the way."

"I'll just get my keys."

The moment Ashwin was out of the room, I glanced over at Lune. "Aw, let him have it. You know that's probably the only time he's going to win."

Lune sighed, his irritation already gone.

Ashwin didn't seem to mind the trip into town. If anything, he was excited to smell the scent Noire and I had talked about for himself.

It was quiet inside the truck; even the old engine barely disturbed the silence. There was an empty space in the dash where there might have been a radio at one time. Despite its age, Ashwin took good care of his truck. The bench seat was comfortable and the upholstery clean.

Unlike his sister, Ashwin didn't like silence when it wasn't absolutely necessary. "I'm going to visit our parents in Faerie in a few days. Would you like to come with me? I bet your parents would like to see you, too."

I winced at the unexpected offer. I hadn't seen my parents or Willow in months. I didn't like the questions, the expectations, that came with being around them.

"I need to keep an eye on Yuti right now. Maybe next time."

Ashwin didn't argue, but we both knew Yuti wasn't the only reason I wouldn't be going to Faerie.

"Will Noire go with you?" I asked.

Ashwin's expression stiffened. "I don't think so."

"This is the third or fourth time you've gone to Faerie since I've been here. She has never gone with you. Why is that?"

He sighed. The silence that followed was so uncharacteristic that I wondered whether he would dodge my question.

"It's not really my place to tell her story," he said finally. "But you're a full pack member now. And if I don't tell you, you may never know. Unlike us, my sister… Noire never completed her rite. She's not a member of Faerie werewolf society."

My mouth went dry. Having been raised to believe that completing my rite was the single most important duty of my life, I couldn't help my unconscious reaction. "Did her bondmate die?" I whispered as if it was some secret we needed to keep from the world.

"Yes. But it was so much more complex than that. Noire…loved her bondmate, was in love with her bondmate."

I froze, the air in the cab suddenly feeling heavy, almost too thick to breathe. "Like Runa," I whispered.

Ashwin nodded. "Yeah… Noire and Heiden planned on eloping in the realm of origin. But he died before they could. He was snatched by a vampire… She couldn't save him."

I felt for Noire. I couldn't imagine losing a bondmate that way, let alone one I was in love with. But I'd seen the desperation, the agony, Runa had felt when Konner had been taken. I'd felt only a small share of it through the promised bond. At the time, I'd been more worried about keeping my promised safe. To me, even to his parents and brother, Konner was dead the moment he was taken.

And though I'd lost the woman I love, I was glad Konner had survived. I'd grown up with him. He was like a brother to me. Sure, he was my rival, but that didn't mean I didn't love him too. And as much as it hurt me to think about it, I knew now that Runa would've been completely crushed if he'd died, a nightmare Noire had actually endured.

16

shwin parked a block away from Yuti's building in a place where no one would think twice about two guys leaving their pickup truck in the middle of the night. We walked the rest of the way, moving silently from shadow to shadow in just the way a vampire might. I was glad to see Yuti's little, yellow car parked on the street.

Once we'd reached the building, I pointed to where a pathway led around to the back.

The insistent chirps of crickets sounded loud in my ears as I listened hard to the night. I heard Ashwin's delicate sniffs while we slipped through the darkness.

There was no chance a human with normal sight would see us among the trees of the backyard near Yuti's window. But we stood still and quiet just the same.

The light in her apartment glowed softly behind pink curtains. I sniffed the gentle breeze. I smelled earth and trees, but the scent was warm and dry and directly related to the fact that we stood amongst a group of thick oaks and maples.

Just as I was about to suggest to Ashwin we leave, Yuti opened her drapes, and light spilled into the darkness. She lifted her window with a little effort and stared into the night, lingering as if to enjoy the fresh air.

Her dark hair was damp, and she wore a thin-strapped tank top and boyshorts. I couldn't recall another time I'd seen her without a hat. It was clear she had just gotten out of the shower even before her fresh, clean scent drifted over to me. I breathed deep the tangy citrus smell, my heart jumping out of time. I wondered if it was her shampoo.

Any trace of potential vampire scent she'd carried around with her that day was completely gone.

She sat down to one side of the window, and I inched over to see her better at the new angle. She must've been sitting in front of a mirror because she leaned forward and started to rub cream into her face. Then she rubbed her hands together and trailed them up her arms, spreading lotion on her brown skin.

The strong scent of cinnamon with the slightest hint of beeswax and the zest of orange wafted to me, and I sighed.

Ashwin glared at me, chiding me for the rush of breath I'd failed to silence. He grabbed me by the arm and tugged, signaling that we were leaving.

But when a phone rang in Yuti's apartment, Ashwin and I froze.

"Shit," she murmured, hurriedly rubbing her

palms on her thighs. "Hello?" Her tone sounded clipped in its rush.

"No, not at all. I just had lotion on my hands. What's up?"

Her voice was clear as if she were standing right beside me, but I doubt even her neighbors heard her.

"Actually, can we move it up earlier in the day? I'm meeting Rowan after his shift."

My ears pricked at my name.

"Yeah? So what?"

She paused as her caller spoke. Then she smiled. "I do," she said softly.

Her smile turned to a scowl. "You sound as if I'm not always honest."

During another pause, she balanced the phone on her ear and continued rubbing lotion into her skin.

"How?"

I strained to hear what the person on the other end was saying, but all I could pick up on was the low timbre of a male voice.

"I am not... Am I?"

The caller responded.

"I was surprised when he asked for my help."

My heart thumped. *Are they talking about me?*

"I just can't—"

I shifted my weight self-consciously and accidentally stepped on a twig. Its snap covered the rest of her reply. I froze and glanced at Ashwin, who bared his teeth in displeasure.

There was silence inside her apartment. *Did she hear me?*

She laughed. "Shut up. He does not."

I released my sigh of relief as quietly as I could.

"No, if he meets you too soon, he'll run away screaming," she teased.

Is she talking about me? But why would her friend want to meet me?

"Aw, well, I'll always love you. You know that. Even if you are a weirdo."

Is this her friend or her boyfriend?

"Pff. Whatever. Is there anything else you want to harass me about?"

Another short pause.

"Okay. I'll talk to you tomorrow then. Bye."

After tapping her phone, Yuti got up from her chair and disappeared. A moment later, the light went out.

I frowned at the still-opened window. That little screen wouldn't protect her if someone—or something—wanted to get in.

Ashwin tugged on my shirt, and I followed him through the night, returning to his truck.

"Are you sure you guys smelled what you say you smelled?" he asked as he began to drive home. "Because I didn't smell anything of the sort, just girlie bath products." He curled his lip as if he'd found the scents of Yuti's products unpleasant.

I blinked at his distaste. "I didn't smell it anymore either. But it was definitely there earlier. Noire confirmed it."

Ashwin shrugged. "Strange."

Staring out the window as the night whizzed by, I thought about what it could all mean. And I hoped we would have some idea before it was too late.

I'd planned to head to bed after I told Lia that the scent was gone, at least for the moment. But as I pushed the door of the study open farther, all plans were forgotten. Lune sat on the couch, hanging his head as if he'd been recently scolded.

Lia and Noire looked up as Ashwin and I entered.

"I was just about to call you," Lia said. "It seems we have a bigger problem on our hands."

17

"Tell them," Lia ordered.

Lune glanced up for only a moment before dropping his gaze to his lap. "I was out in the meadow."

"Alone?" Ashwin raised his eyebrows.

The boys were not to run that far out alone.

Lune shook his head almost imperceptibly. "I was with Zoe."

The room went silent. Lune had not only been that far out this time of night, but he'd taken a human girl with him.

"Continue," his mother commanded.

"While we were…out there, I smelled a vampire. I knew it right away even though it's been a long time since I've smelled it." Lune glanced at his mom.

Her expression offered him no comfort.

"A-anyway, we left right away."

"Long time is right. How long has it been since we've had a confirmed vampire in our territory?" Ashwin asked.

"Braylyn was in kindergarten," Noire answered.

Ashwin whistled. "That long, huh? Is it just one?"

Lia sighed. "He doesn't know how many there were, but he said the trail was fresh."

"I guess there's nothing for it then." Ashwin stretched his arms above his head. "Looks like a good ole hunt to me."

"I agree," Lia said. "And we should all go, just to be safe."

Lune sat up straighter and dared to look up.

"Not you," Lia corrected.

Lune flinched.

"Stay here with your bother. Don't wake him up if you can avoid it. And stay inside."

Lia jerked her head at the rest of us. "Everyone else, get changed."

We went to our respective bedrooms to shift and gathered in the kitchen less than five minutes later.

Lune opened the back door, and we trotted out.

Lia moved forward, and Ashwin and Noire flanked her a few steps behind. I brought up the rear.

We started to run through the forest toward the meadow, sniffing the air as we went. After a few miles, we slowed down as we approached the spot. The waxing crescent moon struggled to shine through the clouds overhead, but my wolf's eyes didn't need it to see the meadow, thick with tall grass and yellow wildflowers.

The night was eerily quiet, danger silencing the creatures around us. My ears swiveled as a gust of wind rustled the grasses.

I lifted my nose and sniffed the breeze as we

stalked forward. Finally, I caught the scent of our prey. Lia led us slowly through the brush in that direction.

We paused for only a moment at the edge of the tall grass before entering the forest on the other side of the meadow.

The rank mixture of earth and decay increased with every step, and we picked up the pace as we neared it.

Eventually, our quarries came into view. Two vampires sat on a fallen tree as if they were having a chat on a park bench.

"I'm hungry," one complained to the other.

"You're always hungry," the other said.

The first one shrugged. "Maybe it's the quality of the food. It's unsatisfying."

Its companion frowned. "Where would you like to eat?"

I didn't register the peculiarity of the exchange as we spread out to surround them, so strange was it for two vampires to be not only together but also having a coherent conversation. It went against everything I'd been taught.

Lia moved her head in such a way that I understood she wanted me to break off with Ashwin while Noire was to pair with her.

At Lia's snarl, we fell upon them.

But these weren't the newly turned vampires I'd dealt with the week before. They were quick even when surprised.

The one Ashwin and I went for bolted, slipping right past us. We pursued it, and the chase began.

My heart pounded in the thrill of the hunt, and warmth radiated through me. My paws struck the ground in a rhythmic beat. Wind ruffled my fur. A howl rose in my throat as if I couldn't silence my exhilaration. Ashwin joined me, and so did Lia and Noire, now well behind us.

The scent of our prey shifted, the sweet decay cleansed by the vinegar of fear. It glanced over a shoulder, its eyes looking very human as they widened.

Ashwin pounced not a second later, and I was on it a moment after that.

We ripped and tore at the thing, its joints popping and its bones cracking beneath our jaws. It screamed for nearly a minute before we silenced it.

With its heart torn out and lying beside its mangled corpse, we were satisfied that it couldn't regenerate. We raced back to the others, but Lia and Noire had been as successful as we had, their prey's head chewed off.

Lia shifted to human form, her naked body splattered with blood. "We need to bury the evidence. Separate the parts, and dig some holes."

I didn't sleep well during what was left of that night. If I slept at all, it was the fitful sort where I thought I was awake, but then I'd suddenly jolt into awareness with the realization I'd drifted off. My mind swirled with questions. *Were the vampires we just eliminated the ones who attacked Yuti? When and where was she attacked?*

And then there were the darker thoughts that stalked the others. *Is she too far along in her transformation? Is it too late for her?*

I didn't want to think about that possibility, didn't want to think about my teeth tearing into her flesh, especially not while the taste of vampire still lingered at the back of my throat. If it was too late, if she was already well on her way to being turned, then we'd have to make sure she didn't take anyone else's future.

As the scent of fresh air from the open window shifted with the approach of dawn, I stopped trying to sleep. I had work in a few hours anyway. Though

I knew the other wolves would hear me moving around, I tried to be as quiet as I could when I went to the bathroom and took a shower.

The water, cool and refreshing, washed away the last traces of drowsiness.

After getting dressed, I sat down at my desk and took out a sheet of paper.

Dear Runa,

My hand froze, the blank paper suddenly too big a space to fill.

Leaving the unfinished letter on my desk, I took the pen and went to the front hall. A vase of sunflowers sat on a long table, which was pushed up against the wall. A few of the yellow petals had fallen onto the table, and the rest were looking sort of droopy.

The table also had a collection of postcards with pictures of the resort and the town. I grabbed a postcard, the picture a night scene of Beyahish Mountain, the sky bright with stars. Then I picked up the vase and brought everything to the kitchen.

After filling the vase with water from the tap, I sat down at the kitchen table with my pen and postcard.

Dear Runa,
I'm still here.
Rowan

On the smaller space of the postcard, my words didn't seem so inadequate. I made out the address and put a stamp on it.

I stared at what I'd written. Never had I been so short with Runa before. I clenched my jaw. *Maybe I should write a full letter after all. But what else is there to say?*

Before I could make a decision, Lia came into the kitchen.

She moved around me as I stood before the stamp drawer. "I've been thinking about what you and Ashwin told me last night after we got home. And the more I think about it, the surer I am. Rowan, are you listening?"

I flipped over the postcard and looked at her. "Yes. You have an idea of what's going on with Yuti?"

She nodded as she took the pot from the coffee maker to the sink and held it under the faucet. "I don't think she's been bitten, and I don't think she's been fed any vampire blood."

My attention sharpened. "So she isn't in any danger?" I asked once she'd turned off the faucet.

"No, I didn't say that." She poured water into the coffee maker, then pulled the coffee tin down from the cupboard. "I think the reason the scent seems stronger sometimes and other times it's not there at all is because it's coming from someone she has contact with."

I frowned. "You think someone she knows is a vampire?"

Lia scooped coffee grounds into the reusable basket. "Or someone she knows has been bitten or fed vamp blood."

"The scent of those two last night wasn't the same as what I smelled on Yuti."

After pressing the brew button on the coffee

maker, Lia turned her full attention to me. "They might have attacked someone she knows, or they could be unconnected."

My mind swirled. *Back to the beginning then.*

"The easiest way to know what's going on is to keep close to her, find out who she's been around lately."

I took in a fortifying breath, then sighed it out all at once. "All right."

Lia watched me for a moment, meeting my eyes, then nodded. "Good. Now help me make breakfast."

I helped Lia in the kitchen, but my mind was still on the questions at hand. *Where is the smell coming from? Who could it be? And how long before Yuti becomes a target?*

Lia dropped me off at work that morning, and I slipped my postcard into a mailbox on my way in.

Camille was even more persistent than she had been the previous day. She wanted to know why Yuti and I had left together. She wanted to know every detail of what we did. But I didn't give her what she asked for.

"How am I supposed to help you if you won't let me?" Camille complained, scattering sugar onto the counter as she flung out her arm while holding the sugar dispenser.

I didn't respond, my mind too full of the problem at hand to indulge her silly fantasies. I just grabbed a rag and wiped the spilled sugar into my hand.

"Rowan," she said, her tone mischievous.

I emptied my palm over the trash can, then looked at her.

"Go open the door." She was grinning.

I glanced at the clock. "We still have ten minutes

before we open. The coffee isn't even finished brewing. And I still have to — "

"I'll take care of it," she snapped. "Just go open the door."

I scrunched my eyebrows. But as I turned to the glass door, I saw why she was being so insistent. Yuti sat on a picnic table, her legs dangling off the side.

My heart thumped and kept thumping the closer I got. *Will she smell like vampire today?* She wore short overalls, the sides of her midriff bare where her crop top stopped and the waist of the overalls began. Today she had on a wide-brimmed hat with a round crown.

She looked over at me when I started to turn the lock.

"Are you opening early today?" she asked with a smile as I opened the door. "I was ready to wait."

Her dark eyes sparkled in the morning sunlight, and I took a deep breath, trying to quiet the beating of my heart. Her scent was clear and clean. Cinnamon and citrus with a slight hint of sandalwood. Purely Yuti.

19

"Yeah." The tightness in my chest eased when I saw that she'd made it to morning unscathed. "I guess we're opening a little early today. Come on in."

"First in line before everyone else? It must be my lucky day," she commented as I held the door open for her.

"How was your night?" I asked. "I assume you got home all right."

"I did. It was good. And yours?" Her tone was friendly and easy.

"Good," I lied.

She stared at me sidelong for a moment. If she saw the circles under my eyes, she didn't acknowledge them.

"What can I get you this morning, Yuti?" Camille asked when Yuti stepped up to the counter.

"I have an early class, so I'm in a bit of a rush. Just an iced coffee with sugar, and leave space for cream. Thanks."

Camille went about getting Yuti's drink. But I could see her smile as she turned her back to the counter. "In a rush and still came all the way here so early—I appreciate the customer loyalty."

My skin prickled at Camille's insinuation, and I hoped Yuti was unaware of it. We had just found a friendly rhythm. I didn't want Camille mucking it up by insisting we should be more.

"The coffee at the cafeteria can't compare to The Rapids for sure," she said to Camille.

Camille's only response was to place the iced coffee on the counter. Her grin was a little too wide, and it was making me self-conscious. Yuti didn't seem to notice. Then again, her gaze was preoccupied, and I felt it on me like the breeze on my bare skin.

"Well, I, uh, have to run. But I'll come back this afternoon when you get off."

I nodded and hoped my smile didn't seem forced. "Right. Okay. See you later then."

My gaze clung to her, how she tilted her head as she poured cream into her drink until it looked more like a milkshake than a coffee, how her bag tapped against her leg as she hurried to the door. I was interrupted only when Camille leaned her elbow on the counter, forcing me to face her.

"Ah, something changed. Didn't it?" she asked.

"Not really," I said.

"You're a horrible liar. What is it? Are you finally starting to notice our little Yuti?"

I snorted. "You make it sound as though she was invisible this whole time."

Camille raised an eyebrow above her purple sunglasses. "Wasn't she?"

I frowned. It was true. I *hadn't* been paying attention to Yuti. Every day for nearly a year I'd seen her but never really looked at her. I'd talked to her but never really listened. I didn't care to. *Am I paying attention now only because of the mysterious smell?*

My stomach clenched. These thoughts made me uncomfortable. But I didn't have to sit with them for long because the morning rush started with our official opening time.

Somehow my shift seemed to last forever despite the fact that it was unusually busy even during normally slow times. But at two in the afternoon, Max took over, and I was free.

Yuti wasn't in the café when I got off work. But as I stepped outside, I saw her car parked on the street. I bent down to look through the closed window. Yuti gestured for me to get in.

The moment I opened the door, all of my nerves stood at attention. It smelled as if Yuti had just crawled out of a fresh grave.

"Get in," Yuti called from the driver's seat.

I didn't want to. I didn't want to be trapped with the scent. Still, I forced myself to climb in and even closed the door.

"What's up? You've got a really weird look on your face."

"Do you mind if we turn off the air and roll down the windows?" I asked while trying not to breathe.

"I guess not." She reached out and turned off the air conditioner.

I cranked the window handle on my side, and she did the same. Fresh air rushed into the car, and I breathed a little easier.

"Thanks."

"No problem. I've got a great place to practice. You ready?"

I nodded. And as she started to drive, I analyzed her. "So...what did you do today?" It took all my self-control not to sound urgent.

"Hmm? Oh, let's see...I went to my morning class. Um...did a little grocery shopping and some homework."

"That's it?" My self-control slipped with every word. "Did you meet up with anyone or see anyone you've been seeing a lot the last few days? What did you do *right* before you picked me up?"

Her shoulders tensed, and she shot me a glance. "I had lunch at my apartment. Why the sudden interest in my exact movements?"

I sucked in a breath. Her tone was a warning. I'd asked too much too soon. It was clear she didn't like her new friend demanding to know where she'd been, whom she'd seen. But when I'd smelled that dank stench muddling her scent—smothering it—I had to know where it came from. I had to know where the potential danger was.

I wanted to shrug and play it off, but I knew I wouldn't be able to do it convincingly. So I bluffed a little.

"It's nothing," I said. "I just... Remember those guys that were being dicks yesterday when we were at the Student Union?"

She nodded. "Warren and Dustin."

"Well, I was on campus the other day—just relaxing in the quad—and I overheard them talking. I'm not sure it was about you, but it could have been. Anyway, Warren doesn't seem to be the kind of guy who takes 'no' for an answer. Last night, I couldn't place where I'd seen them. But once I did, I guess…I just wanted to make sure they didn't bother you today."

Yuti sighed, then pursed her lips a little.

I couldn't discern her reaction, couldn't tell whether she was irritated or something else.

"I didn't run into them today if that's what you're asking. I appreciate the concern, but I'll let you know if I need help with them."

"All right." I cursed myself internally for having fucked up my best lead.

20

It took about ten minutes for Yuti to drive to where we were going. I was silent the whole time. I couldn't think of how to broach the subject again, especially since I'd given such a plausible excuse.

"Here we are," she said as she pulled into what was probably an old parking lot.

If there had ever been a building on the site, it wasn't there anymore. Any parking lines had long since faded, and the asphalt was cracked. I eyed the three light poles.

"Are you ready?" She turned the engine off.

I made a noncommittal grunt, and her answering laugh cleared the remnants of tension.

"Seriously though, you can stop anytime you're uncomfortable." Her eyes met mine.

I unbuckled my seatbelt. After getting out, I walked around the car to switch places with her. The late spring air seemed hot and heavy, an unusual sensation since I was used to the mountain breeze.

I opened the door and slid into the driver's seat. My feet caught under the pedals, and my knee banged against the base of the steering wheel as I tried to adjust my legs.

Yuti giggled at my struggle. "Okay. You're obviously taller than me, so you're going to want to adjust the seat and mirrors. Make sure they're angled so that you can tell whether something is coming up beside you or behind you."

I rummaged around for a lever that would adjust the seat, but I couldn't find it. "How do I move the seat back?"

"There's a bar underneath."

I reached between my legs and felt under the seat. "Where?"

Yuti rose on her knees and leaned over, reaching her hand between my legs and under the seat. With a sharp jerk of her arm, she turned her head to look at me.

I froze, not expecting her to suddenly be so close. With my heart pounding, I took a shallow breath. Her natural scent washed over me. And though I could still smell the vampire scent, our drive with the windows down had aired much of it out. My thoughts couldn't gain traction with her dark eyes staring at me like that.

Her cheeks took on a warm undertone, and I realized she was blushing. It looked so different on her compared to Runa. Then again, she seemed the exact opposite of Runa in every way. Hair dark instead of white, eyes brown instead of light gray.

And her skin was a dusky wheat instead of a fair cream.

"Push with your legs." Her voice was hushed.

It took me a second to comprehend her words, her proximity filling most of my brain. But then I complied, and the seat slid back.

Yuti retreated. She cleared her throat, glancing past me out the driver's window. "Now the mirrors."

"Right." It took me a few minutes to get the mirrors just right, and I felt more and more embarrassed the longer I fumbled around. But I eventually got it.

"Okay. Before we start the car." Her voice became clearer, less uncertain, as she went on. She carefully explained the pedals, the turn signal, and the gear shift.

She paused and I glanced over at her. Eye contact seemed to be what she was waiting for.

"Are you ready?" she asked.

"Maybe?"

Her response to my uncertainty was calm, gentle. "We aren't going to do anything hard today, okay? You don't even have to worry about pressing the gas. We can just coast and steer."

"Okay."

"All right," she said brightly.

I turned the key and let it go as the car roared to life. The engine seemed much louder than it had when Yuti had been driving.

She directed me through each step, and I followed her instructions with precision. With every turn, I felt a little less anxious. And with every turn, my smile got a little wider.

"Okay. Let's try braking. You're going to want

to ease your foot down gently. Don't just slam it down."

I tried my best, but we still jerked to a stop. "Sorry," I muttered.

"It's fine. It takes a bit of practice." She reached out and shifted into park. "So do you want to try something a little more difficult?"

I looked sidelong at her. "Like what?"

"We could try weaving through these lampposts."

"I don't know…"

"You've got a lot of space between them, and you've done well at steering so far."

I bit my cheek but nodded.

A half an hour later, I was grinning like an idiot as Yuti pulled out of the parking lot. Her car had made it through unscathed as had the lampposts.

"Thanks for today," I said.

"You did good. You'll be on the road in no time."

I didn't argue with her even if I couldn't agree. After a few moments back in the passenger seat, the thrill and anxiety from my drive eased, and I settled back into my normal mind-space. I watched Yuti as she concentrated on the road. Someone she knew, someone around her, was putting her in danger. And I needed to stop it.

"Do you have plans for tomorrow?" I asked.

She glanced over at me. "Why? What's up?"

"I was thinking about that foreign film you mentioned. And I was wondering if you had time to watch it with me."

"Tomorrow is Friday. Isn't it open-mic night at The Rapids? You guys are usually packed. Don't you have to work?"

"I do. So I thought maybe…before my shift?"

She was quiet for a moment, and I worried I'd screwed up again.

"Sure." She smiled. "I have a morning class, but why don't you come over after that?"

"When?"

"Like ten? Bollywood movies tend to be pretty long, but that should give us enough time before your shift."

"Cool. I'll be there."

21

*A*fter updating Lia on what had happened that day, I took a shower and slipped into bed. I wanted to run. I wanted to clear my head of the vampire scent that had clung to Yuti. But I hadn't slept the night before, and I was tired. Unfortunately, I found no rest. My dreams were twisted mixtures of memory and fear.

The solstice moon was full and bright, illuminating the dirt road. The fields of crops rustled in the new summer breeze.

Despite knowing that there were other wolves around me, I couldn't help but be on edge. I sniffed the air out of habit, and what I smelled was anything but natural.

Dark earth, damp and rich. And the sickly sweetness of decay. My jaw ached as I clenched my teeth together. A growl rumbled in my throat. A vampire was near.

"Stop!" Konner's voice echoed into the suddenly hushed night, the sounds of crickets and owls silenced.

My skin tingled as my hackles rose. I jerked my head around to Wilhelm to see how the other wolves were responding.

Wilhelm wasn't there. Konner, Runa, Keita, Lars, Anyte, and their faelings—they weren't there. Only Yuti stood on the dark road.

Wearing a summer hat, Yuti tilted her head and smirked at me. "What's up? You've got a really weird look on your face."

Panic seized me and I ran toward her. My heart pounded and my muscles strained as I pushed my body to its limit. Adrenaline pumped through me, my desperation burning like bile in my throat. *Why isn't she getting any closer?*

Then I saw it. A shiver made my tail twitch. My strong legs—my very soul—began to quake. Its eyes shone in the moonlight. Its skin was pale and lifeless. Sharp and stained, its fangs glinted with saliva. But I couldn't see its face.

It lurked over Yuti's shoulder. She didn't look behind her. I called out to her to watch out, but the human words sounded like huffs and whines from my wolf mouth. I howled until my throat was raw, aching with every breath. She just stood smirking at me.

The creature wrapped its arms around her, its bloodless skin stark against hers. She didn't notice. She didn't squirm or fight. My heart screamed in my chest. *Don't touch her!*

I froze as the wet tearing of the soft flesh of her throat made my ears twitch. Horror. Disbelief. Anguish. I couldn't move to save her. I'd already failed.

She didn't have a chance to scream. A small gasp escaped her lips, and then she was dragged into darkness.

I slammed awake as if I'd fallen onto my bed from a great height. I gasped for air, my face and neck slick with sweat. My heart still raced in my chest.

I took a controlled breath, then let it out in a ragged sigh.

A cool night breeze drifted in through my window. And the crickets and owls still sang their songs.

I tried to swallow, but my mouth was too dry. Closing my eyes for only a moment, my stomach lurched—the image of Yuti being drained of life was still on the backs of my eyelids.

My eyes flew open, and I sprang up in my bed. I took a few more deep breaths and got up to get a glass of water.

By the time I stood in the kitchen with half of the glass drained, my heartbeat had evened out, and my sweat had dried.

I returned to my room, hoping I hadn't woken anyone else. I glanced at my alarm clock. It was two in the morning. I thought about trying to go back to sleep, but I was afraid of reentering the same dream.

I went to my desk and turned on my computer. After pulling up the second *Back to the Future* movie,

I took the laptop to my bed and placed it beside my pillow so I could watch while lying down. But I was too tired to pay attention. I drifted off to sleep during the first half.

Dawn had long passed by the time I awoke the next morning, and I was grateful that the rest of my night had been undisturbed by nightmares.

I shuffled into the kitchen. Breakfast was over, so I grabbed a box from the cupboard and settled for cold cereal.

Lia entered a few spoonfuls in, stomping her rain boots on the mat just inside the door. "Ah, you're up."

I looked over at her. "You could have woken me."

"Nah. You've been working hard, and it sounded like you had a nightmare last night."

I wasn't surprised Lia knew. I'd likely been making sounds in my sleep, and she was the alpha after all.

"I'm heading into town to do some grocery shopping in a bit if you'd like to catch a ride." She filled a glass with water from the tap.

I swallowed another spoonful of cereal. "It's still a little while before I'm supposed to meet with Yuti, but I can occupy myself until then."

After taking a drink from the glass, Lia said, "All right. Well, you should probably go and take a shower before we leave. You smell like stale fear."

My appetite faded as the horrible images from my nightmare flashed in my mind, but I shoved another spoonful into my mouth.

22

I had Lia drop me off at the university. I thought about sitting in the cafeteria to practice, but the moment I sat down at a table, I knew I wouldn't be able to be still for long.

Instead, I walked around campus searching for the scent. It was a real possibility that whoever the scent was coming from was a teacher or student. After all, Yuti went to campus every day. It was the most likely place she would be exposed.

The university wasn't huge, but sniffing around every floor of every building took longer than I'd expected. And the morning rain had bogged everything down with a wet sort of smell. Even inside, people had tracked their wet shoes up and down the stairs and all over the carpets. And though it was different from the strange scent coming from Yuti recently, it was similar enough to make things difficult.

I started with the creative arts building and

moved on to the liberal arts, but I couldn't find that particular smell.

I did, however, catch a whiff of Yuti's unique mixture of cinnamon and citrus in one of the buildings with large lecture halls. I peeked in through the little glass window in the door. Yuti sat in the front row, her brow furrowed in concentration as the professor spoke in a language I wasn't familiar with.

Though I was thorough, I found no vampire smell in that building.

I hadn't even reached the science or engineering buildings when my phone chimed in my pocket.

It was my first text from Yuti.

> Hey, I'm going to be a little late. My class went overtime. I'm heading there now. Sorry.

The clock on my phone said it was a little past ten. Instead of heading straight to her apartment, I moved toward the building I'd seen her in.

I found Yuti near the clock tower, walking at a brisk pace in the direction of her apartment. She stared down at the ground as if she needed to concentrate on executing each step. She didn't notice me tailing her, and I frowned at the implications. I followed close behind her for about fifty feet, hoping she would notice and turn around.

Finally, I slid up next to her, matching my pace with hers. "You really should pay more attention to your surroundings," I chided lightly.

She whipped her head around, her eyes wide with surprise, and a little gasp escaped her lips.

My stomach dropped at the sound, so close to the one from my nightmare.

Her shock abated, and she sighed. "God, you scared me."

"I've been following you since the clock tower."

She looked over her shoulder. "Really? I didn't notice."

"I know."

She lifted an eyebrow, her lips quirking in that playful smirk. "Are you stalking me now?"

Stalking. Hunting prey. Ready to pounce at any moment. "No, but if I had been, you'd be an easy target." My tone didn't match her teasing one.

She clicked her tongue, her smirk gone. "You think so?" She stopped in her tracks and shoved her hand into her bag. "I don't think I'm so helpless." She produced a small, pink tube from her bag and held it out flat in her hand.

"What's that?" I asked.

"Pepper spray."

I didn't know what that was, and it must have shown on my face.

"For deterring anyone who doesn't take 'no' for an answer. You spray it in their eyes, and it burns like hell. Oh, and this." She lifted her bag and showed me a little, white keychain about the size and shape of a flash drive. "It's a rape alarm. If I pull it, it makes an ear-splitting beeping sound."

I stared at the little, plastic stick. "Smart."

She started walking again, and I kept pace with her.

"I also pack a mean punch. Think about that next time you try to surprise me. You never know. I might swing first and ask questions later."

All of that did reassure me a little. I wondered whether she was really unaware or whether I'd been able to surprise her only because I was a werewolf. On the other hand, a vampire could be just as silent. *Does pepper spray work on vampires? The alarm certainly will draw attention to her if she's attacked though her punch isn't likely to be very effective against a supernatural enemy.*

She glanced sidelong at me. "Do you still want to watch the movie, or would you like a demonstration?"

I thought about it for a moment. A demonstration would likely make me feel more at ease, but I decided her tone said only one of those choices was really an option. "What movie are we going to watch?"

"*Dilwale Dulhania Le Jayenge.*" A little twinkle lit her eyes as she smiled, and the pitch of her voice rose with excitement the more she went on. "If you're only going to watch one Bollywood movie, it needs to be DDLJ. It's a must. It stars the king of Bollywood, Shah Rukh Khan. Plus, it's referenced in tons of other Bollywood movies. So if you do watch any others, you'll get those references."

Her enthusiasm washed over me, quickening my pulse. "Okay. I'm convinced. What's it about?"

"You'll just have to wait and see."

I chuckled. "Well, I do love a good surprise."

As we walked across campus, I shoved my chilled hands into the pocket of my hooded sweatshirt. It was colder today. The early rain had cooled any chance of heat. And though it had stopped for the moment, the gray skies promised more. I watched Yuti dodge a puddle, her canvas shoes an impractical choice on such a wet day.

"The class you had this morning," I started, not bothering to avoid the shallow puddle in my hiking boots. "Do you have it every day?"

"No, just Mondays, Wednesdays, and Fridays," she answered lightly.

I didn't smell the scent around her classroom, and she didn't smell like vampire on Monday. But she did on Tuesday and Wednesday. Thursday morning she didn't, but Thursday afternoon she did. It doesn't appear to be that professor or someone in that class.

"Have you looked at the course catalog for fall semester yet?" she asked.

"Not yet, no. But I will."

As we approached her building, I took a deep breath. I didn't smell anything unusual. Yuti dug into her bag for her keys and unlocked the front door. As she pushed it open, the scent I'd been searching for, the scent I was never pleased to smell, filtered out.

23

My senses were on high alert, and my skin itched as I fought the sudden urge to shift into wolf form. *The vampire was here in this house, in Yuti's den. Is it a neighbor? Did it break in? Did she* invite *it in?*

The scent wasn't strong. The thing wasn't there now. But it had been there and fairly recently too.

I followed Yuti through the front hall, trying to distinguish if the scent was stronger in some places more than others. I couldn't tell. But as Yuti opened a door labeled *2,* I knew right away that the vampire had been in her room.

I froze on the threshold as she went inside.

She glanced over her shoulder at me. "Come in," she said. "I won't bite."

I flinched at the word but entered her studio apartment, surveying every inch while trying to appear nonchalant.

The bathroom, the little kitchen along one wall, the nook that served as a desk, my eyes swept the apartment, taking everything in. The short couch, the square table and chairs, and a wall full of hooks —a different hat on each one—my mind blurred with sights and smells.

The primary scent was Yuti's cinnamon and citrus. But there was also a strong concentration of sandalwood coming from the corner where a low shelf held a little plate, a clay bowl, and a statue of a fat man with an elephant's head and four arms.

I clenched my jaw, my teeth aching to elongate, when I realized that the vampire scent was strongest in the loft cubby above a few stairs, the cubby that held Yuti's bed. *Did it visit her while she was sleeping? Did it sleep with her?* I thought about the man she'd talked to on the phone, the one she'd said she loved. *Is the vampire her boyfriend? Are vampires coherent enough to hold telephone conversations? Then again, we did hear those other vampires talking, and the scent isn't a full vampire scent anyway. Perhaps he has just been bitten or fed blood and hasn't fully turned yet.* With a deep breath through my mouth, I forced my limbs to relax. *Whatever—whoever—it is isn't here anymore. I need answers, but I can't approach it like last time. Take it nice and easy.*

That's when I noticed Yuti's art. The walls without the hats were decorated with canvases of varying sizes. Some of the paintings were watercolors, and others had been done in brighter acrylics. It was clear they had all been done by the same artist. Yuti's style was airy and strange, dominated by fantastical images not of this world. There were creatures I couldn't identify, weird and wonderful. Some had big eyes and bulbous heads. Others had tentacles. They were doing various things that average people do: drinking tea, dancing, all manner of activities.

Yuti shifted her weight from one foot to the other and cleared her throat. I'd been listening so hard that the sound almost made me jump. *She's uncomfortable. Is she picking up on my tension? Or is she embarrassed of her space? Of her art?*

"Are these all for school?" I asked lightly, gesturing to the paintings.

She looked at her work. "No, these are just for fun. We don't get to do stuff like this for school."

"They're really interesting. Where do you get your ideas?"

Yuti crossed her arms over her chest, glancing around at the walls. "Um…I like to imagine what life is like elsewhere. You know, like other planets." Her eyes met mine for the first time since I'd entered her space. "Do you…believe in aliens?"

"Aliens?" I searched my memory for the "right" answer. I remembered Runa and Konner discussing some book about human beliefs in the supernatural. There had been a chapter on aliens, but I couldn't remember the substance of the conversation. "I guess I never really thought about it."

"Really? I think about it all the time."

That's right. Keep her talking. Keep it light and natural. "You believe in them then?"

"Of course I do. The universe is huge." She flung her arms out for emphasis. "It would be far stranger for us to be the only intelligent life in all that vastness. Whether they've come to Earth or not, that's a much bigger discussion."

I smiled at her sudden outburst of enthusiasm. "Well, I like the paintings either way. Have you shown them to anyone else?" *Who else has been in your apartment?*

"Not really. I mean, Adrian has seen them. I don't post them online. And I don't take them anywhere to show them. He's the only other person who's really been to my place."

"Adrian?" I repeated. I couldn't place the name.

"Yeah." She smiled gently as she thought about him. "I'm going to make some popcorn if you want to take a seat. Would you like anything to drink?"

"Whatever you're having is fine," I answered almost impatiently.

As she went over to her kitchenette, I lowered myself onto her couch, breathing out slowly to steady myself.

"You were telling me about Adrian?" I prompted.

"Oh, right." She poured popcorn kernels into a brown paper bag and then put it in the microwave. "We met first year of college. He's been studying abroad for a while. But he came back earlier this week."

My heart raced, the hair on the back of my neck rising. I barely managed to keep my voice under control. "He just came back? So I haven't met him?"

If she'd noticed my strained tone, she didn't show it. She just took a jar, a cup, and a large bowl down from a shelf. "No, not yet."

"So…is he…your boyfriend? Or…?" *Has he been sleeping in your bed?*

Her shoulders jumped as she flinched. "What?" she yelped, turning around to face me. "Of course Adrian isn't my boyfriend. What makes you think I have a boyfriend anyway?"

I can't exactly say, "Well, a combination of how your bed smells and listening in on your private conversations." Her words made sense. If she had a boyfriend, she likely would have mentioned him by now. And would he have left her so unprotected from mundane dangers like a night walk or a human like Warren? I mean, it was possible, but I wouldn't have. Then again, she seemed to be the willfully independent sort, so maybe he did.

"So you don't have a boyfriend?" *Then why does your bed reek of vampire?*

She sighed more to herself than at me. "No," she said. "I don't have a boyfriend, and before you can even wonder, I also don't have a girlfriend or any other romantic partner."

"Are you into girls?" I wondered. The thought hadn't even occurred to me.

"No, are you?" she shot back.

I blinked at the question. *How did this turn back on me?* I thought she was just being cheeky, but she raised her eyebrows at me, clearly expecting an answer. "Uh, yeah. I guess you could say that." *Runa is female after all.* My heart twinged at the thought. *Is it accurate to say I'm into girls?* It was true to say I was attracted to women prior to Runa. But after her, I'd given up the thought of ever being into anyone again.

"Okay…" Yuti trailed off, turning her attention back to her task.

The only sound in the room was the popping of the corn. *So Adrian isn't her boyfriend, but he's still the only other person she's had over.* "Okay," I said, keeping my tone light. "So you and Adrian are just friends then."

"He's my *best* friend," she corrected.

I forced a smile, and I was glad her back was to me in case it looked more like I was baring my teeth. "If he's your best friend, I'd like to meet him."

She stilled at the counter, then reached for the microwave when it beeped. "Sure. When he gets back, I'll introduce you."

"Gets back? I thought he just got back."

She took the bag from the microwave and dumped it into the bowl. Then she scooped a spoonful from what looked like a jar of butter into the cup and put that in the microwave. "He did. He came back to town to set up his place and get stuff ready for fall semester. But then he went home to visit his mom for the summer."

Can I push for a little more? "Oh? He doesn't live on campus either?"

"No, he lives up on Wren Avenue."

"That's pretty out of the way. It must be inconvenient with him going to the university."

She laughed. "That's what I always say! I encouraged him to rent the apartment upstairs, the one Kyo is in now, but he says he likes it out there in his little cabin. He's the type who needs a lot of alone time though so…" She shrugged.

I marveled at how open she was being, how easy it had become to talk to her. Emboldened, I continued. "When did he go home?"

"He left this morning."

"Did he visit to say goodbye at least? You haven't seen him in a long time. I'm sure you'll miss him."

Her eyes flicked to my face before she turned her back to me to pull open the small fridge built into her counter. She took out two cans of root beer. "No, he just sent me a text. I'll see him in a few weeks. And it's not like he's as far as he was before."

As I took the can of pop she offered, my mind spun with implications. *The vampire very well could be Adrian. The scent didn't show up until earlier this week. And she would have seen him even if they didn't have class together. But why is the scent in her apartment so fresh if he wasn't here today? Maybe it isn't him at all. Maybe it's the owner of the building or a maintenance worker or something that visited her while she slept.*

Yuti took the cup of honey-colored liquid out of the microwave, and a warm buttery scent with a nutty undertone wafted toward me.

"What's that?" I asked.

"Ghee," she answered. "It's the best for popcorn. You get all the buttery flavor, but ghee doesn't melt the popcorn the way butter does." She poured the ghee over the popcorn and shook the bowl. Then she crossed the room and offered it to me. "Try it."

I took a piece into my mouth. It tasted even better than it smelled. "It's good."

"Told you. Popcorn and root beer is the best movie snack."

As Yuti settled on the couch beside me, I managed to get the prickling under my skin to subside, but I couldn't just let go of the knowledge that a potential vampire had been in her apartment.

"I talked to Lia about you coming over to draw," I said.

"What did she say?" Yuti handed me the bowl of popcorn.

I picked through Lia's words carefully as Yuti searched for the remotes. "She said she didn't see how it could hurt. Why don't you come over after my shift tonight?"

She froze for a moment. I doubt I would even have noticed if I hadn't been watching so closely. Then she pressed the remote to turn on the television. "The café closes at eleven. And don't you have to stay after to clean up and everything? Isn't the best time to see wolves at dusk and dawn?"

I fumbled for an explanation, opening my pop with a crack of the tab. "Out in the wild, sure. But they know by now it's a safe place to come at night. I know it'll be late. So…you could stay over and head home in the morning."

Yuti stared down at the second remote as if she couldn't read the buttons.

I bit my cheek and thought of what might have made her hesitate. "We have free rooms, so you'll have your own place to sleep. And we won't be alone either. The boys will be there for sure. And either Lia or Noire will be there, too."

She listened carefully, then nodded. "All right. I can come pick you up from work, and we can drive out there. Thanks."

I didn't like this option, taking my eyes off her when the vampire had been so near. "Aren't you coming to open-mic night?" *She always comes.*

"Sure, but you don't want me to hang around the café all day, do you?"

Until I find out what's going on in your apartment, I don't want you out of my sight. "I wouldn't mind," I said.

Her eyes flicked to my face, her complexion warming, then she gave her full attention to the disc-player remote.

Satisfied that I'd be able to keep an eye on her for a while, I took a sip of my root beer and leaned back on the couch. Yuti was safe for the moment, and we were one step closer to finding out what was going on. I relaxed into the cushion, looking forward to distracting my mind with a movie.

24

I could already tell from the menu screen that this movie would be a romance. My stomach churned, and I regretted drinking the sugary beverage. It hadn't taken me long after coming to this realm to learn that romance movies didn't sit well with me. But this was the film Yuti had chosen for me, and she seemed excited to share it. So I took a deep breath and settled in to endure.

A few minutes in, I pointed at the screen. "Oh! That guy! I know him. He was in *Indiana Jones and the Temple of Doom*."

Yuti smirked. "Yeah, it's hard to forget those glaring eyes."

Unlike the movies I'd seen thus far, I couldn't make comments or small conversation during the film. I couldn't look away from the screen unless I wanted to miss the subtitles. That meant I was paying very close attention to everything that happened.

As I watched Raj and Simran fall in love, my

chest tightened in that all-too-familiar feeling. She was promised to another. They couldn't be together. You could go so far as to say their love was forbidden. The pain of that knowledge grew with every scene. *This is how Runa must have felt. It wasn't just society telling them they couldn't be together. I was also standing in their way.*

I tried to keep it to myself, the sorrow, the guilt. As the intermission started, Yuti turned to me.

"Do you need to use the bathroom or—what's wrong?"

"Nothing," I murmured, still attempting to force the feelings down.

Yuti frowned, her eyebrows puckering in the center. "You don't like the movie?"

I was going to tell her the movie was fine, that nothing was wrong at all. But that's not what came out. "I don't really…like romance movies."

"Oh."

"Do you… Remember the other night when you asked if I'd ever had a girlfriend?"

Her gaze dropped to her laced fingers, which rested in her lap.

"I have…sort of. I was…engaged." Once I'd started, I couldn't seem to stop. "You could say I was the 'right' choice." I used air quotes to punctuate the word. "But she never loved me. And I knew that even when I asked her to spend her life with me. Despite the relationship being taboo, she ran off with my childhood friend. And I can't really be angry at her, at him, at anyone but myself. You can't help who your heart wants and… If I ever truly loved her, wouldn't I want her to be happy? Even if it isn't with me?"

I hesitantly glanced at Yuti. She still stared at her hands.

"At least you were brave enough to take a chance." Her voice was hushed but clear. "I was in love with the same guy for years, but I never even told him. And then I lost my chance." She exhaled through her nose and shook her head.

"Yeah," I muttered, looking vaguely toward the television. "I was brave enough, but it didn't do me much good."

Yuti placed her small hand gently on mine, and a tingling brushed over my skin.

"You were honest with your heart, with her. That honesty can never be wrong. And even if it didn't work out, at least you know you did everything you could. You can live with no regrets."

I met Yuti's gaze, her eyes warm and compassionate.

My lips twitched into a little smile. "Thanks, Yuti."

"Hey," she said softly. "What are friends for?"

I looked down at her hand on mine—dark and delicate, with fingers that had the talent to bring her imagination to life. Such a small thing to provide such comfort.

"I'm sorry about the movie," I said. "Do you mind doing something else?"

She suddenly grinned. "Well, there is one thing I'm always ready for."

My heart skipped at her tone. But before I could ask her what she had in mind, she pulled her hand away and bounded across the room. On a shelf beside the television, she grabbed a thick case, then turned around and held it up in triumph.

"*The X-Files*," she announced.

"*The X-Files*?"

Her mouth dropped open. "You haven't seen that either?"

I shook my head.

"Oh God, then we *have* to. Right now."

I huffed out a laugh. "What's it about?"

She smiled again. "I thought you liked surprises."

"All right. You got me. Put it on."

"Wait. Before that," she said seriously. Moving toward her wall of hats, she removed the paperboy hat she was wearing. Then she took down a gray baseball cap and put the paperboy hat in its place. "In honor of the occasion, I have to wear my special X-Files hat. Also..." She went to her kitchen shelf and pulled down a jar of what looked like sunflower seeds.

She wiggled excitedly, shaking the jar as she pulled the hat, which was embroidered with *NICAP* in yellow letters, onto her head. "Okay," she said with a sigh of satisfaction. "I'm ready."

After putting the disc into the player, she sat down beside me on the couch.

"What's NICAP?" I asked.

"You'll find out soon enough." She cracked a sunflower seed between her teeth.

As the opening credits rolled, she hummed along to the theme song. I couldn't help but smile, her excitement infectious.

I was all in on watching another by the time the first episode had finished. Unfortunately, it was almost time for work. I pursed my lips.

Yuti laughed at my pouting. "We can watch

another next time. It's not going anywhere. It's an old show. Didn't you see how dated their tech was?"

"I know but...I have so many questions."

"That feeling will only get more pronounced as you keep watching. But we don't have time to watch another one. And you don't want to leave in the middle of an episode, do you?"

I thought about it. "I mean..."

Yuti laughed again. "You don't. Believe me. How about this: there are a lot of filler episodes. When we have time to watch another one, we can hop around so you can get the main storyline faster."

I sighed dramatically. "Fine."

She turned off the television and looked around her room. "If I'm not coming back here today, I should probably pack a few things."

I smiled to myself, and the anxiety I'd felt at the thought of leaving her alone disappeared. I hadn't been sure she'd take my suggestion until she started to pack.

It didn't take her long to collect her overnight things and the art supplies she needed. We were soon driving to the café for my shift, and I arrived with time to spare. Once Yuti was chatting with Max, I slipped into the break room and pulled out my phone.

Lia answered almost immediately. "Everything all right?" she asked.

I instinctively ducked my head though she obviously couldn't see the gesture. "I made a judgment call. I hope it was the right decision."

"What happened?" Lia's tone was tense and serious.

I hurriedly explained to her about the scent in Yuti's apartment, about her friend Adrian, and about my invitation to the resort. It was a heavy second or three before Lia responded.

"It's not ideal, but we can make it work. Bring her here after your shift. I'll send Ashwin to her place to really get a lock on things. If he can't follow the scent, he can go up to Wren Avenue and sniff around up there. As for the art session, I think Noire deserves a nice steak for all her hard work. Don't you?"

"I understand."

With a plan in place, I hung up and started my shift.

Open-mic night was always packed even during summer semester. Students gathered to read poetry, play guitar, and even act out scenes from plays or movies. Despite the constant demand for refills, I was able to keep a close watch on Yuti. Sometimes she was on her computer; sometimes she would get up and chat with the other regulars. Once the event started, she watched and clapped or snapped her fingers—whatever reaction was called for.

As closing time approached, I pulled Camille aside. "Yuti is coming over to my place after my shift. Do you mind if she hangs out inside while we clean up? It seems silly to make her wait outside all alone."

Camille gave me a toothy grin. "You're not losing any time are you, bud?"

"She's just coming over for an art thing," I explained, bristling at Camille's suggestive tone.

"Uh-huh. I bet that's the excuse Jack and Rose

used. 'Draw me like one of your French girls,'" she quoted in a breathy voice.

Heat rose in my cheeks. That reference I understood.

Camille chuckled. "I'm only teasing. Of course she can stay, but thank you for asking."

After we closed for the night, and Camille and I had cleaned up, Yuti and I climbed into her car. I told her I needed to make a stop at the 24-hour grocery to make sure our wolf friend would show up for her. I knew Noire preferred venison but no such luck. She would have to settle for beef.

25

Lia and the boys were there to greet us in the front hall when I returned with Yuti. They were curious, curious about the mysterious scent. They hadn't yet smelled it firsthand. But they would be disappointed on that front. Yuti hadn't come into contact with whoever it was that day, and the scent from her apartment had faded after a long day at the café.

Yuti bowed her head, her smile self-conscious as everyone stared at her. "Hello. I'm Yutika, but you can call me Yuti. Thank you for letting me use your home to wolf watch."

Lia smiled her welcoming-mom smile, the same smile she used on customers. She introduced herself and the boys, and offered Yuti something to drink.

"Rowan," Lia said, "Why don't you show Yuti to her room?"

"I'll do it," Braylyn insisted, his eyes bright and eager. He even offered to carry her overnight bag for her.

Yuti thanked him.

Lune scowled as his brother and Yuti headed up the stairs. "I should have thought of that. He's going to get a good sniff of her bags."

Ignoring his complaints, I handed Lia the steak. "Ashwin and Noire?"

Lia started toward the kitchen and I followed. "Ashwin is already en route. He was waiting in his truck as you pulled up. And Noire is awaiting her treat in the woods."

When Yuti and Braylyn joined us in the kitchen, I handed her a glass of iced tea and led her to the back porch, where lawn chairs were already sitting out. I pointed her to the chair that would have the best view. "Best seat in the house."

She stood beside the chair, staring out at the small patch of grass separating us from the forest. "Are we really all right to sit this close?" she asked, her voice hushed.

Her soft words didn't disturb the chilled night, the cool breeze blowing them into the darkness.

"I thought you weren't afraid anymore?" I smirked down at her.

She frowned. "I'm not. I'm worried about the wolves. If we're this close, will they come out?"

"How about this: if we set the food out and a wolf doesn't come, we can go inside."

"All right." After settling into the chair, she pulled out her sketchpad and pencils.

"Do you need more light?" I glanced back at the dim porch light behind us.

"No, this should be enough."

I stared at Yuti more closely. She hunched her shoulders in her chair, the sleeves of her hooded sweatshirt covering most of her hands. Her expression, her posture, seemed to want a warm fire and a cozy blanket, not an uncomfortable lawn chair on a cold, wet night. "Would you like me to make you some hot coffee instead of that iced tea?"

Yuti glanced up at me. "Sure, thanks."

"Coming right up."

Lia was just placing the steak onto a plate when I entered the kitchen. She handed it to Lune, and he went outside, trailed by his brother.

I could feel Lia's gaze on me as I went about making Yuti's coffee and sweetening it the way I'd seen her do a thousand times.

"We're getting close now," Lia said. "By the end of tonight, Ashwin will likely know where the scent is coming from."

I nodded but didn't speak.

"You've managed to get pretty close to her in just a few days."

I flinched, guilt gurgling in my stomach. If it hadn't been for that mysterious scent, I would never have felt anything but irritation toward her. I wouldn't have known how patient a teacher she was, how willing she was to help others. I wouldn't have seen her excitement over her favorite television show. I wouldn't have seen the expression of her imagination on the walls of her apartment. I would never have heard the warmth in her laughter. To me, it would always have felt sharp-edged, like it was pointed straight at me.

"What are you going to do once we find it? Once she's no longer in danger?" Lia asked.

I stared down into the beige coffee, its scent the perfect mixture of the richness of roasted beans, the sweetness of sugar, the lightness of cream. I thought of the warmth she'd given me earlier that day. I'd felt very alone—and then she'd rested her hand on mine.

"I don't know," I murmured.

I closed the back door behind me.

Yuti thanked me for the coffee, took a sip, then placed it on the deck near her feet.

It was cold out tonight, and Yuti was only a small human. I unfolded a blanket I'd taken from the linen closet. "Here..." I wrapped it around her shoulders.

Her dark eyes clung to mine in the dim light. "Thanks." She smiled softly, her thin fingers pulling the blanket closer around her.

Lune's shoes thumped on the wooden steps as he returned from setting out the "bait." I moved closer to Braylyn, who sat in the lawn chair beside Yuti. I motioned for him to get up.

"Aw, but I want to watch Yuti draw," he complained as he stood.

"If you want to watch me draw, you'll see a lot better looking over my shoulder than sitting beside me," Yuti said.

I knew she was trying to be nice, but I didn't

want Braylyn to interfere with her process. "Are you sure?" I asked her. "That won't distract you?"

"It's fine. Besides, I'm always glad when someone shows an interest in art, especially kids."

"I'm not a kid." Braylyn stationed himself behind Yuti. "I'm fully grown."

Sure, your wolf form is.

"I'm sure you have a lot more growing to do," Yuti countered. "You want to be at least as tall as your brother someday, don't you?"

At sixteen, Lune was already taller than his mother though he still hadn't hit his human growth spurt yet. Lune had also settled behind Yuti to watch, leaning his elbow on Braylyn's shoulder.

Yuti looked behind her. "You guys are lucky to have each other. I always wanted a sibling."

"You're an only child then?" I asked.

She nodded. "My parents had a hard time conceiving. They had a lot of miscarriages before they had me." Her voice got quieter as she went on. "And apparently I was a hard pregnancy. The doctors told my mom not to have me at all. So they see me as sort of a miracle.

"But," she added, her voice reaching its regular volume and dispelling the solemn atmosphere, "being a miracle has its upsides. I got away with a lot of stuff I might not have. And they let me do pretty much whatever I want with my life, like study art, for instance. For first-generation Indian parents, that's no small thing. What about you? Are you an only child?" Yuti looked over at me.

"No, I have a younger sister."

"Really? How much younger?"

"A year. Willow turned twenty a few months ago."

"It must've been nice having a playmate growing up."

Considering we were only together for a few years before I went to the Fireleaf farm, I couldn't really say we grew up together. Still, those first six years with Willow did hold some fond memories. And it wasn't as if I'd finished growing up alone. I had Wilhelm and Konner, though werewolf society in Faerie would have considered me grown the moment I was bound with Wilhelm. *Did we really grow up together? Or was I just there to protect them while they got their childhoods?*

When Isla had turned up alive and told Runa and me about how the werewolves in the realm of origin lived, I couldn't believe it. It was so foreign to me, and Isla had had a lot of harsh words for the fae and fae society. She'd challenged everything I'd ever been taught about duty, about society and where I fit into it, about family and what pack really meant.

And when I finally decided to leave Faerie after my unbinding, it was partially to escape those expectations. I also wanted to learn how to be a better wolf, to learn everything I could from the werewolves of the realm of origin.

Once I was here, once I saw how differently Lune and Braylyn were being raised compared to how I had been, I couldn't help but feel a little cheated. Even though I'd been proud to do my duty, even though I was still glad to have seen Wilhelm through his awakening, I wondered how different my life could have been had I not been given away by my parents to near-complete strangers. *Would*

Willow and I have been as close as Lune and Braylyn are? Had our childhoods not been so focused on training to protect fae from vampires, would we have more sibling memories?

As things were, it wasn't worth thinking about. That hadn't been our childhoods. Even so, I had a few warm memories of what it was like to live at home with my parents and my little sister, to live with my pack.

I caught a familiar scent on the breeze and scanned the trees for the dark lines of Noire's wolf form. And there she was, moving slowly, cautiously, in the shadows.

I knew the moment Yuti's human eyes saw her. Her breath hitched as Noire slunk toward the plate, her yellow eyes glowing in the light from the porch.

"Beautiful," Yuti whispered. "Look how it moves."

Noire was putting on quite the performance, moving exactly the way one would expect a wary animal to, one that wasn't a part-time human. But when she reached the plate, she started to eat the steak slowly.

After studying Noire for a few more minutes, Yuti's pencil started to drift across the paper, and it was as if no one else was there but Noire. Yuti's expression was smooth and open. Her lips were parted slightly, giving the impression that a very small smile was her natural state. Her dark eyes were focused as if she saw the truth of the world, saw something no one else could see.

"Pff, what a ham," Lune muttered under his breath.

I looked over at Noire. Her black fur was

groomed and fluffed to perfection. Done with her snack, she stood completely still, staring into the distance as she posed. After about a minute, Noire threw her head back and howled.

Yuti jumped in her chair and gasped. Then she sighed out a laugh, shaking her head at herself for being the only one startled. She watched Noire closely, seemingly trying to memorize her every move. Then Noire turned her back to us and returned to the trees.

Yuti didn't say anything for a while. She just concentrated on her sketchpad, flipping the pages as she deemed necessary. Finally, she clicked her tongue. "I should have had you take a picture," she said. "But I got the basic lines down."

"Can I see?" I asked.

"No, not until it's finished."

I frowned. "But the boys watched you the whole time," I complained.

"I guess you should have had a better vantage point then," she countered with a smirk.

27

"All right, boys." Lia stepped onto the porch. "I think it's time for bed."

"Mom, I'm sixteen," Lune reminded her, "and it's a Friday night."

Lia stared blandly at him. "Funny. Because I recall a certain sixteen-year-old wanting to begin his driving lessons tomorrow, a certain sixteen-year-old who broke the rules not so long ago and *begged* me not to let it affect his driving lessons. But maybe—"

"I'm *going*," Lune interrupted.

Lia didn't bother to hide a smile of satisfaction as the boys wished us goodnight and went inside. "I'm going to head up, too," she announced, turning back to us. "I've got some early checkouts tomorrow." She looked at her watch. "Today actually."

Lia rested her hand on Yuti's shoulder. "If you need anything before morning, Rowan should know where it is."

Once Lia had shut the door, the night closed in around us.

I pointed to the closed sketchbook in Yuti's lap. "Aren't you going to work on your sketches? You said you only had the basic lines down."

She tapped her thumb against the eraser of her pencil. "I don't want to be rude."

"It's fine. I'm sure you want to finish while it's still fresh in your mind."

She reopened her sketchbook. "Thanks."

I watched her for a moment before turning my attention back to the trees. The steady stroke of Yuti's pencil on paper was punctuated by the natural sounds of a late spring night. The crickets, the owls, the wind in the trees, and the soft reminder that I wasn't alone lulled me. It was pleasant, still, and calm even in the midst of activity. And for a few seconds, for a few minutes, for a few hours, there were just me and Yuti and that spring evening.

In reality, it was probably only three-quarters of an hour before our companionable silence was interrupted by someone opening the back door. Yuti and I both turned around as Ashwin and Noire stepped outside.

"Hello again," Yuti greeted Noire. "I was wondering if I'd see you."

"My brother and I had some things to take care of. I'm Noire by the way." Noire held out her hand.

Yuti stood from her chair to shake it, her pencil dropping to the porch. "Yuti."

Ashwin retrieved the pencil.

"And this is my brother, Ashwin."

Yuti thanked him for the pencil he offered and said hello.

I could tell just by looking at Ashwin that he had

the answer to our inquiry. He wouldn't have been nearly as relaxed if his hunt had been fruitless.

Noire's gaze drifted to the sketchbook clutched to Yuti's chest. "You said you were an artist before. Are you working on something?"

"Oh, right." Yuti looked down at her sketchbook. "I actually came in hopes of being able to draw a wolf."

"And did you see one?"

Yuti smiled. "I did, and I got some really great poses from it, too."

"Do you mind if I look?" Noire asked.

"Sure. I mean, they aren't finished yet, but this one is mostly done. I just have to do the background and the shading and stuff."

Yuti offered the book to Noire, and I stood to look as well. The drawing was of Noire howling, her eyes shut and her head thrown back in a graceful arch. It was a wolf fully giving herself to what it meant to be a wolf, and Yuti had captured it beautifully. I smiled at the image.

Yuti had no way of knowing that Noire's smile was the best compliment she'd ever get. "It's gorgeous," she said. "And not a bad-looking wolf either."

"It was stunning. I didn't do it justice," Yuti answered.

Noire's eyes warmed as she looked back at the artist.

"I think you did a great job," I said, defending her piece against her own criticisms.

She lowered her head, the brim of her hat obscuring most of her face. "Thanks."

"I have an idea," Noire said. "Why don't we go

inside for some ice cream? Have you ever tried maple-nut ice cream, Yuti?"

Ashwin and I both stared at Noire, our eyes wide and our mouths agape. Noire guarded nothing so well as her maple-nut ice cream. I'd never seen her share it. If I had to rank it by importance, I'd say maple-nut ice cream, then Ashwin, then the pack—though some days her brother was in absolute last place.

"No, I've never had it, but it sounds good," Yuti answered.

Noire grinned, and my brain almost didn't know how to process an expression so foreign to her face. "It's the best there is. Come on."

Yuti put her sketchbook and pencils back into her bag and followed Noire into the house. Ashwin moved to go in as well, but I grabbed him by the arm.

"Come on, man," Ashwin protested, "I want to see if she'll really share it or if she'll snarl by reflex."

I glared at him. I didn't want to wait any longer. He took in my expression and sighed. Then he closed the door.

My heart began to pound. "You found it?" I whispered, my lungs unable to get enough air to make my voice any louder.

Ashwin nodded. "Yeah, it was really strong up on Wren Avenue."

My stomach rolled and I clenched my jaw. *It's her best friend. It's Adrian.*

28

Knowing the identity of the potential vampire did nothing to make me feel more at ease. Sure, I didn't have to track it down anymore, but Yuti was in way more danger with it being someone so close to her.

After we had ice cream, and after we all said goodnight and went to our respective rooms, I lay on my bed, staring at the ceiling, my gaze unfocused.

Is Adrian a vampire or hasn't he completed his transformation yet? Was he attacked while abroad? Now that he's back, will the vampire let him go?

It was possible that, removed from the situation, Adrian's system just needed time to flush out the potential transformation. Eventually, the blood he'd ingested or the blood he'd lost would return to human normal. As long as it was only one or the other; both was another story.

Yuti had said he was going home for the summer. *When will he be back? If he's only half-turned, then the taint should be gone by the end of summer. Or he could be fully turned by then, and Yuti could be in even more danger. If he comes back a vampire, we will have to kill him.*

I turned my head toward the wall that separated my room from the one Yuti was sleeping in. *She'll be devastated if her best friend disappears or turns up dead. And even if she never knows it was us—never knows it was me—how will I be able to face her? Will knowing that I only did it to protect her, to protect everyone, be enough for my conscience? Will it be enough when I see the sorrow in her eyes, when I wipe her tears away?*

My chest squeezed at the thought of Yuti's pain. Lia was right. I had gotten close to her in just a few days; I'd let her in. I may not have liked her before, but even then, I hadn't wanted to see her hurt. On the other hand, if she had been the vampire, I would've had to eliminate her the same as her friend. They're my natural enemy—I wouldn't have thought twice about it.

I wondered if that made me a monster just like the human stories said. *And what now? What if Adrian comes back and attacks Yuti? What if he turns her? Will I be able to spill her blood now that I know her better?*

My stomach wrenched. *I can't let it come to that. I won't have Yuti's life cut short. I won't let her be turned. If Adrian comes back a vampire, I'll end him without hesitation. I* will *protect her.*

Protecting someone from vampires was what I'd been raised to do. It was only in the last year that any other purpose for my existence had even been an option. And in making a vow to protect Yuti, I felt comfortable, anchored. Guarding was something I did well. I'd protected two faelings most of my life, an unheard-of feat. I knew I could protect one small human without any trouble.

What I hadn't taken into consideration was that Wilhelm and Konner had *wanted* protection. They knew what was out to get them. They knew they couldn't fend off a vampire on their own. They didn't mind being followed, never being alone except when in the safety of their own home.

Yuti, on the other hand, was a human. She didn't know the dangers that stalked her. As a college student, she was just tasting independence from her parents. And she would not be used to, or appreciate, being monitored.

Those thoughts crashed down on me after breakfast while Yuti prepared to leave. Anxiety tingled in my shoulders and down my arms. It wasn't the full-blown panic I would've felt if she'd been my bondmate or my promised, but I recognized the start of apprehension nonetheless.

"Thanks for inviting me. Really. It was great," she said while I watched her pack her few things from the doorway of her room.

"You could stay longer if you want," I offered.

"Thanks, but I really should get back. I have a lot of homework to do before Monday."

I wanted to argue, but she hadn't taken kindly to my insistent prying the other day. If I wasn't careful, she might end up avoiding me.

"When can I see you again?"

She licked her lips ever so slightly; I likely wouldn't even have noticed if I hadn't been watching her so closely. Her complexion warmed, and she focused her attention on zipping her bag. "If

I'm very diligent today, I could probably meet up tomorrow afternoon."

Adrian isn't around. And even if he was, that doesn't mean he'll attack her. She saw him all week and she's fine. Tomorrow will have to be good enough. It's fine.

"Sounds good," I said. "Keep me updated."

"I will."

Five minutes later, she was gone. I leaned my back against the front door, my eyes closed.

"You made the right decision," Lia said.

I opened my eyes and looked at my alpha, who was arranging lilies in the vase that so recently had held sunflowers.

"Yuti isn't the sort of woman who would take kindly to an overbearing man. And even if it's your instinct to protect her, she won't see it that way. Now you see why there aren't so many human and werewolf matings even in the realm of origin. Our instincts come off as possessive. If you push her too much this early, she'll cut ties with you. How will you protect her then?"

"I know," I muttered.

Lia frowned slightly, leaving the lilies and turning fully toward me. "We all want Yuti and everyone else to make it through this safely. We'll do everything we can to ensure that happens. But one human life isn't worth potentially exposing all of werewolf kind to humanity. We must tread carefully. Do you understand?"

Dread twisted my gut. "I understand."

I managed to wait forty-seven minutes before texting Yuti, asking if she'd gotten home all right. Then I paced my room while waiting for a reply. I was just arguing for the merits of going into town when my phone chimed.

Yuti had sent me a picture of herself. The lower half of her face covered with a blue and yellow box, her eyes shining between the brim of her hat and the box.

> Look what I found!

I stared at the unfamiliar logo, then texted back:

> What's a Jaffa Cake?

> (☉.☉) Only the best snack ever.

> Adrian gave it to me.

> Well…more like Adrian sneaked into
> my apartment before he left and hid
> it under my pillow.

My stomach dropped. *He sneaked into her apartment? That must've been why her room smelled like vampire even though she said he hadn't been there to say goodbye and why her bed smelled like him.* I took a deep breath.

> …?

> Haha that must sound pretty weird,
> right?

> It's sort of a game we play. I don't
> know how he does it. It doesn't
> matter if all my doors and windows
> are locked; he always seems to find
> a way in. He hides little treats for me
> so I know he was here.

I tried to swallow around the tightening of my throat. *Is she crazy? Why is she laughing about this?* But my own answer came immediately. *Because she trusts him. Protecting her just got a whole hell of a lot harder.*

My phone chimed again.

> (¬‿¬) If you're very nice to me,
> then I may share some of my Jaffa
> Cakes with you.

My thumbs moved over the touch keypad despite my rising panic.

> I better be on my best behavior then.

And then the conversation stalled. I knew she had work to do, and the sooner she got it done, the sooner I'd be able to see her again.

But as the hours slowly ticked by, I couldn't settle my racing mind. He had been in her apartment. He had broken into her apartment without her even knowing, and that danger didn't seem to bother her.

By late afternoon, I was climbing the walls. And when Lia and Lune returned from their driving lesson, I greeted them at the door.

"Lia, would you mind taking me into town?" I asked.

Lia stared at me for a moment, and I wondered how frazzled I looked to her. She nodded without saying anything and went back through the door she'd just entered.

On the drive into town, I told her what Yuti had texted me about Adrian and his habit of breaking in. She listened, letting me rant about how ridiculous, how foolish, the whole thing was. When we arrived in town, I asked to be dropped off at the café.

The café was just busy enough that Camille couldn't question me as much as she would've no doubt liked to. Carl made the blended chai latte I ordered, and I was out the door in less than fifteen minutes.

Since we were already in town, Lia had gone to pick up a few things from the grocery. So I made my way to Yuti's apartment on foot.

The temperature was chilly again. I eyed the

dark clouds rolling in as a zing in the air raised goose flesh on my arms. A storm was coming.

Finally reaching Yuti's building, I hit the doorbell for apartment two. I counted each second. I waited a full twenty-three seconds before the building door opened.

Yuti tilted her head at me but gave me a smile. "Hey. What's up? What are you doing here?"

I shrugged. "Well, Lia had to come into town for some things, so I thought you could use a break." I held the latte out to her. "I come bearing gifts."

She took what I offered with a little huffed chuckle. "I suppose I could take a break, at least until Lia comes to pick you up. Come on in. The wind is really starting to howl out here."

I followed her through the hall and into her apartment. Breathing deeply through my nose, the tightness in my chest eased when I failed to detect the slightest trace of vampire smell. *He must really have just hidden those cakes here before he left for the summer.*

"Thanks for the drink," Yuti said over her shoulder as we stepped into the main room. "Please excuse the mess."

The apartment wasn't as tidy as it had been the day before. There were unwashed dishes in the sink, books sprawled out on the floor, and Yuti's overnight bag still sat unpacked near the stairs. It was far more comfortable than it had been. It was clear she was relaxed in her own space, which—combined with the lack of vampire scent—made me relaxed too.

"So how much work have you gotten done?" I shoved my hands into my pockets.

Turning toward me, she took a sip of the latte. "Oh, I've finished my exercises, but I still need to write a paper. I was just starting to do research when you buzzed."

"I hope this isn't a bad time." I shifted my weight from one foot to the other as I suddenly cared about inconveniencing her now that I knew she was safe.

"It's fine." She smiled. "As long as I buckle down tonight and tomorrow morning, we can still hang out in the afternoon."

I dipped my head in acknowledgment, my gaze drifting around her apartment.

"So do you want to try a Jaffa Cake?" I could tell from the tone of her voice she was excited to share it with me.

My phone chimed with a text from Lia.

Are you ready?

I shared my location with her so she knew where to come get me. Then I gave Yuti a smile. "Have I earned one already?"

"Well, you came all the way here to bring me a latte, and you were worried about me taking a break. I think you deserve a reward for all that."

My heart gave a little flutter. I wasn't used to someone being so easily pleased by small gestures. Her dark eyes twinkled as she handed me the round, yellow cake with chocolate on one side.

I brought it to my lips.

"Wait, what the heck are you doing?" Yuti challenged.

I froze. "What's wrong?"

"You can't eat it with the chocolate down. That's just unnatural."

"Does it matter?"

"It matters," she said firmly.

I chuckled. "All right. Okay. Chocolate up then." I turned the thing over and took a bite. It had a sort of fluffy, spongy texture with the tartness of orange and rich sweetness of chocolate. I didn't like the combination, but I shoved the rest in and swallowed.

"You don't like it," she observed.

"What? No, it's good."

She laughed. "You liar. You don't have to like it just because I gave it to you."

"You're right." I smirked. "I hate it. Who puts chocolate and orange together?"

"Whoa there. Just because you don't like it doesn't mean you get to bash it. I will defend the Jaffa to the death."

I raised my hands in surrender. Then my phone chimed.

"Well...I better go. And you've got to get back to work." The grin slid off my face.

She sighed. "I do. But thanks for stopping by. And thanks again for the latte."

"Anytime."

As I walked to the car, I wasn't nearly as worried as I had been when Yuti had left that morning. I knew, that for now at least, she was safe.

30

It rained all the next day, so Yuti and I decided to watch more episodes of *The X-Files* rather than practice driving.

When I arrived home later that night, Ashwin was just returning from his visit to Faerie. He dug into his bag and handed me an envelope. "Picked this up for you at the post office near the portal. I have no idea how long it's been there. Do you know where Noire is? Our parents sent some stuff along for her."

I shook my head, and he left to look for her.

Sighing, I went to my room and sat on my bed before breaking the letter's seal.

Dear Rowan,

We haven't heard from you in a while, and we haven't seen you in even longer. Are you well? Are you eating enough?

I understand how you must be feeling after losing

your promised. But did you really have to go all the way to the human realm? We worry about you.

Should I assume you didn't attend the Wolf Moon Festival this year? I really wish you had. The pup population in Faerie is suffering. There are even rumors that they're considering revisiting the treaty with so many faelings going unprotected.

Won't you come home soon? If you came home, we wouldn't even have to talk about it if you didn't want. You could start working at the dojo immediately. The pack would be glad to welcome you back.

Willow will be unbound next month. She'd like you to attend. I've included the invitation with this letter. I really hope you'll come. I hope this letter reaches you in time.

Love,
Mom

Also in the envelope, there was a little card.

Feather Bayberry & Willow of the Lowlands Clan invite you to the ceremony and celebration of their unbinding and Feather's awakening Saturday, the twenty-seventh of July at sunset 1653 East Everly Avenue, Mysraina

I frowned at the paper. It was the right thing, the proper thing, for family members to attend an unbinding ceremony. Willow and Feather had been at my unbinding. With Adrian gone for the summer, it would likely be all right for me to visit Faerie for a day. And if I was really worried about it, I could ask

Ashwin to keep an eye on Yuti or Noire to hang out with her.

I crossed the room and tucked the letter and invitation into my desk drawer. The unbinding wasn't for another seven weeks. I didn't have to think about that, or the emotions my mother's letter had evoked, right now.

The following day, and every other day that week, Yuti taught me to drive. By the first week of July, I was comfortable on a public road.

Yuti was a very patient and encouraging teacher. She let me take things at my own pace. And every hour, every day, every week, I got to know her a little better. I watched her smile, the sound of her laugh becoming familiar and gratifying. I watched her cringe and hide under a blanket when a scary or gross scene in *The X-Files* came on, despite having seen them all before. I watched her lose herself in her art, her clear eyes giving me a sense of peace.

One day blurred into another until it became the norm to hang out with her every day. We grew comfortable with each other, no longer plagued by awkward silences or uncertain words, especially when it became clear Adrian wasn't coming back anytime soon. We laughed and teased. Being with Yuti became effortless, but over the last few days, this sense of easy friendship had started to shift as my mind went to places it had never gone with Yuti before.

I was just wondering how Yuti's exam had gone one Friday afternoon when the door to the café opened, and the wind carried her familiar cinnamon and citrus scent my way. I didn't have to look over to see that Yuti was coming in, but I did anyway.

She wore a particularly wide grin under the brim of her bucket hat.

I returned her smile as she skipped to the counter. "I take it your exam went well?"

"What?" She waved her hand. "Oh yeah. That was fine. But guess what?"

"I wouldn't dare to try. What's up?"

"I got an email during class from the astronomical society. They're having a special talk this weekend about black holes! Do you want to go?"

I wasn't particularly interested in whatever a black hole was, but I was on board with anything that made Yuti this excited. "Sure. Sounds fun."

"Right? It's about an hour drive, but it'll be so worth it. I hope they go into Einstein-Rosen Bridge Theory."

I didn't know what any of that was, but I enjoyed seeing her so enthused.

A woman in line behind Yuti groaned, drawing everyone's attention. "Oh my God! Are you going to stand here all day, or are you going to order something?"

Yuti's eyes widened, and she looked over her shoulder at the woman. "Sorry. I didn't see you there."

"Yeah, well, not everyone has all day to stand around and flirt with the barista," the woman sneered.

A dash of salt entered Yuti's scent, and she put her fist on one hip. "You certainly have enough time to be nasty." Then she turned back to me. "A regular black tea."

I frowned. "Are you sure?" She never took her

tea plain. She'd even told me once that regular black tea tasted like stale mud water.

The brim of her hat jerked as she nodded.

Glaring at the woman behind Yuti, I rang up the order. And then I took my sweet time making her tea. Camille was taking stock in the back before open-mic night descended upon us, so it was only me running the counter. Even though Yuti had ordered her tea plain, I added sugar and topped the whole thing with whipped cream and rainbow sprinkles.

The smile that Yuti gave me was all the thanks I needed.

By the time I was ready to take the rude woman's order, she was fuming. Her face was red, and she practically vibrated with rage. She ordered her drink in a clipped tone, and I did my very best sloth impression while filling it. I was confident that when she stomped out of the café she would never be back.

"So," I said to Yuti, leaning my elbows on the counter to talk to her. "When is this thing we're going to?"

31

The following day, Yuti and I left early. I'd never driven on a major highway before, and we didn't know what the traffic would be like, so Yuti took the wheel. As we approached the city, traffic slowed to a crawl. The summer heat, which had cooled for the last few days, was back with a vengeance. And once again I wondered how far north I had to go to not have to deal with such high temperatures.

The air conditioner was on full blast, and the recycled air blew Yuti's scent directly into my face. I knew from experience that my clothes would smell of her even after we parted.

When we arrived downtown, we left the car in a parking garage. I stared up at the buildings towering over us. I'd seen tall buildings in Lupine City, but they were nothing compared to what the humans had built.

Yuti chuckled. "You might want to close your

mouth. Nothing says tourist quite like that look on your face."

"What's wrong with being a tourist?"

She smiled. "You know? That's a good point. We *are* tourists. We might as well enjoy it."

Standing beside one another on the sidewalk, we stared up at the buildings and the blue sky. As her arm brushed against mine, my heart jumped, and I wasn't so interested in human engineering anymore.

I looked over at Yuti, her upturned face unshaded by the brim of her hat. Her eyes sparkled as she smiled, and her warm skin looked like it would be soft to the touch. My heart screamed in my chest, and an uncomfortable tingling ran up my arm. I wanted nothing more than to reach out and lace my fingers with hers.

Would she pull away? How angry would she be? My mind raced to stop my body from doing anything I would regret. *Yuti has never given me any indication that she likes me in that way. And even if she had, how could I ever be sure? I'd thought Runa had liked me, but she left me without hesitating.*

Runa had told me I was worth the wait. She'd kissed me with such passion and enthusiasm that I was beyond certain of her feelings. But I'd been wrong. Her heart only wanted Konner. I knew she couldn't help that, but the result was the same on my end. I was alone. Abandoned. My promised bond broken and cold.

Looking back up at the sky, I shoved my hands into my pockets to stop them from doing something stupid.

We made our way to the astronomical society—a small building that was clearly an old, converted house—at a comfortable pace. Folding chairs were set up in front of a white screen in a large room with wooden floors. The atmosphere was hushed, more like a museum than a library.

People stood in loose groups, talking about everything from their kids to topics that I wouldn't even attempt to decipher.

"Did you know black holes could be important to making contact with alien worlds?" Yuti whispered as we stood along the wall by ourselves.

"How's that?" I asked.

"It's pretty complicated. But the easiest way to put it is that there's a theory that black holes could be wormholes, like tunnels connecting two points in space. Space travel takes a really long time, and chances are aliens don't live anywhere close to us. So it's sort of like a shortcut."

"Is that what they're going to talk about today?" I asked.

"Mmm, they might touch on it, but more likely they'll talk about how they just took a picture of a black hole earlier this year. They'll talk about event horizons and stuff."

Just when I was about to ask what that was, I recognized an unwelcome face entering the room. Yuti followed my gaze.

"Dustin?" She blinked.

I glared at the man as he looked over upon hearing his name.

"Yuti?" His surprised tone matched hers.

The social pressure of recognizing a classmate seemed to overwhelm my glare. At least he had the decency to hesitate as he approached. I scanned the crowd over his shoulder. He appeared to be alone.

"I didn't know you were interested in this stuff," Dustin said upon reaching us.

Yuti nodded. "I guess you must really have a telescope after all."

He cast his eyes down. "Hey, listen. I want to apologize for that night. I've tried to tell Warren you aren't interested in him. He can be a real jerk sometimes."

Yuti frowned. "You can't apologize for someone else, Dustin."

"I know," Dustin muttered. "But I don't know what else to say. I feel sorry, so I say sorry."

"If you feel that way, maybe you should look at why you're friends with him to begin with."

Dustin looked appropriately scolded, his frown deep and his eyes sad.

"So," Yuti said. "how did you hear about this lecture?"

"I'm on their email list." He answered more confidently now that the conversation had taken a turn.

I was glad when someone announced that we should take our seats. I knew Dustin wasn't a danger to Yuti, and she wasn't afraid of him. But something about the way they understood each other's interests bothered me. I didn't like watching them interact while standing there with nothing to say.

32

The following evening, I couldn't seem to sit still. The sun hadn't completely set, but it had dipped behind the foothills. It was that in-between time, the time just before the night came alive. And I found no peace in it. I needed to move, to run, to do something—anything—that would stop my mind from continuing the cycle of the last few days.

After climbing the porch steps, I opened the back door, determined to shift and go for a run. Noire looked over at me, freezing as if she'd been caught doing something wrong. I took in the eight pints of maple-nut ice cream stacked on the counter beside her and the frozen meat she was neatly placing into the freezer.

"I was just—" she started.

I held up my hand. "I didn't ask. I don't even want to know."

"That's probably for the best."

"Listen, I was about to go for a run. Do you want to join me?"

Noire raised her eyebrows. "This is the fifth time this week. And isn't Yuti coming over in a little while?"

I didn't reply. Letting the freezer door shut behind her on its own, she turned her full attention on me. I couldn't help squirming beneath her steady gaze.

"Grab some ice cream and follow me," she said.

I filled my arms with frosty containers and followed her to the basement door. When she opened it, the musty smell of wet, stagnant air wafted up toward me. The wooden stairs creaked beneath our thudding footsteps. I didn't like going down to the basement. I didn't like the dank scent, the stillness. But that was where the laundry machines were, and that was where the large freezer was.

Noire opened the freezer lid and took a pint from me. "So what's going on?" She didn't meet my eyes as she transferred the ice cream from my arms into the freezer. She just waited, silently, patiently, as if she could wait forever.

"Would you...take another chance if you got one?" I whispered finally, the words seeming to exhaust the last bit of air in my lungs.

Noire slowly closed the lid of the freezer, then looked up at me, her yellow eyes showing through her blue contacts in the dim basement light. "This is about Yuti?"

As always, Noire and I were on the same wavelength. Not only did she know what I was asking her, but she also knew what it was really about.

I lowered my chin.

Leaning her hip against the freezer, Noire sighed through her nose. "Yes, I would." Grief, pain, sadness, all passed over Noire's face despite her words. "Losing Heiden… It broke me. You wouldn't even recognize the person I used to be. And in order to be the person I am now, I had to take all those shattered pieces and try to fit them back together. But once something is broken, it can never go back to the way it was before."

My chest ached at the truths she spoke, not because I wanted to go back to my pre-Runa self, but because I wanted to have just a sliver of that hope that used to come so easily to me. "Then why would you risk that pain all over again?"

"If there's someone out there who can make me feel love again, who can spark that feeling in me, I don't think I could stop myself. When you think about it, humans, werewolves, fae, we really aren't that different. We're all drawn toward warmth. We all want to feel love and happiness. And if this someone saw how chipped and cracked I am and still loved me, then I would know no greater happiness."

"But…what if she doesn't want *me*? What if by taking the chance, I ruin not only that potential but our friendship? What if she leaves me like Runa? How will I survive that again?"

Noire's mouth twitched into a sad little smile, and she rested her hand on my shoulder. "You've already been through it. You've already overcome it. You've even healed enough to feel something for someone else. If the worst happens, you already know how to deal with it. Don't let the fear of death keep you from living your life."

With a squeeze, she dropped her hand. "And, uh, this." She knocked on the lid of the freezer, shaking her head. "Never happened. Got it?"

I stifled a laugh. "Got it."

As always, her words had rung true. But the emotions are never so easy to convince with logic as the mind. And my heart remembered the sting of the blade even if the wounds had scarred over.

It wasn't two hours before Yuti arrived at the resort. I'd promised to take her up the mountain to see the stars.

"You ready?" she asked with a smile when I opened the door. She wore jeans and a hooded sweatshirt against the nighttime temperatures. Her NICAP hat shaded her eyes from the porch light, and a pair of heavy, black binoculars hung around her neck.

My stomach fluttered in the face of that smile, Noire's words still echoing in my ears. But I covered it by stepping out and shutting the door behind me. "Yep, let's go."

Yuti followed me through the night as we made our way to the ski lift. It didn't take us long to reach the control panel in the wooden booth beside where the motor was housed.

First, I turned on the lamps. Bright light flooded the mountain in a straight line to the top.

"But how are we going to see the stars if the lights are on?" Yuti asked.

"I'll turn them off when we get up there," I assured her. Then I hit the buttons to start the lift.

The chairs began moving slowly upward. I

turned to Yuti. She watched the chairs pass, a line of concentration forming between her brows.

"You aren't afraid of heights, are you?" I asked as her head followed a chair up.

"What? No. I just...haven't been on a lift before."

I smiled at her little insecurity; it was just too cute. "Don't worry. I'll help you."

She looked over at me and nodded, her worry-line smoothing out, and my heart skipped a beat to know that even that little reassurance on my part had set her mind at ease, that she trusted me that much.

"All right." I stepped closer to her and placed my hands on her shoulders from behind, my fingers tingling at the simple contact. "Timing is every-thing," I whispered, watching the chairs pass. "Okay, *go*." I nudged her forward and positioned her in the correct place. "Now, the chair is coming. All you have to do is sit down."

We both sat, and I pulled the bar down.

She grinned over at me. "That wasn't so hard."

"I knew you could do it."

The ride up was pleasant and quiet, the only sound the clanking of the chair as we passed a tower. I watched Yuti smile down at the ground far below, her joy spreading warmth through me.

As we reached the top, I lifted the bar and we hopped off. Then I shut down the lift and turned off the lights.

"Whoa," Yuti breathed, her eyes sparkling brighter than the stars she gazed up at.

"Over here," I instructed.

The light of the nearly full moon was bright

enough for even her human eyes to see the ground. I led her to the overlook, and we settled on the bench beside one another.

Yet again, the night closed in around us, but it wasn't nearly as peaceful as the time she'd drawn Noire. The crickets were the same; the night birds were too. I, and my hammering heartbeat, was the only difference.

Yuti leaned her head back, slouching down to rest her neck on the back of the bench. "I wonder how many other worlds there are out there," she mused, her voice hushed.

I mimicked her posture so I could see what she was seeing. "Doesn't it scare you?" I asked. "I've seen enough movies about aliens now to know that most people seem afraid of the idea."

"Scare me? No. If anything, I'd say the idea comforts me." She chuckled, and the sound brushed over my skin like a soft kiss. "People can be so awful sometimes, and I like to think that somewhere out there someone is better. And…how do I put this? It…sort of takes the pressure off. Does that make sense? Like humanity isn't the universe's only chance to get it right."

She turned her head toward me, our eyes meeting in the shining moonlight. Her dark eyes caught the light in such a way that it seemed the whole universe could be found there. And there it was again, that desire to reach out and touch her. My heart screamed in my chest, and I tried to swallow as my mouth went dry.

"Do you know what I mean?" she asked.

"Yeah," I whispered, not even sure what she'd asked me.

She directed her gaze back to the sky. "It's great up here. Thanks for bringing me. Maybe next time we should invite Dustin. He could bring his telescope. I wonder what kind he has."

I frowned. My heart still ached, still pounded at being so near to her, but all I could think about was how she and Dustin had chatted at the lecture the day before. And all I did was stand there with nothing to say, lonely and forgotten.

I flinched at the thought. Reaching over, I placed my hand on hers.

Her breath hitched, and her head snapped toward me.

Our gazes met, my heart exposed and vulnerable. *What have I done? Have I ruined everything? Will I lose her too?*

Her eyes were wide with questions. There was uncertainty. There was wonder. But there was no rejection.

"Is this…okay?" I murmured, unable to hear my own words over the wild beating of my heart.

She moved her hand, and my heart sank.

Then she laced her fingers with mine. Her answering smile was shy but encouraging. She nodded.

33

*E*arlier that summer, I'd looked at the university's fall semester course catalog and hadn't found anything that I was particularly interested in. But after the lecture on black holes, I decided to look again.

I'd learned basic science during school in Faerie, but it hadn't taken me long to realize that what I'd learned was outdated. Not wrong, but incomplete.

I found the lecture we went to interesting, but it was my inability to participate in Yuti and Dustin's conversation that had urged me to sign up for Introduction to Astronomy.

As I walked Yuti home one night a few days after our stargazing, I told her I'd turned in my form to Admissions and mentioned which class I wanted to take.

She squeezed my fingers, laced with hers, gently and smiled up at me. That simple contact had become habitual in only a few days, but that hadn't stopped it from making my heart jump every time.

"I'm glad the lecture sparked your interest," she said as we strolled, in no hurry to reach our destination.

The hot summer day had cooled after the sun had gone down. Yuti's tank top and shorts weren't enough to keep her warm. I felt a shiver run through her.

I stopped and dropped her hand. Her brow crinkled in confusion. I took off my jacket, a light one I kept at the café for drastic temperature shifts, and wrapped it around her shoulders.

"Thank you," she mumbled, slipping her arms into the sleeves.

I chuckled at the sight; the sleeves hung well past her fingers. I motioned for her to hold her arm out. And as I rolled one cuff, I could feel her eyes on my face.

"A friend of mine is having a birthday party tomorrow night," she said.

It didn't seem like a statement that required a response.

"Would you come with me…as my date?"

My hands stilled. *What did she say?* My gaze flicked to hers, certain I'd misheard. But her dark eyes glittered with hope in the light of the street-lamps. She held her breath, and I sensed her nervousness.

I felt weightless, my answer bubbling to my lips as if I had to release the air. "Yes."

Her breath was ragged as she sighed. Then she smiled up at me. Standing in the pool of yellow light, one sleeve of my jacket rolled up over her hand while the other hung loose, her straw hat pushed back on her head, Yuti never looked more beautiful.

My hands started to tingle, and I slowly reached for the brim of her sun hat. The rough straw rubbed against the pads of my fingers when I slid it from her head. Her silky hair glistened in the overhead lighting. Her breath caught, and she froze, her eyes watching me closely.

With a trembling hand, I stroked her hair, the dark strands soft and smooth. And as I took a shuddering breath, her cinnamon and citrus scent intensified. A little telltale undertone had mixed in. It was different for everyone. Yuti's arousal was warm and sweet like maple syrup and caramel.

When that scent drifted into my nose, I had no reason to hesitate. Still, I took it slowly, savoring the aroma, enjoying how it warmed me, reveling in the effect it had on me.

I inched closer to her, her arousal and my anticipation growing with every moment. Her eyelids fluttered and closed, her breath caressing my face. Floating in her scent, I pressed my lips to hers.

My inner wolf stood at attention, memorizing the feel of her against me and the inaudible moan her throat didn't let go of, too soft for normal human hearing. There were conventions, norms, about how werewolves interacted with potential mates, and I'd experienced how my wolf had reacted to Runa. I had no way of knowing how differently he would react to a human, to Yuti.

As we kissed on that cool summer night—her free hand clutching my shirt, pulling me closer—my wolf wanted her. He wanted to lay claim to her, mark her for his own. He wanted every other creature to know that she was his. This fragile human was under his protection, and any harm that should befall her would be a declaration of war. It took all my inner strength to check that compulsion.

A moment that should have been sweet and enjoyable left me with a lot of questions. But as we pulled away from each other, I was glad to see that those instincts hadn't ruined it—at least not for Yuti. She smiled up at me, giddy excitement written all over her face.

"What took you so long?" she asked with a little chuckle.

But my head spun, too dizzy at her words—too stunned by my wolf's reaction, too full of questions—to reply.

It wasn't much farther to her apartment. With goodnight wishes, I saw her safely inside, promising to meet her the following evening for her friend's party. But as she shut the door behind her, leaving me outside, my wolf whined, reluctant to go.

I forced my legs to move, my steps awkward like those of a mechanical windup doll as I returned to the university where Lia was waiting for me.

"I may have a problem," I said, climbing into the parked car. I explained what had happened. "What should I do?" I asked when it was clear she wasn't about to say anything.

She stared at the road, her face giving no hint to her inner thoughts. "What do you want to do, Rowan?"

"I don't know," I groaned. "I feel…mixed up. I like Yuti. I'd like to keep getting to know her. But what my wolf is doing… It's so much worse than it was with Runa. I don't know why."

"Yuti is human. She's more vulnerable than Runa was even without a potential vampire stalking her. Your wolf is only responding in a way he feels is appropriate to that reality. And…" she trailed off.

"And what?"

Lia sighed. "And you've already lost one promised. It's natural for your wolf to try even harder with anyone else you show an interest in, especially if she reciprocates."

The soft reminder that my relationship with Runa had been purely driven by convenience, that I had been the only one truly invested, stung a little.

"Listen," Lia added gently. "We aren't like Faerie. There aren't rules about who you can and can't be in a relationship with here. Still, you need to be careful. If you want a real relationship with Yuti, you're going to have to tell her what you are. It may still be too soon for that. Timing is important. But before you get in too deep, you have to consider how this might end. If you tell her, and she can't accept you, we'll have to call someone in."

My stomach lurched. I knew Lia was only looking out for me, but the thought of a fae completely wiping me from Yuti's memories made me want to vomit.

34

When Yuti had invited me to her friend's birthday party, I hadn't thought there would be so many people. Even standing outside on the porch, I could tell the house was packed as music blared and lights flashed inside.

Yuti wore a short, red dress, its skirt rippling in the breeze. She'd tied a scarf into her hair like a headband, the ends brushing her collarbone. She had a small gold hoop in her nose and red lipstick that evoked memories of the kiss we'd shared the previous night. Her dark eyes drew me in, sultry and enticing with smoky makeup. I felt mismatched with her in my jeans and t-shirt though I had taken particular care to tame my hair while getting ready. From the way her eyes sparkled at me in the dim porch light, I knew she appreciated my effort as much as I appreciated hers. She slipped her hand into mine with a smile and pushed open the door.

Sounds and smells overwhelmed me as we stepped into the chaos, and it took me a moment to push them to the background. The mayhem seemed vaguely organized in sections. There was a space near the stereo where people danced, but most everyone else was just standing around talking and laughing. Nearly everyone had a red cup in hand.

"Let's find Autumn first," Yuti said louder than was necessary for my werewolf ears.

I let her lead me through the crowd, and she eventually approached a woman whose golden hair was topped with a fuzzy, pink tiara. Yuti released my hand to embrace the squealing woman.

"Thanks so much for coming!" the woman said.

"Of course, thanks for the invite." Yuti pulled away. "And happy birthday."

The woman's blue eyes flicked to me, and she tilted her head.

"Autumn, this is Rowan."

"Happy birthday," I said.

Autumn eyed me critically for a moment, then smiled. "Thank you. You must be the one Yuti has been so secretive about. I can see why she'd want to keep you all to herself."

I raised my eyebrows at Autumn's flirtatious tone.

"And why don't we go get something to drink, shall we?" Yuti urged.

Autumn laughed. "Enjoy the party!" she called as Yuti led the way to the kitchen.

The small space was packed with kegs and coolers. A man wearing a top hat seemed to be the de facto bartender because he asked what he could get us when we entered.

"I'll have whatever she's having," I responded, his solicitous eyes on me.

"Just a cola," Yuti said.

The man reached into a nearby cooler and handed us each a can.

"That's Autumn's boyfriend, Kyle," Yuti informed me as we left the kitchen.

I made a sound of acknowledgement.

Yuti led us to a room adjacent the dance floor, greeting those she knew along the way. While we stood against the wall sipping our pops, she told me about her friends, their names, and what they studied. It wasn't ten minutes before I recognized someone, too.

Dustin smiled and raised his hand as he entered the room. Then he made right for us, or rather, right for Yuti.

"I wondered if you'd be here," he said once he'd reached us.

"Yeah, well, here I am," she answered.

"So what did you think of the lecture the other day? You guys left before we got a chance to talk about it."

I frowned, and the sweet syrup of my pop suddenly tasted bitter.

"I liked it," Yuti said. "Rowan liked it, too. Didn't you, Rowan? He even signed up for Intro to Astronomy next semester."

Dustin gave me a friendly smile. "Oh yeah? That's cool. I hope you get Professor Benson. He's much better than Russell. She's a brilliant researcher, but, man, she just can't dumb herself down enough to teach intro classes."

Any amount of warmth I might have shown Dustin in that moment was destroyed when Warren joined us.

"Dude, there you are." Warren held a red cup out to Dustin. And then he saw Yuti and his face broke out in a nasty little smirk that made me clench my teeth. "I see you've gotten me a present, and it's not even my birthday."

Warren's eyes slithered over Yuti's body, and it wasn't long before the tangy scent of vinegar reached my nose. My inner wolf's hackles rose, and I barely managed not to growl.

Ignoring Warren's presence, Yuti reached up and touched my bicep. "Hey," she said cheerfully. "Let's dance. I really like this song."

I glared at Warren until he was out of sight. Yuti's fear lessened as we went into the next room, but it didn't disappear.

"Do you want to leave?" I asked her softly.

"I don't want to let him ruin our fun. Besides, I really do like this song."

I listened to the music. "I don't know it," I admitted.

"'I'm Shakin'' by Jack White? I love it!"

And she really seemed to. Joining the rest of the dancers, she started to wiggle and sway to the music, her skirt shifting in a hypnotic ruffle of fabric.

I was pleased to see that human dancing, at least this kind, was much closer to werewolf dancing than what the fae did. I joined in, moving my body close to hers. Her movements were smooth — sensual — and everything male within me noticed.

Any fear she'd had moments before was replaced as her cinnamon and citrus scent intensified.

By the time the song was over, she was breathless but grinning. I was just fine, but then I had a werewolf's stamina. Again, I followed her to another room, farther away from the music.

She sighed contentedly and took another sip from her pop.

"You want some rum to mix with that?" a man asked, his eyes on Yuti as he stopped in front of us.

The woman he clung to answered on Yuti's behalf. "I don't think she can have alcohol, right?" she asked Yuti in a sympathetic tone. "Muslims can't drink alcohol. It's against their religion."

Yuti stared hard at the woman but sighed. The sharp smell of salt came off of her. Still, she kept her tone polite. "I'm Hindu, not Muslim. And I'm not drinking because I have to drive."

Then Yuti turned to me. "Would you mind holding this for me? I have to go to the bathroom." She held out her drink, and I took it with a nod.

"Jeez," the woman whispered, already halfway across the room. "She didn't have to be such a bitch about it. I was trying to be sensitive to her situation."

Ten minutes passed while I waited for Yuti to return. I just stood there, watching her friends play some drinking game and sipping from my can. Whether she really had to go to the bathroom or she'd just wanted time to herself to cool down a bit, I didn't know. But as ten minutes turned into twenty, and I began considering drinking from her can since I'd already finished my own, I decided to go look for her.

The bathroom wasn't difficult to find; there was a line all the way down the stairs from the second floor. *It could definitely take twenty minutes to get through that.* But as I reached the front of the queue, I still hadn't found Yuti. I turned to the person who was first in line and opened my mouth to ask if Yuti was in the bathroom.

A familiar voice cut off my question. "I've made myself clear," Yuti said firmly from around the corner, and I moved toward the sound. "I'm not interested in you."

"You're really going to choose a pretty boy like that over me?"

Yuti sighed loudly. "My interest in Rowan has nothing to do with my lack of interest in you. Even if he wasn't around, I still wouldn't like you. That's all I have to say."

Yuti walked into view at the end of the hall, and Warren followed close behind, grabbing her by the wrist and jerking her arm to force her to face him.

"Ah!" Yuti cried out in pain.

The scent of her fear spiked, the tangy vinegar aroma so strong it made my eyes water.

"Let go of—"

Yuti's demand was cut off as I launched myself at Warren, catching him by the throat and pinning him to the wall. The splatter and fizz from her pop can hitting the floor, the loud thump of Warren's weight against the wall, the rattle of picture frames that hung nearby, the sudden silence of those around us—I didn't pay attention to any of it. All I cared about was Warren's strangled gasps for breath.

His eyes widened, panicked and glassy.

"Rowan, stop it!" Yuti shouted.

But I could see no good reason not to eliminate this threat forever. He was the lowest type of scum, lower than a vampire. At least a vampire needed to drink blood to survive. I could understand that drive even if it was my duty to stop it.

A growl rumbled in my chest as I squeezed the soft flesh of Warren's throat. Real horror showed in his eyes now; my gaze burned into his.

"I said *stop*!"

The panic, the fear, in her voice reached me even in the depths of my fury.

I released my hold on Warren's throat but pulled him close by the collar. "Don't ever touch her again," I snarled, more wolf than man.

Once I let him go, he leaned against the wall and slid to the floor, coughing and gasping. It was when I turned back toward Yuti that I realized I'd broken some human rule. The music downstairs still thumped, and people partied on. But those near us gawked, wide-eyed and nervous about what I might do next.

Yuti's fear was worst of all. Her dark eyes stared at me, and her breathing was ragged.

"Yuti—"

"No." The vinegar scent turned briny. She shook her head, then turned on her heel and stomped down the hall.

I followed, trailing her down the stairs and out into the cool summer night.

"Yuti, wait!"

Once we were alone in the yard-turned-parking-lot, she spun around to face me.

"I don't want to hear it right now, Rowan." Her voice was low but firm. She paused for a heavy moment. "Find your own way home."

I watched her stomp to her car, frozen in place by her anger. With every step she took, my chest tightened a bit more. By the time she drove away, I could hardly breathe. I don't know how long I stood where she'd left me. If I had been in wolf form, I know my ears and tail would have hung low.

The lights and sounds of the party still hummed in the background, another world, distant and separate from the one I inhabited. Eventually, I dug into my pocket and pulled out my phone. With numb fingers, I pressed and held the two on the keypad.

The ringing was loud, harsh in my ear, and it seemed to take forever for Lia to pick up.

"Rowan?" Lia called when I didn't respond right away to her greeting. "Are you okay?"

"I need a ride," I said, my voice thick and uneven. "I think I fucked up."

"You were right," I admitted after telling Lia what had happened. I stared out the car window, my eyes losing focus in a blur of dark trees. "I...I scared her. My every instinct told me to eliminate the threat, to protect her... Maybe... Maybe I shouldn't have left Faerie. Maybe I'm just not a good fit for this realm."

"I'm not going to stand in your way if you want to go back, but I do want to point out that you've done remarkably well in adjusting so far," Lia said.

I shook my head. "That has nothing to do with me. I've heard Konner prattle on about human stuff most of my life. I was bound to pick up some things here and there. But having basic knowledge and living amongst them are totally different."

Lia kept her tone even and reasonable. "That's true. But this is only your first real mistake so far. Even werewolves who've lived here all their lives mess up sometimes. And given the circumstances, it's understandable."

"Is it though? Will Yuti see it that way?"

"Well, Yuti doesn't know about your nature. She might be more understanding if she did. How strongly do you feel about her? Is it worth taking the risk for?"

I frowned, my gut twisting. "I don't know. If it wasn't for her friend suddenly returning and rubbing his scent onto her, I likely wouldn't have ever gotten close to her. I reached out to her because of that, asked her for help under false pretenses."

"Does that matter now?" Lia asked gently. "Just because you befriended her for another reason doesn't mean your feelings aren't real."

I squeezed my eyes shut. My chest felt like it was caving in on itself. "But now, I might not be able to protect her at all. Not just from assholes like Warren but Adrian too. If I just fucked it all up, what's going to happen when he returns?"

"We'll just have to take this one step at a time," Lia said calmly.

The moment I was home and in my room, I texted Yuti.

> Did you get home all right?

I knew she didn't want to hear from me at the moment, but I thought this approach couldn't hurt. And even a small acknowledgment would have given me hope that she would eventually forgive me.

I never got it. I stayed awake as long as I could, staring at the bright phone screen, the only light in the dark room. My eyes were swollen and crusted, and I had to keep my phone plugged in just so it wouldn't die.

At some point, I fell asleep from pure exhaustion. But the little sleep I got was unfulfilling. My head was heavy and my mind foggy when I jerked awake the next morning.

I fumbled for my cellphone and opened my messages.

Did you get home all right?

Read

Yuti had still not responded. I sighed, low and long. *If she read it, that at least means she's okay.*

I managed to get up and eat before giving in to the compulsion to text her again.

Can we talk?

I dropped my phone onto the kitchen table, groaning as I rubbed my hands over my face. The back door opened behind me. I didn't turn around.

"You have to work today?" Noire asked.

"Later," I confirmed.

"Come with me."

I stood from the table and followed Noire outside. We walked around the house and eventually reached the nearest guest cabin.

"I want you to pull all the weeds around all of the cabins before you head to work." Noire pointed at the weeds that grew up near the base of the cabin. "Put them in the wheelbarrow and bring them to the shed when you're done."

Before I could even respond, Noire left. I sighed and lowered myself into a crouch. The prickly weed scraped my palm and fingers as I ripped it up by the roots. And then I did it again. And again. Until the wheelbarrow was overflowing, weeds of various shades of green hanging over the edges and dropping to the ground as I pushed it.

By the time I was finished, I was grateful to my packmate. As ever, Noire showed her kindness, her empathy, in the most roundabout ways. The task she'd assigned was tiring, especially in the midday heat. But I didn't look at my phone once until after I'd finished and showered.

The hard labor had made the time pass more quickly, but it had not paid off. When I opened my messages again, I still had no response from Yuti, just the indicator that my message had been read.

> Please.

My stomach was fluttery and anxious during the ride to work. I concentrated on the wind in my hair, the physical sensation giving just a little respite from my thoughts.

I checked my phone again, sighing for the hundredth time as I put it away in the break room. Still no reply.

I'd never wanted to be at work more than this moment. Yuti would come. Yuti always came.

As I filled an order at the cash register, the bell over the door tinkled. My heart jumped, and my eyes flicked in that direction. And then my heart sank. It wasn't Yuti.

Every time the door opened, I had the same response: hope for the space of a single heartbeat, which was then crushed just as quickly. Yuti never came.

My limbs were heavy and numb when I turned the lock on the café door, closing it to customers for the night. My chest ached, making it hard to take a full breath.

"What's going on with you today, Rowan?" Camille asked as I mopped the floor.

I didn't even have the energy to respond. Mercifully, Camille didn't push. After we had finished, I mumbled a goodnight and went outside to wait for my ride.

A cool night breeze brushed against my skin, raising the hairs on my arms. *Yuti still has my jacket.*

Pulling out my phone, I sat at the picnic table with little hope that I'd received a reply. And I was right, still nothing. I hung my head, taking a deep breath through my nose as my eyes started to burn.

But when the scent of cinnamon and citrus hit me, I jerked around.

Yuti stood in the dim light outside the café. Her face was drawn and her eyes sad beneath the brim of her hat. She wore my jacket, so long on her that it covered the hem of her shorts. She lifted one sleeve-encased hand.

"Hey," she murmured.

36

I resisted the urge to run toward her, to embrace her. "Hey," I echoed. My eyes raked over her body, and I took a little solace in the fact that she seemed physically all right.

"Do you still want to talk?" She shifted her weight from one foot to the other.

I nodded.

"Okay."

I opened my mouth, but now that I had the chance to talk, no words came out. *What can I say? I'm not sorry for protecting her. I'm not even sorry for the way I did it.* I cleared my throat. "I'm sorry for scaring you," I said honestly. "My behavior was not the appropriate response." *For humans.*

Her dark eyes stared at me for a long moment.

"You're right. You went overboard. I know you wanted to protect me — Warren *was* hurting me. And I know that you did what you did because you care about me." She frowned deeply, shaking her head. "But you didn't even give me a chance to handle it myself." Her tone was urgent. This was something she needed me to understand.

"I told you once I could defend myself. If I ever feel like I'm in a situation I can't handle, I'll ask for your help." Her eyes pleaded with me. "Rowan, I'm not too proud to ask for help if I need it. You have to trust me, trust in my abilities. I've survived my entire life without your help. I'm capable of taking care of myself."

My chest tightened at her words. *I hurt her pride. If she were a werewolf, I would've been protective, but I would've given her a chance to deal with it on her own first.* "I understand," I said softly. "If you say you'll ask for my help when you need it, I'll trust you on that."

She gave me a gentle smile, her furrowed brow smoothing out in relief. "Thank you."

My heart warmed as her expression relaxed, my tension finally easing.

Frowning again, she lowered her gaze. "I...I have to apologize, too. I shouldn't have stranded you there. I knew you'd be able to get a ride, but it wasn't a very nice thing to do. And I'm sorry I didn't text you back today. I didn't want to say anything before I'd worked through my feelings. You weren't too worried, I hope?" She glanced up at me, concern lighting her eyes.

"I'm not angry you left me there. But I was really upset you didn't text me back. In the future, could you just tell me you want time to work through it?"

She nodded. "I think I can do that."

I stood up, and we closed the distance between us. As we embraced each other, I shut my eyes and buried my face in her neck, breathing deep her scent. A sense of satisfaction, pride, made me smile when I smelled my own unique scent mixed with hers, still faintly present on the jacket I'd loaned her a few days before.

After a long moment, we pulled apart. I slid my fingertips down her arms to hold her hands. She winced when I reached her wrist. I took her hand gently in mine and pushed the sleeve up to look at it.

Instant fury bubbled in my gut when I saw the dark bruise wrapped around her wrist. Any hope of regret I might have felt for almost killing Warren vanished. He'd marked her with his violence. I shook with rage.

"Hey." Yuti placed her hand on my cheek, forcing me to meet her eyes. "I'm fine."

"You're not fine, Yuti. You have a bruise. And this is your drawing hand!"

"I know," she hushed. "I know. But it will heal."

I squeezed my eyes shut, swallowing my anger, swallowing the pain I felt on her behalf. Then I brought her wrist to my lips and brushed it with a kiss.

A hint of maple and caramel mixed in with her scent, but it was gone in a second as Yuti gasped. She took my hands in hers, looking at my palms.

"What happened?" she demanded.

I stared down at my scratched and irritated hands, suddenly aware of the discomfort now that my mind had calmed. "I helped Noire do some weeding today," I explained.

"Did it occur to you to wear gloves?" she censured.

I shrugged, averting my gaze.

She sighed. "Do you have salve at home? Do you want me to go to my place and get some?"

"I'm fine. They will heal," I said, echoing her.

Yuti squinted at me, pursing her lips. "Put something on this when you get home."

"I will."

Yuti tilted her head to the side, glancing around me. "Well, it looks like your ride is here."

My chest swelled at the sad little undertone to her voice. The truth was Ashwin had been sitting in his truck waiting for a good five minutes, but I wasn't about to tell her that.

I didn't want to leave her either. Now that we had made up, I wanted to revel in the glow her presence gave me. I glanced around, hoping I could offer her a ride home at least. But then I saw her car parked on the other side of the street.

"Yeah…I guess I should probably get going." I started to pull away, but she tightened her grip on my hands.

"*Wait.*"

I gazed down at her.

"There's a cult classic showing at the drive-in tomorrow. Do you want to go with me?"

I bent down and kissed her lightly on the mouth. "It's a date," I answered.

Her eyes sparkled as she smiled. "I'll text you the details."

"Okay."

"Goodnight," she said softly.

"Goodnight."

Reluctantly, we parted ways for the evening. Still, I made sure she was safely in her car before I let Ashwin drive away.

It took quite a bit of effort to suppress my grin as Ashwin drove us back to the resort. It had been a long while since I'd felt this good. But it didn't last long.

He glanced over at me. "Seems like things are getting pretty serious. Are you going to tell her?"

I sighed at the weight of his question, and it took me a while to reply. "You've been here for a long time. Have you ever been with a human?"

"No." He shook his head. "My romantic experience was different."

I waited for him to continue, taking in his sardonic smile, which I'd never seen on him before.

"I fell in love early. Very early. Before we'd even been bound with our bondmates... Maple was a packmate. We grew up together. And even after we were bound with our faelings, we stayed in touch. We were even lucky enough to be able to visit each other sometimes. When the time came, we met up at the Wolf Moon Festival..."

His voice grew quieter. "But when it came to entering into a promised bond, a lot had changed for me. Everything that happened with Noire and her bondmate... I wanted to come to the realm of origin to be here for my sister. I asked Maple if she would come with me. She refused. I think she was more than a little ashamed to be in any kind of relationship with someone whose family had brought such shame, what with Noire not completing her rite. I think she was glad when I gave her such an easy out."

He was quiet for a moment. When he spoke again, his tone was lighter. "In any case, you're asking about werewolf relationships with humans, right? I've never been with a human, not that I'm not open to the idea. But Aryn has."

"And did she tell him?" I asked.

"She did."

I frowned. Considering Aryn was unmated, I guessed that the situation hadn't ended well.

"From what I saw, I'd say be very certain about how much she means to you. I can't imagine anything worse than you remembering everything and her not even recognizing you."

Bile rose in my throat, and I swallowed it down.

"But," Ashwin continued. "I wouldn't say Aryn sees it as a tragedy or anything. She was raised in Faerie, same as us. Not many of us even get to experience love in our lives. She once told me she was grateful to her human for making her feel that way. And who knows? Maybe she'll feel that way again. Maybe I will, too."

He was right. After Runa, I never thought I'd love again. With the way the mating system was set up, it was rare for werewolves in Faerie to mate for love. The priorities were to find a mate and sire pups, to feed the treaty that said our children must protect the fae from vampires. The love—if there is any—comes later, surfaces through the mate bond.

But one thing was clear to me in that moment. My anxiety when Yuti hadn't spoken to me that day, my desire to protect her at all costs, my apprehension at the thought that she couldn't accept my true nature—the fact was that I had fallen in love with Yuti. And now I was fully aware of it.

37

The moment I awoke the next morning, I wanted to go see Yuti. But she had some homework to do, so I dutifully waited until the evening when she was to pick me up for the movie. Dutifully, but not patiently. I was so unsettled that I actually asked Noire to give me some work. She sent me to Lia, who had more than enough to do since the boys had gone off with their friends and skipped out on their chores.

Even while my hands were busy, my mind didn't take a break. I ran through a million different ways of telling Yuti I was a werewolf. If we had any hope of a future, it needed to be done. But finding the right moment, the right words, was imperative. I told myself to start looking for openings. Maybe by the end of the night, I'd have my answer.

By the time Yuti pulled up to the house that evening, I was already waiting on the front lawn. The grass was still wet from the thunderstorms we'd had that afternoon, and the temperature wouldn't likely warm up again until the following day.

She got out before I could reach her. She wore black leggings stuffed into her rain boots, a tank top with a green alien head that said *Believe*, a black zip-up hoodie, and a slouch beanie.

Her clothes were practical and comfortable, and she never looked more beautiful. My pulse raced just from being near her, just from looking at her, and I couldn't help but grin.

I closed the distance between us and embraced her. The dull itch that had crawled over my skin throughout the day subsided.

She gave a surprised chuckle but returned my hug. "Miss me?" she teased.

I didn't trust myself to answer.

Easing away from me, she held up her car keys. "Do you want to drive us there?"

I didn't want to. I didn't want to have to pay attention to the road when she was sitting beside me. But I smiled and nodded because she was showing her confidence in me and my abilities.

Once I was behind the wheel, she gave me general directions to where we were going.

"You really have improved a lot," she pointed out as I changed lanes, using my blinker and everything. "Want to take your driver's test soon?"

I'd put in a lot of driving hours. I even knew how to parallel park. "I feel like I should get some driving time on a major highway before that," I said.

"That's probably a good idea. Let's do that next week."

With no hesitation in her voice, her confidence reassured me. If she thought I could do it, she was probably right. I only had to do what she'd taught me.

Not long after, I saw the marquee for the drive-in: Fri Sat Sun *An American Werewolf in London.*

My stomach dropped, and my fingers went numb as my blood turned cold. I had to concentrate very carefully to pull us safely into the next open parking space.

"*An American Werewolf in London?*" I asked, my voice a little unsteady.

Yuti didn't seem to notice. "Yeah, have you seen it?"

I shook my head. I knew, of course, that there were tons of werewolf movies, but I'd never seen one. The idea had always made me uneasy. Would I be able to live happily amongst humans if I saw what they thought of us? I knew the legends, the old stories—the slander—that the humans had propagated as a way to spread fear, the stories that made us something ugly, something vicious. Not just animals but monsters. It was those stories and the persecutions that sprang from them that had made the treaty with the fae necessary to begin with.

"You like movies like this?"

"Horror movies?" she asked. "Occasionally, I mean some of *The X-Files* episodes are pretty scary, right?"

"No. Werewolf movies."

"I like vampire movies better, but who doesn't like a good werewolf flick?"

I sat up straighter, indignant at the insult.

She laughed. "I guess you like werewolves better, huh?"

"Absolutely."

She grinned. "Well, since you haven't seen it, I'm excited to watch it with you."

She tuned the radio to the station broadcasting the movie's sound. Then, reaching into her backseat, Yuti produced a bowl of popcorn. She took off the lid and the rich, salty aroma filled the space.

"Are you allowed to bring outside food in here?" I asked.

She lifted an eyebrow at me, her smirk irresistibly adorable. "Are you going to rat me out to the popcorn police?"

"I wouldn't dare. They'd confiscate it, and I'm sure yours is better."

"You say the sweetest things." Leaning over, she slipped a piece of popcorn into my mouth.

As it melted on my tongue, I watched her closely. The lines of her body, her smooth movements, the slight gloss left on her lips from the ghee she'd drizzled over the popcorn. *What would she taste like if I kissed her now?*

Her dark eyes met mine, and she huffed a laugh, her tongue peeking out ever so slightly between her teeth and her lower lip. "Screen is that way." She pointed past the windshield.

"You don't say."

"You're going to miss the beginning," she added softly.

My heart pumped hard at the slight breathy rasp in her voice.

"It's still the credits," I argued though I had no idea if that was true since I wasn't looking at the screen, but "Blue Moon" was still playing in the car speakers. "You're beautiful," I said simply.

She stared at me for a moment, her eyes glinting

in the light from the screen. Readjusting her grip on the bowl, she leaned over and pressed a soft, salty kiss to my lips.

Her scent warmed with maple and caramel, and blood rushed to my loins. But she didn't indulge either of us for more than a brief moment.

"Thank you," she whispered, her breath still on my lips. "Now watch the movie."

Pulling back, she returned to her seat as if nothing had happened. But she couldn't fool my nose. The scent of her arousal lingered in the air, making it very hard to concentrate on the film. It wasn't until the werewolf on the moors was tearing into the two backpackers that it fully disappeared.

The movie truly horrified me. It was gruesome. It wasn't that being attacked by a werewolf wouldn't be that graphic and brutal. Of course it would. It was the inaccuracy of it all. The creature depicted was a weird mixture of human and wolf, not one or the other but some freakish form stuck in-between. The werewolf had no memories, and he had the innate desire to just blindly slaughter anything and everything.

If these were the stories humans told centuries ago, I could understand why they wanted to kill us. *Is this how Yuti sees us?*

And then there was the uncomfortable juxtaposition of sex and violence. One moment we were watching pornography, then the screen flashed to his mutilated victims, the erotic sounds of sex loud and arousing as the shredded bodies urged the werewolf to kill himself. I didn't know how to feel, and the whole experience was very uncomfortable. I was glad when the movie was over.

"Is that what you think werewolves are really like?" I waited for the other cars at the drive-in to leave before I attempted to pull out. I held my breath for her response.

She burst out laughing. "Just because I believe in aliens, doesn't mean I believe in *everything*. Come on, there's no way werewolves are real."

I blinked at her. "Why are aliens more plausible than werewolves?"

She rolled her eyes and gave me an exasperated look. "I mean, the universe is huge. It would be stranger for humans to be the only intelligent life out there. It just doesn't make mathematical sense. But werewolves? Don't you think we would know about that by now? How could they live among us without our knowing? Might as well say Big Foot is real."

I didn't know what a Big Foot was, so I didn't argue that point. "What if they could? I mean, how would you know? They have human forms too after all."

"Yeah, but there would be signs, right? Like how can a bunch a people turn into monsters every full moon and no one notices? Not their families? Friends? Neighbors? *No* one?"

I flinched at the word. *Monster.* My heart sank. I knew it wasn't her fault. She'd been fed lies her whole life, the entire human race had been for centuries. Even the point about the full moon wasn't accurate. It still hurt. Maybe, if I came at this the right way, I could get her to see us for who we really were. But I was too shaken to try at the moment.

"Yeah..." I kept my eyes on the road. "You're probably right."

38

With the way my wolf was responding to Yuti, with the way my heart and body were, I knew staying away from her wasn't an option—at least not yet, not when I knew she still wanted me. But I also knew I needed some way of softening the blow, of easing her in, before I told her the full truth.

I decided in order to do that I'd become an expert on human werewolf stories. Well, a targeted expert anyway. I went online and found as much research as I could to support a more accurate view of werewolves.

Some of this research was from old books that had been archived. While they didn't paint werewolves in a particularly good light, they were at least accurate as far as transformational form and timing. I also found some whispers of werewolves seen as friendly or as guardians and protectors.

Each time I hung out with Yuti, I would present these findings to her.

"Wow, you're really getting into this," she said as I read her an article on my phone while she cooked in her kitchenette.

I frowned. "Do you mind?"

She smiled at me over her shoulder. "Not at all. It's interesting to learn about folktales and stuff. Who knew werewolves had so many interpretations?"

My anxiety eased a little. Yuti had proven to be open-minded. And I was starting to have hope though not too much. Hearing various views on werewolves, even accepting the possibility that there are werewolves and they aren't just out to murder you, isn't the same as dating one.

"Here." Yuti approached me on the couch with a spoon in her hand. "Try this."

I eyed the multi-colored food. It appeared to be fried potatoes, pomegranate seeds, green herbs, and some yellow bits I couldn't identify—all topped with a white sauce. "Is it vegetarian?"

"It's aloo chaat. Just try it."

"Mmm, no thanks."

"Come on." She rested one knee on the couch and moved the spoon closer to my mouth. "It's good. I made it myself."

I leaned away from her, turning my head so she couldn't reach it. But she only became more persistent.

"Try it," she growled, practically pinning me as she leaned her weight on her hand near my head.

Between the warmth of her body, inches from mine, and her scent—so intoxicating it overpowered the rich spiciness that filled the air of her small apartment—I froze.

She took advantage of my surprise and shoved the spoon into my mouth.

A complex mixture of textures and tastes rolled over my tongue. It was actually quite good. But I barely spared a thought for the food as I swallowed.

Yuti met my eyes and grinned. But as I let out an uneven breath, her smile slowly faded. The scent of maple syrup and caramel was the only encouragement I needed.

I lifted my head, meeting her lips in a patient but purposeful kiss. She was not so patient, and a jolt of electricity ran through me as she slipped her tongue into my mouth. The soft *tink* of the metal spoon hitting the floor sounded very far away, muffled by our mingled breaths.

She lowered her weight on top of me, her soft body yielding to mine. My heart raced, and my cock stiffened as she pressed her palms against my chest, warm even through the fabric of my shirt.

Slipping her supple thigh between my legs, she pulled back only enough to meet my eyes through heavy lids, her playful smile telling me she knew just how aroused she'd made me. And as she pressed a much more urgent kiss to my lips, I knew she liked my response to her.

Every breath, every rustle of fabric, sent tingles across my skin. Lust raged in my veins, and I could be submissive no more.

Switching our positions, I watched her response as I looked down at her. She felt too small beneath me. But she wrapped her arms around my neck, pulling me toward her.

Every kiss on her mouth, on her neck, released a

little more of her arousal scent. I was swimming in it. I was drowning in it.

She moved against me, her motions encouraging, always asking for more, until she panted in my ear. "Please, Rowan," she begged, her breath hot and her words only a whisper.

I met her eyes, dark and clouded with desire.

"Touch me, please," she said, and there was no misunderstanding what she was asking for. Her face was warm, flushed, but there was no embarrassment in her gaze.

My cock throbbed, and my wolf wanted her. He wanted to mark her as his. His promised. His mate. His alone.

I squeezed my eyes shut, swallowing hard. My stomach dropped, then clenched at what I was about to do. "I can't," I said.

Her brow furrowed. "What?" Her tone was thick with confusion. But the bewilderment swimming in her eyes soon changed. She wiggled beneath me, an attempt to free herself rather than entice. I moved away from her, giving her space to sit up.

The scent of her desire disappeared; only the stale aftermath hung in the air.

"Did I do something wrong?" she asked.

"No," I reassured hurriedly. "No, you didn't do anything wrong."

She frowned. Her eyes were focused on something behind me as if she were thinking intently and I was a distraction.

"Do you…not find me attractive?"

My brain fully stopped working at her words. I had no idea how she could have come to such an outrageous conclusion. Had I not been clear somewhere along the way? "Huh?" I grunted, no words to express my stupefaction.

But she didn't clarify. She lowered her eyes, withdrawing from the conversation.

How could I tell her that I wanted her, that there was nothing in the world I wanted so much as her? It was I who was the problem. It didn't feel right to have sex with her, to connect with her in that way, when she didn't even know who I was. She had no way of knowing what she was getting into. It felt like a violation. And though she might not have thought that at the moment, she might feel differently once she knew the truth.

This wasn't a frivolous coupling of two wolves having a good time at the Wolf Moon Festival. This merging mattered to my wolf. He'd had one promised snatched away, and he wasn't about to let his second chance go. If I had sex with her—if I let her in—and she rejected me later, I didn't think I could recover.

"It's not that," I told her.

Her expression was entirely unconvinced.

I knelt beside the couch, taking her hand in mine. I stared at her, compelling her to meet my eyes. "Yutika, you're *beautiful*. You're attractive. I *want* to make love to you."

"But?" she prompted.

"But...I'm not ready." That wasn't quite the truth, but I didn't have a better way of putting it.

She was silent for a while, analyzing my face. "Are you a virgin? Is that why?"

That wasn't why. Werewolves, especially werewolves raised in Faerie, put no such sacred emphasis on virginity. But technically, it was true.

"Yes, I'm a virgin." I answered only her first question.

Yuti placed her free hand over mine. "That's okay. So am I. But you know what?"

"What?"

"I trust you, Rowan. I feel safe with you."

I'd never been so moved—so proud, so miserable—by any words said to me.

"I'll wait until you're ready," she promised. Then she leaned forward and pressed a kiss to my lips. It was sweet with only the hint of her earlier desire. "But I hope you don't make me wait too long."

39

I stared up at my bedroom ceiling, then squeezed my eyes shut and groaned. "You're a fucking idiot," I told myself.

I couldn't believe I'd walked away from Yuti when she had been so open, so willing. Leaving her apartment had taken all of my inner strength. It was like playing tug-of-war with my wolf.

The distance I'd put between us had done nothing to diminish my desire. *"Touch me, please."* I shivered as though Yuti were still whispering in my ear.

I puffed out my cheeks and blew out a heavy breath. Then I rolled over on my side and reached for the drawer of my nightstand. I didn't find what I was looking for.

After getting up from my bed, I went to the bathroom. In the cabinet under the sink, I opened the jar of no-questions-asked condoms that Lia kept stocked for the pack.

I remembered being surprised by them when I'd

first come to stay. Not because they were shared so openly. Everyone there was a werewolf, and we all knew about werewolf sex drives. I'd never seen a condom before. They weren't exactly necessary in Faerie. I was amazed at human engineering and how it drastically reduced the mess of self-service.

Taking a few of them back to my room, I put all but one in my nightstand drawer. And after I rolled it on and closed my eyes, I was right back in Yuti's apartment.

I could still feel her slipping her thigh between my legs, her firm flesh pressing against me. I shuddered, a jolt running through me as my fingers wrapped around the shaft of my cock.

Her eyes clouded with lust. *"Please, Rowan."* My breath became ragged, the warm pressure from my hand gliding smoothly up and down while I stroked.

I could still smell her scent on my clothes. Cinnamon and citrus. Maple syrup and caramel. My heart hammered in my chest.

"Don't make me wait too long."

My body seized and then jerked, my breath coming out in a rush as the proof of my desire for her spilled into the condom.

I let my arm drop to the bed, my limbs heavy with relief. After a few deep breaths, I pulled off the condom and threw it into my bedroom trash can. Then I closed my eyes and drifted off to sleep.

The summer night was alive with the sounds of nocturnal creatures singing to each other. We sat atop the ski hill. I'd turned off the lift and all the lights to give Yuti a better view of the stars. Even in the dark, I could see her smiling at me.

"It's pretty isolated up here." Her voice was low, almost a whisper. "The closest people are at the resort. And they're way down there."

Her suggestive tone elicited an immediate response from my manhood.

She leaned toward me, and my heart squeezed. I didn't move, but I didn't need to. She closed the distance between us, her lips voracious and insistent.

My body flushed, my heart pumping hard.

Smiling mischievously, she pulled away. "Have you ever wondered what it would be like to have sex in the wild like this? Just two more animals merging on a summer night."

My wolf was fully ready to make that fantasy a reality this very moment, and I agreed with him. But I frowned. "Yuti, I have to tell you something."

She wasn't deterred by my tone. Shifting her weight, she climbed smoothly into my lap. The feel of her thighs straddling my hips made me question how important it really was to tell her the truth. *Do I really have to tell her* right now?

"Right now?" she asked, slipping her arms around my neck and pressing a feathery kiss to my lips.

I clamped down on my impulse to give in. "Yes, it's important."

She kissed me again. "Okay. Tell me," she whispered against my mouth.

Her fingers playing with the hair at the nape of my neck, her weight pressing against me, her every breath on my face—my mind grew foggier and less resolved with every passing moment. I swallowed, my throat dry. "I'm a werewolf."

Before I could muster any concern about what her reaction would be, she said, "I know. Is that what was so important? Because I have something far more *pressing* to address." She ground her core against my cock.

My control snapped. Wrapping my arms around her, I crushed her to me, and she was all too willing as she moaned against my lips.

But just as I slid my hand up the smooth skin of her back, a horrible buzzing screamed in my ear.

My eyes flew open at the sound of my alarm clock. My body was flushed and my erection throbbing.

I slammed the snooze button. Closing my eyes, I sighed heavily. *This can't go on.*

With the images and sensations from my dream still swirling in my head, I reached for another condom from my drawer. I was finished before the snooze on the alarm clock expired.

It was Friday, and I had to work the morning shift. But as I showered and brushed my teeth, I made a resolution: I had to tell Yuti the truth. I'd call into work if I needed to.

I knew she wouldn't respond the way she had in my dream, but the longer this hung over my head, the worse it would be.

I entered the kitchen as the pack—minus the boys, who slept in during summer break—was about to sit down to breakfast.

"I'm going to tell Yuti," I announced.

They all looked at me.

"When?" Lia asked.

"Right now," I said. "If someone will give me a ride."

Ashwin grabbed two pieces of toast from the table and tossed one at me. "Let's go." He bit into his slice as he made for the door.

40

My leg shook with impatience the entire drive into town. I didn't know exactly what I was going to say, but I had to tell her.

Ashwin stopped at the end of Yuti's street. "Good luck. Let us know how it goes."

Let us know if we need to call a fae to come wipe her memory. But when I started to answer that I would, I realized that I'd forgotten my phone. In fact, I'd been so worked up last night that I couldn't even remember if I'd plugged it in to charge.

"Uh…I left my phone in my room."

Ashwin shrugged. "Take mine." He reached into his pocket and handed me a small flip phone.

"Thanks."

I got out of the truck and shut the door behind me, flinching at the sound, too loud in the predawn hush.

Ashwin gave me a thumbs-up of encouragement from inside the truck.

I straightened my back and strode forward with

confidence, but every step I took was a chisel strike, chipping away at my resolve.

Finally standing on the front porch, I took a deep breath—swallowing my pounding heart—and reached for Yuti's doorbell. But before my finger even touched the button, the door opened.

Yuti's eyes widened in surprise.

I froze, staring at her as my breath rushed out of me. She wore a long skirt, carnation pink in the early morning light, that somehow wrapped around her waist, then over one shoulder. Her emerald shirt was short, exposing her full midriff.

She looked down at herself, then she smiled with a soft huff of a giggle. "Yeah, I always wear a sari when my grandparents visit. It's a whole thing. So did you come to see me off? How come you didn't answer me last night?"

I focused on her face. Her hair was uncovered by a hat, and she wore an emerald stud in her nose.

"Last night? I never got anything. I think I forgot to plug in my phone. Are you…going somewhere?"

"Yes, I'm going home for the weekend. My grandparents are visiting from India."

My chest tightened. "And you're leaving right now?"

She nodded. "My bags are already in the car. I was just checking to make sure I hadn't forgotten anything before I left."

My sorrow must have shown on my face because she reached out and stroked my arm, her eyes gentle and reassuring. "I'll only be gone a few days. I'll be back Sunday."

Now is not the right time to tell her I'm a werewolf. It's much too big a conversation for such a short amount of time.

"So what brings you here before work? If you didn't get my messages, you must've wanted something."

Her dark eyes met mine, expectation swimming in her gaze.

"I just had something I wanted to tell you, but it can wait until you get back."

"Oh, come on. You can't do that. Now the curiosity is going to be gnawing at me all weekend. Tell me." Her eyes pleaded with me.

I took her hands, the thin, green bracelets on her wrist tinkling as I brought her hands to my lips. I kissed the knuckles of each, my lips trembling while my heart quaked within me. Her gaze never wavered from mine.

"I love you," I whispered, my throat too dry to say it any louder.

Her breath rushed out of her, and her face flushed with that warm undertone. Then she smiled, and her eyes sparkled. "I love you, too, Rowan."

I swallowed against the emotions rising in my throat. My hands shook and a shiver ran through me, raising the hairs on my arms. I felt relieved, warm, light, and terrified to my core. In that moment, I knew that not only had I long given up on ever hearing those words, but I had felt unworthy of them.

I slipped my arms around Yuti's back, pulling her into an embrace. Burying my face in her neck, I breathed in her scent. The fabric of her sari was delicate and soft as it brushed against my cheek. I stroked the smooth skin of her back with my fingertips, and she quivered against me.

"Thank you," I murmured, pressing my lips to the sensitive skin where her neck met her shoulders.

Maple syrup and caramel swirled into her cinnamon and citrus scent. She pulled away gently. "You're naughty," she scolded with a smile. "You know I have to leave, and you tease me like that."

"I'm sorry," I lied.

She was not convinced, squinting up at me. Then she sighed heavily. "Ugh, now I wish I didn't have to go."

"Me too."

She pursed her lips. "Actually, wait here a second."

Leaving me on the porch, Yuti went back inside and came out a few minutes later, a sketchbook in her hand. She held it out to me. "Don't look at them until I'm gone. Okay?"

I nodded, itching with curiosity.

"And you can't keep it. I want it back. Okay, you can keep one. But don't pull it out without me approving which one you picked."

"All right."

Yuti clicked her tongue. "I really do have to go now, and you'll be late for work if you don't run. You want me to drop you off?"

As much as I wanted to stay with Yuti for even a second longer, I needed time to think before starting work.

"No, thanks. I could use the walk."

She was clearly disappointed.

"Hey," I said, wiggling her hand to get her to

meet my gaze. "I love you," I declared again, much more clearly and with more confidence.

The declaration immediately brought the smile back to her face. "I love you, too."

Wrapping her arms around my neck, Yuti stood on her toes and kissed me. It was soft and sweet, but our parting gave it a bitter aftertaste.

"You can text me anytime," she said.

"I will. As soon as I get home. Be careful on the roads. No texting and driving."

"I'll be careful," she promised. Then she gave me another peck. "I'll see you on Sunday."

Nodding, I reluctantly let her slip from my arms. Then I grabbed her hand, and she led the way to her car, every step echoing in my heart. Too soon, we stood by the driver's side door.

"Well..." she muttered.

"Enjoy your visit. I'll be here waiting for you."

Throwing herself against me, Yuti kissed me deeply, and I felt the force of it in every ounce of my being. It was a kiss of declaration. It was a kiss that my wolf recognized all too well. I had been claimed.

Breaking away, Yuti smiled as if she were proud of a task she'd completed.

I stood, stupefied, then blew my breath out in a loud rush. I had no words.

"See you Sunday," Yuti repeated. Then she got in her car and started the engine.

It took every bit of strength I had not to run after her, not to chase her car down the street like a dog who can't control its instincts.

41

A dull ache settled in my chest, and I knew it wouldn't be gone until Yuti returned. My heart was warm, still glowing from her declaration, but heavy. She loved me. And the only thing that could ruin that was the truth I'd kept from her: she couldn't really know if she loved me or not if she didn't really know who I was.

I told myself that, trying to temper my exhilaration with a hearty dose of reality. But my wolf was not to be reasoned with. As far as he was concerned, he had been claimed. And he jumped and wagged like a yearling after spring's thaw. All he wanted was to make this woman his promised, to make her his mate.

I knew I needed to tell her as soon as possible before I made things worse for myself. But it couldn't have been helped. It hadn't been the right time. For now, I could only hope that when she came back and when I told her, her love for me would be strong enough.

As I walked across campus, I pulled out Ashwin's phone and called Lia.

"Hey, it's Rowan. Ashwin gave me his phone because I forgot mine."

"How did it go?"

"I didn't tell her. She was on her way out of town. It didn't seem the right time."

"How long will she be gone?"

"She's coming back on Sunday. Maybe it's a good thing I didn't get to tell her. Maybe I got too far ahead of myself. She has finals next week. She said they're mostly projects and papers, and she's got most of them done, but she does have one exam she'll want to study for. What I had to say would have distracted her from that."

Lia hummed her acknowledgment, no doubt hearing the stress of being away from Yuti in my voice. "Didn't you say your sister's unbinding was this weekend?"

"What's the date?"

"July 26."

I thought about the letter and invitation, still in a drawer of my desk. "Yeah, I guess her unbinding is tomorrow."

"Why don't you go? It sounds like you're already uncomfortable with being away from Yuti. Perhaps a change of scenery will distract you. You haven't seen your family in a while. And it's tradition for family members to go to an unbinding, isn't it?"

"I'll...think about it."

"You do that. And if you decide not to go, we can keep you busy. Braylyn has been asking to go camping. It might be nice to head off into the wilderness for a few days."

At the moment, nothing sounded appealing to me, nothing but sitting on Yuti's doorstep and howling until she came back to me. "Anyway, I'm almost at work now, and I'm running late. I'll see you later."

When I entered the café, Camille looked over at the door. I could tell just by the set of her mouth that she was going to scold me. I must've appeared truly pathetic because she asked me what was wrong instead.

"Sorry I'm late. Yuti's going home for the week-end, and I went to see her off."

"Ah, so that's why your face looks like that. As your boss, I should tell you not to let it happen again. But as your friend, I hope you had a nice goodbye."

"Thanks, Camille."

"You're lucky I'm such a romantic at heart."

I went to the break room to put Ashwin's phone and Yuti's sketchbook away.

"So did you?" Camille asked as I tied my apron strings.

"Did I what?"

"Did you have a nice goodbye?"

"Yes." Despite the warmth in my chest and the smile on my face, my voice sounded sad even to my own ears.

Camille stared at me, the bag of coffee beans she was about to open forgotten. "Would you like to elaborate on that?"

Normally, I didn't tell Camille such intimate details no matter how much she asked. I had excellent deflection skills when it came to dodging her questions. Plus, it was just fun to tease her, regardless of what topic she was asking about. But she was sort of my friend, and she had been supporting Yuti and me since before there was a Yuti and me.

"I…told her I loved her," I admitted.

Camille gasped, squeezing the bag of beans between her hands. "And?"

"And she said it back."

Camille grinned, a little squeak of delight escaping her throat. "I knew it! *Finally*. Ugh." Her eyes softened behind her blue sunglasses. "I'm so happy for you two, really."

"Thanks."

Because I'd been late, I had to work extra hard to get the café ready before the doors opened. And on a Friday morning, it was packed. I didn't even get a breather until my lunch break.

Sighing just to get off my feet, I sat down at the round table in the break room and unwrapped my café sandwich. As I took my first bite, my eyes drifted around the room and landed on the sketchbook Yuti had given me that morning. I took another bite and retrieved the book.

The sketchbook seemed normal enough. It had a blue cover of thick cardstock. But as I opened it, I clamped my lips together, trying not to spew bits of food onto the page.

The first sketch was of me. She'd drawn me offering a cappuccino cup, the only color the arctic blue of my eyes. My stomach fluttered. I felt her love in every line. The drawing was dated around the time when I first began working at the café.

And it wasn't the only one. Every page had a

picture of me. Sometimes I was at the café. Sometimes I was leaning against a tree in the quad. I looked playful, peaceful, irritated. I laughed. I frowned. She'd captured every face I'd ever shown her. Some of the later pages were more recent. My heart pounded as I saw my own desire staring back at me. And on the last page, she'd even captured my love for her in the light of my eyes, in the lines of my mouth.

She'd seen it all, knew it all. *Well, almost all.* There weren't any pictures of wolves in the book.

42

The moment I got home, I raced up the stairs and plugged in my phone. I tapped my fingers on the case for the full thirty seconds the phone took to charge enough to turn on. Once I unlocked it, it was one chime after another as half a dozen text messages from Yuti finally came through, informing me that she was going home.

> Did you get home all right?

In less than a minute, I received a photo of Yuti and a much older woman, who I assumed was her grandmother. They both smiled brightly, clearly happy to be reunited, their faces pressed cheek-to-cheek to fit into the frame.

> Dādī says hi.

> Hello, Dādī.

Dādī says you're handsome.

My chest warmed. *Yuti is telling her family about me? But does she have any pictures of me? Maybe she showed them one of her sketches.*

(≚ ‿≚) Thanks, Dādī.

I was glad she was having fun with her family. It made being away from her a little more bearable and a little more lonely. My gaze drifted to my desk, and I sighed.

Hey, I think I'm going to go home tomorrow, too. My sister has a sort of rite of passage thing going on, and I should really be there.

Oh! That'll be fun. When will you be back?

I'll be here on Sunday for sure.

But...there isn't cell service where I'm going, so you won't be able to reach me.

(┳_┳) I understand. Be careful, and let me know when you get back. Okay?

I will. (^ ‿ ^)⊃ ♡

(^ 3 ^) ~♡

I smiled when I received her response. Then I left my phone plugged in and went to tell Lia of my plans.

The next morning, as Ashwin drove me toward the nearest portal to Faerie, I couldn't manage to sit still. My skin tingled—an itchy sort of sensation—and I kept moving my shoulders to relieve it.

"I'll be in the area all day, okay?" Ashwin said. "As soon as you call, I'll come pick you up."

I nodded, his words calming me a little.

Ashwin pulled off the narrow road that wound up the mountain and stopped at an overlook. "Do you need me to show you the way?"

"No," I said. "I remember it. Besides, it's marked, isn't it?"

"Yeah." Every so often, Ashwin would come out here and mark the path in case a werewolf from Faerie lost the way. "All right then. Good luck."

"Thanks." I got out of the truck.

Gravel crunched under the tires as Ashwin pulled away.

Staring at the trailhead across from the overlook, I took a deep breath and crossed the street. The packed-dirt path of the trail was soft under my boots, and the early morning mountain air was fresh and crisp. The sensations of being out in nature settled my nerves.

I got to be a wolf around my pack, of course, but I was still around humans much of the time; the realm of origin was dominated by them. I'd had to be careful to act appropriately while living among the fae when bound with Wilhelm, but I didn't have to hide who I was. Living in the realm of origin was a trade-off, freedom in some ways and restrictions in others.

The prospect of being openly werewolf in public again, even for a day, put a hop in my step as I hiked toward the portal.

Half a mile along the trail, Ashwin's path to Faerie diverged. I stepped off the trail and followed the scent for another mile. Finally, I reached a pair of trees, twisted and misshapen as they grew together. There was an opening near the ground, a small space where the trees didn't meet at their bases. The door to Faerie didn't look like anything out of the ordinary. If you didn't know it was there, you'd never find it.

I took my phone from my pocket, turned it off, and dropped it into a water-tight bag. Then I stuck it under a hollowed-out rock that Ashwin had put near the trees.

Taking a deep breath, I got down on my hands and knees and crawled through the opening and the veil.

I came out near a small, still lake.

Even this early in the morning, it was hot in this part of Faerie. The cicadas were loud and insistent, and gnats and mosquitoes buzzed around my head. I didn't delay departing the stagnant lake, not wanting to be eaten alive.

It took another thirty minutes before I reached the nearest town. It was small as all border towns were. I'd never spent more than a few minutes in it, but I knew where the depot was.

The depot was dead. The fae conductor was the only resident, and she sat slouching on a bench reading a book.

I cleared my throat as I entered. She looked up from her book, eyeing my human attire.

"Where are you headed?" she asked.

I paused, frowning. *It's a long while before Willow's ceremony starts. Should I show up this early?*

"Avton." I stepped into the only transportation circle. *I might as well stop in at the Fireleaf farm to see how they're doing.*

The conductor muttered her spell. The circle glowed, then flashed yellow, and I stood in a familiar depot.

Robin, the conductor at the Avton depot, smiled upon recognizing me. "Coming for a visit?"

I nodded. "Just a short one. I'll be back in a couple of hours."

"I'll be here."

43

My feet carried me down the road out of town toward the Fireleaf farm, each step familiar from the many times I'd walked it. Despite the liveliness of summer all around me, it felt unnaturally quiet. This was the first time I'd walked this road alone. Even after my unbinding, Wilhelm had walked beside me, talkative as ever.

I readjusted my shoulders, trying to relieve the foreign feeling. Then I picked up my pace until the farm finally came into view.

Slowing my steps, I took in the fields of lush herbs, the fields I had spent the majority of my childhood running and playing in. I breathed deep the summer air and flinched when I could no longer smell my scent marking the boundaries of my former home.

A high-pitched scream pierced the air, and my easy stride turned into a sprint. My heart pounded in my chest, panic crawling across my skin, as I raced around the house.

I skidded to a halt.

Wilhelm and Arete, each with a bucket and ladle in hand, splashed water on each other. Arete squealed again, dropping her bucket and running from her mate. Wilhelm caught her easily and wrapped his arms around her waist. She giggled and spun around in his embrace. Then she kissed him deeply; he didn't hold back either.

My eyebrows rose at their blatant lovemaking. Even between mates, fae didn't usually show such public signs of affection although their own yard was hardly public.

"Should I come back at a better time?" I grinned.

Both of their heads whipped toward me.

"Rowan?" Wilhelm's delighted surprise was apparent in the tone of his voice.

"Who else?"

Releasing each other, they moved toward me. Wilhelm reached me first, embracing me as he would his own brother.

"Welcome." He pulled back and took me in with his eyes. "How have you been?"

"We can talk about that in a bit," I said to my lifelong friend before turning to his mate. "It's nice to see you again, Arete."

Her hazel, woodland eyes were warm and welcoming. Then she too embraced me. "Welcome back. You'll stay for lunch?"

"I will. Thank you."

"I'll go let Kat and Ed know you're here," she said.

Wilhelm watched her walk away, his eyes sparkling with love and admiration.

"You seem to have settled into mated life quite well," I observed.

Wilhelm's grin broadened as his face flushed. "You, uh, caught me at an interesting time."

I laughed at my friend, clapping him on the shoulder. "It's good to see you so happy. So what have you been up to?"

"Same as always, I suppose." He shrugged. "Not much has changed really. Arete and I work the farm with Mom and Dad. Her family has developed a few new spells to help our plants become hardier so we have a better yield. But other than that, things are pretty quiet. About the same level of activity as when Konner and Runa left and it was just the four of us."

Wilhelm clamped his mouth shut, realizing his misstep too late. I frowned, but the sound of her name no longer gave me the heartache it once had. Sadness, sure, but not the soul-wrenching pain of loss.

"I'm so—"

"It's fine." I cut off his apology. "I'm fine. But thank you."

Wilhelm eyed me, leaning back as if that would help him see me better. "Something has changed. What's up?"

I chuckled. It seemed that even with a dissolved bondmate bond, I couldn't get away from Wilhelm's knowledge of me. Wilhelm was a chatterbox, a fun-loving troublemaker, and he could be a little dense sometimes, but he'd always known what I was feeling as well-matched bondmates ought to.

"I guess I can't pull one over on you. I met someone—a human."

Wilhelm blinked at me, at a loss for words for the first time in this life. Though it didn't last long. "And you care about her?"

I nodded. "Very much."

"And she…?"

The echo of Yuti's words warmed me, and I couldn't help but smile. "She loves me, too."

"Rowan, that's great! Congratulations!"

I couldn't return his enthusiasm. "There…may be a slight problem."

He sobered up. "What?"

"She doesn't know I'm a werewolf…and her best friend may be a vampire."

Wilhelm's mouth dropped open. "Okay, you're going to need to start at the beginning. Let's go get the others, and you can tell us the whole story."

It took the rest of the morning, but I finally explained my situation and everything that led up to it to the Fireleafs. They hung on my every word as though I were telling a ghost story around a campfire. They laughed, they gasped, they leaned forward in their seats — completely enthralled.

"What are you going to do?" Kat asked from the kitchen counter while she prepared lunch.

I leaned my elbows on the kitchen table, resting my chin on my fist. "Well, I have to tell her, right? I don't have a lot of options."

"But Konner said humans can react violently to things they don't understand." Wilhelm, sitting across from me, looked worried.

I gazed out the kitchen window at the blue summer sky and answered his concerns in a far-off voice that didn't seem to belong to me at all. "The wolves in the realm of origin have a network of fae they work with, fae that also live in that realm. If someone…if Yuti can't handle it, or reacts badly, they'll wipe me from her memories. That's…the kindest of their potential responses."

Arete gasped, grabbing Wilhelm's hand on top of the table. "How awful!"

The more I thought about it, the more my chest tightened, my heart struggling to pump in the constrained space. "It's the price we pay, I guess."

Ed sighed heavily. "There's always a risk when it comes to love, but it also comes with the greatest rewards. You don't want to build a relationship on lies, Rowan. It will rot what you have from the inside out."

"I know."

The tense silence lasted only a moment, broken as Kat announced lunch was ready. It was much too hot to stay in the house any longer, so we all took the food outside.

My mouth watered as I bit into a juicy berry. As much as I enjoyed food in the realm of origin, nothing could compare to the pure magic of the food in Faerie. And the berry bushes on the Fireleaf farm were the sweetest I'd ever tasted. I hummed my appreciation. "Wow, I'd almost forgotten how good it can be."

Kat smiled, her lips still red with the juice from the berry she'd just swallowed. "I'll pack some up for you to take back."

I thanked her and shoved another into my mouth. My eyes drifted over the familiar yard as we ate and chatted. I'd had so many happy memories here. My gaze landed on the step where Runa and I had shared a glass of tea, where we had shared our dreams, where we had almost kissed. *I also have some bittersweet memories.*

I forced my attention away, then tilted my head when I saw something unfamiliar. "How long has that been there?" I pointed at a vine of ivy climbing up the side of the house.

Everyone looked.

"Oh," Arete said. "My parents gave that to Wilhelm and me as a mating gift. It was the first plant they tried their ever-love growth spell on."

I smiled to myself. "Too bad we don't have things like that in the realm of origin. Yuti said everything she tries to grow dies."

"Would you like a clipping?" Arete asked. "We can propagate it, give you a little part that will grow on its own. Ivy is easy to take care of. And even better, this magic grows with love. The more love a person has, the healthier the plant will be."

I thought of Yuti's eyes sparkling with joy as she looked at her healthy, green ivy. "I think I will take some back for her. Thank you."

44

---

*L*ater that afternoon, laden with a basket packed with berries and a potted ivy clipping, I headed back to Avton's depot.

Robin asked me where I wanted to go.

"Mysraina," I told him.

"Whoa, really? All the way to the capital? It's a big place, and there are a lot of depots. Do you have an address?"

I handed him the invitation to my sister's unbinding, and he walked toward his directory book, which sat on a tall bookstand against the wall.

After a few minutes of searching, he returned the invitation to me. Then he motioned for me to get into the transportation circle.

"Say hello to the queen for me," he said with a smile before uttering his spell and sending me on my way.

The depot I arrived in was large and bustling even though it wasn't Mysraina's central depot. I quickly stepped out of the circle and made for the exit.

Out in the street, my mouth dropped open. I'd been impressed with the human city Yuti and I had visited, but I'd never seen anything as glorious as Mysraina. The focal point of the city, what everyone's eye immediately went to, was the mountain. It rose up at the center, the city surrounding it on all sides. A road spiraled upward, leading to the fae royal palace, where the same family had been ruling Faerie for centuries.

On this clear summer day, I could see the palace —all silver and green in the sunshine—which was usually shrouded in mist. The winding road was dotted with temples and sanctuaries of various sizes and purposes.

At the foot of the mountain, the city proper began; homes and shops squeezed together as if trying to shove each other out of the way to get a glimpse of the royal family.

Yuti's voice echoed in my mind, *"You might want to close your mouth. Nothing says tourist quite like that look on your face."*

I smiled to myself, wondering what Yuti would think of a place like this. I'd never been to Mysraina though my sister had lived here since she'd been bound with Feather. In fact, I hadn't seen Willow in over a decade before she and Feather attended my unbinding.

Walking along the busy street, I took in the buildings around me. Most were no more than two stories. Some were cobblestone with thatched roofs, some brick. Some were smooth and gleaming white while others were more modern, wood constructions. Mysraina was the oldest and biggest city in Faerie, and the buildings reflected the many eras it had seen.

Coming to a crossroads, I stood on one corner, looking around to decide which way to go.

"Are you lost?" someone asked from behind me.

I turned around and faced an elderly fae who was coming out of a flower shop.

I smiled sheepishly. "I think I might be."

"Where are you headed?"

I handed her the invitation.

"Ah. East Everly." She nodded. "You're heading in the right direction. You just go two blocks farther, then it's three blocks to your left."

I thanked her.

"You're going to an unbinding?"

"Yes, my sister's."

"Wait here for a second." She went back into the shop.

A few moments later, she returned and held out a wreath of fragrant, yellow flowers and small, orange ones.

"For your sister." She smiled. "Freesia and milkweed."

I reached into my pocket, glad I'd brought a little Faerie money with me. But she held up a hand to stop me.

"Knowing that another faeling will make it through her awakening because of the protection your sister provided is payment enough for me."

"Well, if you won't take money, would you like some berries? I just came from a farm in Avton."

The woman accepted a handful of berries, and she waved her goodbye with a smile.

Her directions soon brought me to a square, two-story house, its smooth, white façade embellished with a front portico.

My knock on the door was promptly answered by a fae woman dressed all in white.

"You must be Rowan." She smiled. "I'm Lillia Bayberry, Feather's mother."

I bowed my head.

"Willow told me what you look like. Please, come in. Your parents are already here. They're in the courtyard with Willow."

I followed Mistress Bayberry into her home, which had an open floor plan. Standing in the entryway, I could see the kitchen, dining area, and sitting room, all the inner walls opening into a courtyard.

My family looked over at me as I approached. Though I'd seen them at my unbinding, I couldn't get over how much my parents had aged. Most of my memories of them were from when I was quite young. Over a decade later, my father's ashen hair was streaked with white, and my mother's eyes had wrinkles in the corners as she smiled at me.

If seen together, one would never know Willow and I were even related. She was shorter and leaner than I—though that was to be expected—with amber eyes and long, gray hair, which varied in hue as the light and shadow played in it.

The welcome I'd received at the Fireleaf farm was much warmer than the reunion with my own family. It wasn't that we didn't love each other; it was more that we didn't really know each other anymore. We could only share so much of ourselves in letters, and not much at all when our letters were infrequent.

As my mother embraced me, I realized just what the bondmate system cost the wolves.

45

After I'd embraced both my parents and my sister, my mother inclined her head to the only other occupant of the courtyard.

"You remember Saige, don't you?" she asked.

I looked at the werewolf in human form, her speckled, cream-colored hair familiar somehow. Her copper eyes smiled sadly at me as she nodded in greeting, and I remembered how they used to shine when we'd played as children.

"My old packmate," I said. "Of course. How are you, Saige?"

"I'm all right. Thank you," she replied softly.

My mother dropped her voice as if Saige's wolf ears couldn't hear her anyway. "Saige is also unmated."

Saige flinched, but my mother continued.

"You didn't go to the Wolf Moon Festival again this year…?" She raised her eyebrow at me.

I confirmed her suspicion with a nod.

"As I thought. Well, then I'm glad I invited her."

I suppressed a sigh. *I knew something like this would happen. I shouldn't have come.* I looked away from my mother for anything that would calm me. The courtyard around us had been decorated for the occasion. There were summer flowers tied to every column, and bright ribbons streamed across the open space. This was the biggest day of my sister's life so far; she was completing the rite that would make her a full member of werewolf society in Faerie.

"Mom," I began, pleased my tone was even and patient, "this is Willow's unbinding day… Don't you think we ought to be concentrating on that?"

She scowled, little wrinkles forming around her pursed lips. "Who said I was neglecting Willow's day? And why wouldn't she want a packmate to attend? You don't mind, do you, Willow?"

My sister's eyes widened, flicking between our mother and me. "I…better go up to my room and see if there's anything I have left to pack. Would you like to come with me, Saige?"

They made their escape without another word, heading up the stairs to the gallery, which wrapped around the courtyard.

My mother sighed, turning helpless eyes on my father. "Talk to your son," she pleaded. "I'm going to see if Lillia needs any help."

My father watched her go, then turned to me. Though I hadn't seen him for most of my life, I couldn't mistake the worry in his face.

"Your mother means well," he assured me. "We understand how hard it must have been for you. But to go to the human realm? We never taught you to run away from your problems."

Sudden anger made me flush, and a shiver ran

through me. "And what *did* you teach me, Dad? If you cared so much about how I would turn out, then you would've raised me yourself. You wouldn't have given me away to practical strangers to act as their guard dog."

I knew I was being unfair. I loved the Fireleafs. They'd been my family for most of my life. And I knew that what my parents had done wasn't only conventional but had been agreed upon between two governments by treaty. But in that moment, I didn't care. "If pack is so important, you wouldn't have let me go in the first place."

As my harsh words hung in the air, I could see I'd hurt him. Regret made my stomach drop. Not because what I'd said wasn't true—it was—but for how I'd said it.

"I have something for Willow," I grumbled, walking in the direction I'd seen my sister go.

On the second floor, I found Willow and Saige in a bedroom, the door ajar. Saige brushed Willow's long hair before a mirrored table situated between two beds.

I knocked gently on the door. "I brought something for you." I pulled the flower wreath from my basket.

Willow smiled. "It's beautiful. Thank you. Saige, will you help me put it on?"

"Of course."

I passed the wreath to her. The atmosphere in the room was thick and uncomfortable while Willow handed pins to Saige, who secured the wreath in her hair.

Just as Saige finished, Willow's bondmate, Feather, entered the room. Feather was tall and lean, with wispy hair that was nearly as light as the whitest parts of Willow's speckled gray.

She smiled affectionately at Willow, and anyone would be able to see they were well-matched.

"Ooh, I like that, where did you get it?" Feather asked.

"Rowan brought it for me."

"What a good brother you are." She smiled at me before turning her attention back to her bondmate. "They wanted me to tell you that your alpha is here."

Saige and I blinked, then exchanged glances. It wasn't that alphas weren't welcome at pack members' unbindings; it was just that it was pretty unusual for them to actually attend. Invitations were sent out of courtesy, but no one expected the alpha to come.

"Well, I'm off to meet with Zeb and the fae priest to go over the final details of my awakening. See you in a bit." Feather flitted from the room.

I met Willow's eyes in the mirror. She wasn't nearly as surprised as Saige and I were that the alpha had come to her unbinding.

"You know why Efren is here," I said with certainty.

Willow frowned. "I have a suspicion," she corrected.

"Which is?"

My sister sighed, staring into her own eyes in the mirror. "I don't want to say anything before I'm certain. I'll tell you later." Then she stood up and left Saige and me alone.

I glanced over at Saige, but her gaze was fixed on the floor.

"Hey. I'm sorry my parents dragged you into this. I hope they didn't give you the wrong expectations."

Saige's mouth twitched into a sad smile, and she looked up at me, her eyes swimming with tears. "I'm relieved," she breathed.

I froze, not sure how to respond.

She sniffed hard and huffed out a sound that could have been a laugh or a sob. Wiping her face with the backs of her hands, she apologized. "I'm sorry. I'm sure none of this makes sense to you. The truth is I was promised to someone else until a few weeks ago."

My heart squeezed at her predicament. "Did he break the bond?"

She shook her head. "No, he…died."

The sorrow in her voice was raw, fresh, and I cursed my parents for forcing this meeting on her.

"Keir is…was a private investigator." She went on in starts and stops. "He was passionate about what's going on with the vampires. He wanted to know why their behavior had changed after all this time. Why are they hunting together when they've never been pack hunters? Why have they been hunting down wolves specifically when they'd always just gone after faelings before? Things like that. He was killed during one of his investigations." Her voice quivered then dropped off.

"Vampires?" I asked.

She shook her head. "Humans. He was in wolf form. Apparently, humans still aren't fond of wolves."

I wasn't going to argue with her. There were enough humans that felt that way to make her statement correct. And any contradiction on that point would have only made her feel worse.

I reached out and rested my hand on her shoulder. "Listen, you don't have to do this. You don't have to be mated if you aren't ready. You probably don't want to come to the realm of origin to be with the packs there, given what happened to your promised, but you are welcome. You have to give your heart time to heal. Don't rush it. Okay?"

"Thank you." Tears spilled down her face.

When Saige and I went back downstairs, we were greeted by Efren, the Lowlands Clan alpha. As his sharp eyes fell on us, Saige dropped to her knees and bowed her head. And for the first time in my life, I stayed on my feet at his arrival, only lowering my eyes as a sign of respect. I felt his power, the presence that all alphas had, but I felt no overwhelming need to submit. He was an alpha, but he wasn't my alpha anymore.

Efren released Saige with a touch on her shoulder, but his eyes were on me.

"Rowan…" He held out his arm. "You're looking well."

I grasped his forearm. "I am well, Efren. Thank you. And you?"

"I am well also," he answered formally, releasing my arm.

Efren had never been an overly approachable or affectionate alpha, but he was fair and cared about the pack members in his own way.

Before I could ask him why he'd decided to come to Willow's unbinding, a fae man—who I assumed was Master Bayberry—escorted the wolf mystic into the courtyard. Efren turned his attention to the new arrival.

And that was only the beginning. Over the next half-hour, more visitors arrived every moment, the vast majority fae.

As evening approached, food was brought out, and guests stood around eating and talking, congratulating Feather and praising Willow. There was a great deal of chatter about Mistress Bayberry being a fae matchmaker, and many of the fae mothers there were hoping she would find their children as good a match as she had found Feather.

When the sky began to dim with the softening light of dusk, the fae priest and the wolf mystic started their preparations in the courtyard for the unbinding, and the gathered crowd hushed to a lull.

As the sun dipped below the horizon, someone lit the courtyard with yellow fae lights, which drifted around like so many fireflies. Finally, the priest and mystic took their places beside one another.

"I call forth Feather Bayberry," the fae priest said.

Feather entered the courtyard and stood facing the priest.

"I call forth Willow of the Lowlands Clan," the wolf mystic said.

And Willow entered the courtyard, joining Feather before the clergy. At the signal, Feather and Willow faced each other and clasped hands.

"Feather, the nineteen-year cycle is complete,

and the time of your awakening is upon us. Are you ready to unbind from your bondmate, Willow?" the priest asked.

"I am," Feather answered.

"Willow, you have executed your duty with honor. You have upheld the treaty, and your faeling will awaken because of your devotion. Are you ready to unbind from your bondmate, Feather?" the mystic asked.

"I am," Willow answered.

Together the priest and mystic pronounced, "In this moment of unbinding, let what once was one be put asunder. One mind to two minds. One heart to two hearts. One spirit to two spirits. So it is and so it will be."

Each with a teary smile, Feather and Willow embraced each other, and their bond was severed.

Then the priest made a gesture with his hand, and a young fae man stepped into the courtyard.

"Now the guide will commence with the awakening ceremony," the priest announced.

Lacing his fingers with hers, the young man brought Feather's hand to his lips. She smiled and blushed in the drifting fae lights as he led her upstairs.

Once he'd closed the door, the hush over the gathering broke, and people began talking and moving about the courtyard.

I looked at Willow, but when she met my eyes, I froze. A shiver ran over my skin, and my stomach quivered.

Power, untamed and raw, simmered in my sister's gaze, fully released when she was no longer bound in fae magic.

"I knew it." Efren stood beside me, a rare smile on his face. "She's an alpha."

Efren and my parents strode toward her, and I was not far behind.

"Congratulations, sweetheart." Our mother embraced Willow. "Efren's just confirmed. You're an alpha. Oh, I'm so proud of you."

But Willow didn't look happy about the news. Her shoulders slumped, and her lip stuck out ever so slightly in a pout that I still remembered from our early days.

Efren either didn't notice or didn't care. "We can start your training as soon as we return."

"No," Willow said softly.

No one spoke.

"No," she said louder. "I'm...I'm going with Rowan back to the human realm."

Her eyes met mine, and they reflected what I'd felt not so long ago. Confused. Sorrowful. Lost.

"What—?" I started.

"I'm going with you," she said firmly. Her eyes hardened.

I flinched. "Okay." I was unsure whether it was her pain—and my responsibility as her older brother—or her alpha presence that had convinced me.

"Now wait just a second—" our mother protested.

"It's already late," Willow interrupted. "We don't want the depot to close before we get where we're going. I'll grab my bag and meet you outside."

As Willow rushed up the stairs, our parents and Efren turned their displeasure on me.

"What did you do, Rowan?" my mother demanded.

I held up my hands in surrender. "I swear, I didn't do anything. I had no idea she was planning any of this. I didn't even know she was showing alpha tendencies."

My mom turned her eyes to my dad for help. "Do something," she pleaded.

But as my father met my gaze, I knew that my words from a few hours before still echoed in his mind. "What would you have me do?" he asked. "They're adults. How can we control their lives?"

My mother's eyebrows puckered, and she made one final effort by looking at Efren. "Efren, you were her alpha. Surely, you can still compel her to stay in Faerie."

Efren shook his head, disappointment lining his face. "Willow needs to learn how to use her power effectively and ethically. Forcing my will on her will not be the first lesson I teach her as an alpha."

With no one else to turn to, my mother burst into tears, and I had no words of comfort to give her.

47

The streets of Mysraina after dark were lively and festive, lit by a combination of flame and fae lights. Fae laughed as they walked and chatted with their companions.

But the only thing festive about my sister at that moment was the wreath of orange and yellow flowers still in her hair. Her gaze was fixed straight ahead, and she frowned severely, her eyes cold and hard.

"What's going on?" I asked as we headed toward the nearest depot. "Why did you suddenly want to come with me?"

She didn't answer until after we'd been transported to the depot closest to the portal I'd come through earlier that day. Finally, standing in the empty street of the slumbering border town, she sighed. As her tension eased, I realized that my own eased as well. I wondered if that was because she was my sister or an alpha.

"I don't want to be an alpha."

I tugged on my earlobe. "Um… It's my understanding that you don't have much of a choice. It's something you're born with."

She growled in a sound that was pure frustration, and my shoulders tightened. "I don't care. Just because I was born with alpha power doesn't mean I have to use it. I don't want to lead a pack. I don't even like people."

"What do you mean?"

"Can we just get going?" She looked around. "We can talk about this on the way."

I led her out of town toward the portal.

"Don't you ever just feel like you want to be alone?" Willow asked.

"Sure, that's pretty normal."

"Well, alphas don't get that luxury," she grumbled. "When you need time by yourself you probably go for a run or whatever. Your alpha probably knows when you need that and when to step in. But you know you have that assurance, that even alone you're in a pack, under the alpha's leadership and protection."

"Don't you think we would come to Lia's aid if she needed our protection?" I asked.

"It's not the same." Her tone urged me to understand. "When you're an alpha, you're always…on. You're always the leader. You have to be or things fall into chaos. You don't get the privilege of doing selfish things. I mean, you were bound with a fae—did you get any time alone in all the years you were bound?"

I thought about it. "Not really, no."

"Exactly. And then the minute I think I can

finally do what I want with the rest of my life, it's snatched away from me." Her voice, laced with bitterness, barely carried into the darkness, despite her volume. The air was thick and humid, and the night sounds seemed eerily close.

"But things were different for me." Unconsciously, I lowered my tone. "I was in a border town. Surely, you got to go to the Wolf Moon Festival?"

"I did. And it was nice to get away from all things fae for a few days. But then I wasn't alone, was I?"

"I suppose not. So…what? You just want to go to the realm of origin and avoid being an alpha altogether?"

"Are you saying I'm not welcome there?" she snapped.

"I'm not saying that at all. I'm just saying that it's not like we don't have werewolves."

"Yes, but there will be far fewer of them."

I couldn't argue with that, but I still felt like she didn't know what she was getting into. "That's true, but…adjusting to the realm of origin is a big change. Are you sure you want to do this?"

She snorted and smirked, an expression I recognized as reflective of my own. "You don't think I can?"

"Well, we're about to find out," I said as we came upon the stagnant lake near the portal.

The waning moon shined off the glassy surface of the lake, illuminating the lily pads that grew at the edges. The pulsing chirring of cicadas was punctuated by the bellowing of bullfrogs.

Willow followed me to the twisted trees, our steps soft on the narrow path. I went first.

A moment later, she crawled out from the space between the trees and took in her surroundings. "It doesn't look that different," she muttered. The thick atmosphere that had dampened the sound of her voice in Faerie was not present on this side of the veil.

"Just wait," I said.

I retrieved my phone from the hollowed rock and turned it on.

"What's that?" Willow stepped close to get a good look at the phone.

"It's a cellphone." My phone chimed with multiple messages from Yuti. But instead of reading them, I opened my contacts and called Ashwin.

"You ready?" he asked.

Willow's eyes widened at the sound of his voice.

"Yeah, still at the portal, but I wanted to give you time to get here."

"Okay. See you in a bit."

"Ashwin?" I asked, stopping him from hanging up.

"Yeah?"

"I've, uh, got someone with me."

"Call Lia." Then he disconnected.

"What…what was that?" Willow demanded as I pulled the phone from my ear.

"This way," I said, following Ashwin's marked path. "A phone allows you to talk to someone at a distance, sort of like a messages table. You can send written messages, talk by voice, and most newer phones even let you see the person face-to-face."

"Wow…"

"You've never read any books on humans or their technology? Never heard anyone talk about it?"

"No. Should I have?"

I shook my head. "It would've made things easier for you."

We started hiking toward the trailhead, the temperature much cooler on this side of the veil. It must have just finished raining because our shoes splattered water as we tramped through the under-brush. I called Lia along the way.

"Rowan? Are you and Ashwin on your way back? I need to talk to you."

"No, I haven't met up with Ashwin yet. I'm still headed that way. He told me to call you. I hope it's all right, but my sister is with me."

"Oh? Of course it's all right. You know friends and family are always welcome here."

I hesitated. "She's uh… Well, we just found out she's an alpha."

Silence answered my statement.

"Is that…okay?" I knew that an alpha coming into another alpha's territory, even a newly discov-ered and untrained one like Willow, came with a set of issues nonalphas didn't really understand.

"I will hear her story when you arrive," Lia said finally.

"All right. See you later."

I hung up and slipped my phone into my pocket. "How much do you know about being an alpha?" I asked Willow. "Do you know the etiquette and stuff?"

"We've suspected for a while," she admitted with a sigh. "Efren found me at the Wolf Moon Festival a few months ago and gave me a pamphlet about what I might expect."

"A pamphlet," I said flatly. "Great."

48

"What is *that*?" Willow jumped back as Ashwin pulled up to the overlook in his truck.

I never truly appreciated just how much living with Konner and his obsession with humans had prepared me for the realm of origin until that moment.

"It's a…carriage." I opened the passenger door. "Get in."

"Hi, I'm Ash—" Ashwin stiffened, and I knew he'd recognized Willow's alpha nature. He cleared his throat. "I'm Ashwin."

Willow gingerly climbed into the truck, scooting toward Ashwin to sit in the center seat. "I'm Willow, Rowan's sister."

Ashwin met my eyes in the dim overhead dome light. "Rowan, you've, uh, told Lia about this?"

I nodded, got into the car, and shut the door. After helping Willow with her seatbelt, I buckled my own, and we started toward home.

On the drive, Willow wanted to know all about how the truck moved without being pulled. But once we were on the main road, she had a million questions about every little thing she saw. Ashwin patiently explained it all.

I pulled out my phone and checked my messages. It felt like I'd been gone for a week; so much had happened since I'd seen Yuti last. She hadn't sent many messages, just a few texts telling me she hoped I had a good time with my family and to text her when I got back. There was also a picture of her face from the nose up, her eyes wide and a table packed with food behind her.

> They think I'm really going to eat all this.

I smiled down at my phone, warmth spreading from my chest. I was glad to be back in the same realm as her and even happier to know I'd see her the next day.

> I'm back.

> Did you miss me?

My phone chimed a moment later.

> Ask me again tomorrow.

Willow leaned over in her seat and looked down at my phone. "Who's Yuti?"

Ashwin snickered. "That didn't take long."

"Yuti is...very special to me."

I could feel my sister's eyes analyzing me. "Your mate? Your promised?"

The weight of her questions, the weight of the still-unspoken truth, pressed on my chest. "One day...I hope."

Willow smiled and bumped me with her shoulder. "Aw, look at you. That's adorable. But what are you being so cautious about? If you like each other, why don't you just ask her?"

I frowned. "It's not that easy. Werewolves live by different rules here. We have to be careful to keep who we are quiet. Yuti is human, and she doesn't know I'm a werewolf."

Willow quirked her mouth. "I can see why that might cause a problem. So when are you going to tell her?"

I didn't want to get into the whole story of how I'd wanted to the day before but now I was thinking about Yuti's exams that week. "Soon."

Lucky for me, there was no more time for Willow to ask questions because Ashwin pulled into the resort's drive.

Lia was on the front lawn before we even got out.

"That's Lia," I told my sister as I unbuckled her seatbelt.

"Your alpha," Willow said seriously.

Out of the truck, Willow and Lia stared each other down for a tense few seconds that made my skin itch. But the moment passed when Willow bowed her head, acknowledging that this was Lia's territory and she would submit to her authority.

Lia smiled warmly in response. "You are in the territory of the Northern Pack, and you are welcome." Then she strode forward, and the two women clasped forearms.

"Thank you for having me," Willow said.

Lia took in Willow's attire, so different in style and material than what most humans wore. "You've never been to the realm of origin before?"

Willow shook her head. "I have not."

"I'd like to hear your story. Come in, and you can tell me all about it."

Lia turned around and entered the house first. Willow followed.

"This ought to be interesting," Ashwin said to me before we both went inside.

Noire had taken the boys on that camping trip Braylyn had been asking for, so it was only the four of us in the kitchen as Willow told Lia everything she'd told me. Willow and Lia sat at the table while Ashwin and I sat on stools nearby, observing the exchange.

Lia listened carefully, impassively, her fingers laced together on the table in front of her. But once Willow was finished, she frowned. "I think there's something you aren't taking into consideration. I've lived in the realm of origin my entire life, so correct me if I'm wrong, but isn't there a formal training program for alphas in Faerie?"

"Yes. It's more like an apprenticeship though. Most new alphas train with their birth pack alphas though sometimes they're assigned a different mentor by the Wolf Council."

Lia nodded. "Not so different from how we do it here. And that's my point. An untrained alpha is dangerous in that she is undisciplined. The innate power you have can have a major effect on other werewolves. So far, you've only come into contact with wolves that already fully belong to a pack. But if Ashwin or Rowan had been unclaimed, that would've been a completely different story. Even if you decide to become a lone alpha, you need to learn how to control your abilities, not to mention the ethics and rules that go along with them."

Willow sighed and hung her head, wiping her face with her hands. Lia's eyes softened with sympathy.

"Can't you teach me?" Willow looked up at Lia. "If I go back to Faerie, Efren will want me to take over the Lowlands Pack, or other alphas will seek me out. I just know it."

Lia gazed at Willow for a long time before she sighed through her nose. "I can teach you."

Willow smiled, her amber eyes warming as they lit up.

"But," Lia added, "I want you to go back to Faerie first."

My sister opened her mouth to protest, then clamped it shut when Lia silenced her with a glance.

"From what you've told me, you left under… less-than-amicable terms. I don't think it wise to start your training this way. I think you should go back and make peace with your former alpha and your parents. The alphas of the realm of origin may not be governed by the same rules and treaties as our counterparts in Faerie, but we do have…an understanding. I don't want your negative feelings to get in the way of your training. Also, I think you need a transition period. From what I gather, you don't know much about this realm or about humans. I think you should spend some time, even a short time, learning about humans and our way of life here before you come to stay. It'll make your transition easier."

Willow's face fell. "If you think that best…" she said in a defeated tone.

Lia smiled gently. "I do. Now, you can stay for the night, but I think you should go back tomorrow. I'll send some books back with you, books written by both fae and werewolves that will help with your transition."

"They offer human studies classes at Faerie universities." I remembered Konner talking about them. "That might help you prepare even better than a book."

Lia looked over at me. She frowned seriously but dipped her head at Willow. "I agree. But you're going to have to be careful around other werewolves your age if you go that route."

"What about a fae university?" I suggested. "There won't be many werewolves there."

Willow nodded once, agreeing despite her expression of displeasure. "I'll look into it."

49

I showed Willow around the house into the early morning hours, explaining everything from the toaster to the computer. She was a bottomless well of questions. By the time I finally crawled into bed, I had to agree with Lia—Willow needed to gain a better understanding of the realm of origin before she moved here.

Ashwin and I took her back to the portal the next morning, but I had to admit I was sad to see her go. Having her here, even for such a short time, made me feel a little more whole. We hadn't grown up together, and in a lot of ways we didn't really know each other. But she was my family, and I looked forward to her coming back to stay with us.

Still, I breathed a steadying sigh after Ashwin and I had gotten back into the truck and started toward the resort. It had been an eventful few days, and the only thing I wanted to do was see Yuti. She'd sent me a text that morning promising to let me know when she was back.

"Do you know if there are any chores that need to be done?" I asked Ashwin while he pulled into the drive. "I want to—who's that?" I pointed at a silver car parked in front of the house.

Ashwin leaned forward in his seat to get a better look. "I don't know. Maybe a guest parked in the wrong place?"

I went inside first. Striding through the front hall, I called out. "Hey, Lia, there's—"

I halted like I'd hit a wall; my breath rushed out of me and my stomach rolled. At the kitchen table, Lia knelt before Runa, smiling as she touched her pregnant belly.

"Rowan." Konner greeted me from behind them.

But I didn't look at him. My eyes were focused on Runa. Her long, white hair was tied to one side, the gathered tresses lying over her shoulder and chest. Her light gray eyes met mine, and she smiled.

My heart exploded in my chest, and my hands trembled. "I…have to go." My voice was uneven and entirely too soft.

"Rowan—" Lia started.

"I have to work today." My brain supplied the lie with ease.

Lia knew I didn't have to work. It was Sunday, and I never worked the weekends except on very rare occasions. But she didn't argue.

"All right. Ashwin will take you. Call me on your break, okay?"

I think I might have nodded. I only know I left the room without another word. On my way out the door, I grabbed the basket the Fireleafs had given me and Yuti's sketchbook, which I'd placed on the hall table so I wouldn't forget them. I had taken most of the berries out of the basket to share with the pack, but I'd left some berries and the ivy plant for Yuti.

I was already in the truck and buckled in by the time Ashwin opened the driver's side door. I could feel his eyes on me, but I just stared straight ahead.

Once we were on the road, he asked, "Are you okay?"

"Did you know?"

He didn't respond immediately, and my eyes flicked to his face.

"I didn't. I swear."

"Why are they here?" My voice was flat, cold, and it was all I could do to keep it from raging.

"I don't know."

I sighed, trying to control the turmoil inside me. "Why didn't Lia warn me?"

He shook his head. "I don't know."

My mind spun but didn't gain traction. Then my phone chimed. Sure it was a message from Lia explaining herself, I pulled it out of my pocket.

Back safe and sound.

My unsteady heart latched onto the knowledge. "Drop me off at Yuti's."

I closed my eyes against the wind blowing through the open window, letting the sun warm my skin. But the image of Runa's smiling gray eyes—the image of her pregnant with Konner's child—was burned into the backs of my eyelids. My eyes flew open. I leaned my head against the door and watched the many shades of green blur together as we drove.

It didn't take any longer than usual to get to Yuti's street, but it felt like every breath was squeezed out of me. My fingers were cold as I pressed her doorbell, and I counted the heartbeats it took before she opened the door.

Her dark eyes lit with delight as she smiled up at me. I wrapped my arms around her and buried my face in her neck. Her cinnamon and citrus scent washed over me. I breathed deep. *How long has it been since I smelled her?* I only knew that it had been too long. The chill that had numbed my limbs, that had made my heart shiver, warmed as she returned my embrace.

"I missed you, too," she whispered into my chest, tightening her arms around my waist.

By the time we pulled apart, I was much calmer, more balanced. I smiled down at Yuti, this human who had showed me that my heart could love again.

"You're here just in time," she said.

"In time for what?"

"I'll show you. Come on."

Picking up my basket, I followed her through the hall and into her apartment. She gestured toward her small kitchen table, where food storage containers were stacked on top of one another.

"As you can see, there's no way all that food is going to fit in my tiny fridge. I tried to tell my mom and grandma, but they wouldn't listen. So…are you hungry?" She turned to me with a grin, but then it faltered. "What's wrong? You can't hate vegetarian food *that* much."

"Nothing," I murmured. "I'm fine."

Yuti quirked an eyebrow. "Come on, Rowan.

You think I don't know your face by now? Something is bothering you."

I frowned. The moment I was in Yuti's presence, my response to Runa and Konner's surprise visit seemed silly. *I love Yuti. Why should Runa showing up affect me?*

I latched onto Yuti's gaze. "A lot happened over the last few days. I went home yesterday, and my sister decided she was going to run away to stay with me. Lia convinced her to go home, but when I got back from dropping her off this morning…Runa was there."

50

Yuti eyed me. "I'm going to assume Runa is your ex-fiancée…?"

I lowered my chin.

Yuti mimicked the gesture, wrapping her arms around herself. "Do you…still love her?" She averted her gaze.

My chest ached, and I winced at the pain. Closing the distance between us, I rested my hands on her shoulders. She looked up at me, her eyes vulnerable and uncertain.

"No," I said. "I don't love her. I love *you*, Yuti." Despite the pain, the sorrow, the surprise I felt at Runa's sudden appearance, I knew I spoke the truth.

"Yeah?"

"Yeah."

Her mouth twitched into a small smile. She unfolded her arms, relaxing, and I released her shoulders. "Okay. So why do you look so upset then?"

I sighed, a frustrated breath rushing out of me. "I don't know. I guess… I had no idea she was coming, for one." The more I spoke, the more the words tumbled out of me in what was beginning to sound like a rant. "Then she shows up out of nowhere, pregnant. I mean really pregnant, like could-go-into-labor-any-day pregnant. It's not like I didn't know she and Konner were…married. And I knew they were expecting, too. But seeing it all…"

I sighed again, deflating. "I guess it sort of made me feel like I never had any place of consequence in her life. She moved on so thoroughly. All the feelings I'd felt at the time were really only on my end. I was nothing to her."

Yuti reached out and laced her fingers with mine. "I can understand that feeling," she said gently. "But if she's that pregnant, why is she here? I mean, why would she travel? Isn't it normal for doctors to tell pregnant women not to go very far when they're that close to giving birth?"

I shook my head. "I don't know. I think I said four words before I got out of there. And they said even less."

She squeezed my hand. "Do you know how long they'll be here?"

"No, I should probably call Lia and get all the particulars. But I'm not ready to talk to her right now."

Yuti was silent for a moment, her gaze drifting around the room before she met mine again. "Do you…want to stay here tonight?"

My heart stopped, and any thought of Runa and Konner flew right from my mind. I analyzed Yuti's eyes. *What does she mean exactly?*

"That's not me trying to pressure you into doing something you aren't ready for," she said quickly though not quickly enough for me to temper my desire. "I just thought…you might not want to go back tonight."

I thought about her little apartment. I thought about her exams and how she still didn't know who I was. I thought about whether I'd be able to handle her ready, willing, and well within reach. "I don't want to be in the way."

She smirked. "Hey, if you promise to eat enough food that those containers can fit in my fridge by tonight, I'd say you've more than earned your keep."

I glanced over at her table, stacked with dishes she'd brought from home, and pursed my lips. "You drive a hard bargain."

"I'll get you a spoon." She grinned.

As much as I teased Yuti about her being a vegetarian, the food her mother and grandmother had sent home was truly excellent. I even told her as much. By the end, my stomach was uncomfortably full, but we did manage to fit the containers into her small fridge.

"Ugh, I'll never eat again." Yuti slouched beside me on the couch. "It hurts so much."

I had to agree, but I didn't say so.

"Shhh, don't say anything. It hurts for me to hear sounds right now."

I chuckled, the motion making my stomach even more uncomfortable. "I didn't even say anything."

"You were going to. I could tell."

Yuti's head was pushed forward, her neck at an awkward angle; she looked like she'd been poured onto the couch. I smiled at the sight, at what it said about where we were in our relationship.

"Other than your family trying to put you into a food coma, did you have a good visit?" I asked.

"Yeah." Her eyes lit up with a gentle fondness as she smiled. "It was good to see my grandparents. I miss them a lot."

Reaching over, I rested my hand on hers, her fingers small and warm in mine. "I was really happy to know that you'd told them about me."

Maple and caramel mixed in with Yuti's cinnamon and citrus scent. "Don't tempt me when I can't move. That's just rude."

I chuckled again. "I'm sorry. I'll try harder next time."

"You better," she grumbled, squinting at me. Then she sighed. "How was your visit? I mean besides your sister running away. That sounds like a whole big drama. Did you tell your family about me?"

I tried to come up with an easy way to describe my family situation. *How can I tell Yuti my parents effectively gave me to another family when I was young? Without understanding the treaty and the way our societies are set up, she won't get it. Is this a good time to tell her the truth? Will it mess with her exams?*

Yuti's face was slack, her free hand resting on her full stomach.

"My visit with my parents…didn't go that well. But remember when I told you Runa ran off with my childhood friend Konner?"

"Yeah."

"In a lot of ways, Konner's family—his parents and his brother—were more like my family than my parents and sister. So before I went to my sister's thing, I stopped in to see them. I did tell them about you. I even brought you presents."

"You brought me presents?" She perked up. "I was wondering what was in the basket."

"Would you like to see?"

"Yes." She straightened from her slouch.

I brought her the basket, which I'd put near the door upon coming in.

She opened one side. "Berries?" she asked.

"These aren't just any berries. Try one."

Despite complaining about having eaten too much, Yuti popped a berry into her mouth. Her eyes widened, and her face lit up. "Oh my God, what did they *do* to these? I've never had anything this good."

"I know, right? There's something else, too."

Flipping open the lid on the other side of the basket, she pulled out the little ivy plant.

"Aw, look how cute it is," she cooed.

"I know you said you kill everything you try to grow. But they told me this type of plant is really easy to take care of."

Getting up, Yuti took the pot and placed it on the windowsill near her vanity.

"Please don't die," she told the plant. "I will talk to you every day and only water you when I'm supposed to. I'll give you just the right amount of plant food and sunlight. So please don't die on me."

hen Yuti got into the shower later that evening, I called Lia.

"Rowan, I'm sorry," she said immediately. "I meant to tell you I got the call from Runa's alpha, Layton, while you were in Faerie. But then everything happened with Willow, and I didn't get the chance."

I recalled Lia saying she had something to talk to me about when I'd called her upon returning.

"Why are they here?" I was glad my voice was controlled and even.

"There's a lot of vampire activity where their pack is. Runa's too far along to shift, and the baby's already showing signs of fae magic, so Layton thought it safer if they came up here to stay until Runa gives birth. Even with our recent incidents, it's much quieter here. I've put them in one of the rustic cabins since we can't have Konner and the baby's magic accidentally shorting out anything in the house. And Layton sent Andi to look after them, so we probably won't even see them any more than we see any of our customers. I wanted to talk to you about it first, but you were gone and—"

"It's fine," I said. I could hear how upset she was. She always tried so hard to look after the pack. I sighed. "Really, Lia, I was just surprised. Of course I want Runa and the baby to be safe. But listen, I'm going to stay at Yuti's tonight. I just need to prepare myself to come home, you know? I have to work tomorrow morning, but I'll be back tomorrow afternoon."

"I understand."

I wished Lia a goodnight and hung up the phone just as Yuti came out of the bathroom.

She wore an oversized, gray t-shirt and shorts, which just peeked out below the hem. Her warm scent filled the room as she rubbed her wet hair with a towel.

My eyes followed her, taking in her every motion. My cock stiffened as my body flushed.

"Check out this shirt my grandparents brought me," she said, clearly unaware of my desire.

The logo on the shirt was orange and blue with words I couldn't read. "What is it?" I asked, my voice a little thicker than I would've liked.

"It's the Indian Space Research Organisation." She laughed. "I think they're still hoping I'll change my major to aerospace engineering. Anyway, the shower is yours if you want it."

The shower was not what I wanted.

"Rowan?"

"Thanks. I'll just be a bit," I said, smashing my lust down. I needed to keep a tight leash on my wolf and his impulse to mark Yuti as his own if I had any hope of making it until after Yuti's exam to tell her the truth.

A cold shower took care of the immediate problem but not the cause. When I came out of the bathroom, Yuti lay on her stomach on the floor, her books and notes spread out before her.

"Hey, sorry. My exam is coming up, and I was just refreshing my memory." She sat up.

I waved my hand at her. "I don't want to take time away from your studying. Don't mind me. Just do what you need to do to prepare for your exam."

"Thanks."

It was another couple of hours before Yuti looked up from her books again. I spent my time on the couch, sometimes on my phone, sometimes just watching her. I watched the little crinkle between her eyebrows, the column of her neck as she tilted her head. I watched her place her pen between her teeth as she frantically turned pages.

Finally, she looked up, her eyes easily finding mine. "What time is it?"

I looked at my phone. "It's pretty late." I showed her the time.

"Oh, shit. Yeah, we better get to bed. You have to work tomorrow. You could've gone to sleep before me."

I gave her a gentle smile. She would never know how much I'd enjoyed just watching her study. "It's fine."

She glanced at her short couch and then at me. "You...don't mind sharing a bed, do you? I guess I didn't think my invitation through. That loveseat isn't really big enough for either of us, is it? I can behave. I promise."

But can I? "I don't mind if you don't."

"Okay. Good. Then, uh, I'm just going to go to the bathroom one more time, and you can head up first." She closed her books and stacked them neatly. Then she got up and went to the bathroom.

I climbed the stairs to where her bed was. The space was only big enough for the bed; there wasn't even room to walk on either side. At the foot of the bed, there was a shelf built into the wall, which was stuffed with books and little trinkets. I turned on the overhead light and climbed onto the bed, scooting until I was near the wall.

More than anyplace else, this small space smelled of Yuti. Lying on my back, I breathed deep.

"Do you want me to set an alarm?" She hovered in the doorway.

"Yeah, thanks. A half hour should be enough with your place so close."

"Okay." Crawling across the bed, she set her alarm clock and put it back on the shelf. But when she turned back around, she hesitated, her limbs stiffening as she tried to decide how to lie beside me.

I opened my arms to her. "Come here," I said gently, despite my pounding heart.

She accepted my offer without hesitation, snuggling her head against my chest.

In that space, her body pressed up against mine and, surrounded by her cinnamon and citrus scent, I'd never wanted her more. But the gentle weight of her head on my chest, of her arm on my stomach, made me content to live in this comfortable moment. "Can I ask you something?"

"Hmm?" she hummed, not looking up at me.

"Your sketchbook, the one you gave me before

you left. There were drawings in there from over a year ago, almost right when I started at the café."

She waited for my question.

"If you liked me for that long, why didn't you ever say anything?"

She raised her head and propped it up on her elbow. "Do you not remember when you first started at the café?"

I squinted in thought. "I think I do."

"I don't think you do. I was always trying to get your attention. I'd ask you about yourself. Once I even suggested we hang out. That took a lot of courage for me, you know. But you were so…uninterested. And I learned pretty quickly that the only way to get you to pay attention to me was to goad you. That wasn't the type of attention I wanted from you, but it was better than being ignored."

I swallowed with difficulty. "I ignored you?"

"You did."

"Okay, but did you have to goad so hard? You didn't even call me by my name until that time we went to the library."

She snorted, then smirked. "Do you remember what I used to call you? Jaaneman. It means darling or sweetheart."

"It does not," I objected.

"It does. I promise." She laughed.

"You're telling me that for a whole year, when I thought you hated me for no reason, you were just flirting with me every chance you got?"

"Yep."

"Then why did you hesitate so much when I started to reach out to you?"

Yuti's face warmed. "What did you expect? I'd

already fallen into a pattern of behavior by then, and you went and changed your tune so suddenly. And the first time you were over here, you were so sad about Runa. It was clear you still loved her. You never showed any interest in me as more than friends until you held my hand up on the mountain, and I couldn't really be sure even then. Plus…" She looked away.

I guided her eyes back to mine by trailing my thumb along her jaw. "Plus?"

She pursed her lips. "I didn't think it would work, okay? Trying to get someone out of your league to pay attention to you, even just a little, is totally different than having them actually turn around and talk to you. Crushing on someone is different than having it be a real possibility. I didn't know how to react. I never expected the hottest guy I've ever seen to suddenly start paying attention to me."

I smirked. "Am I the hottest guy you've ever seen?"

She clicked her tongue. "Well, that was before I knew you."

"Oh yeah?"

"Mm-hmm."

Gathering her in my arms, I drew her to me and kissed her gently on the lips. "And now?"

Despite my desire pulling at its leash, I kept the kiss short and sweet. Yuti may have promised to behave herself, but if I smelled maple and caramel at that moment, I knew I wouldn't be able to say no to her.

She squinted, her eyes twinkling. "What will you give me if I say yes?"

I chuckled. "A pat on the head and a kiss on the cheek."

She jerked her head to the side, lifting her chin in disdain. "No deal."

I kissed her on the cheek anyway. "Goodnight."

Yuti sighed, reached over and turned out the light, then cuddled in close to me. "Goodnight," she murmured in the dark.

Wrapped in Yuti's scent, I slept better than I ever had. Even so, I awoke before dawn.

"Are you awake?" Yuti whispered.

"Yeah." My voice was still thick with sleep.

She moved closer to me, squeezing my middle with her thin arms. "I didn't wake you, did I?"

"No."

"Good…" She paused, and the resulting silence was heavy. "I like waking up with you."

My chest swelled, and I grinned a silly grin. Thankfully, she couldn't see my expression in the dark, but my werewolf eyes could see her. I stroked her hair with my fingertips. "I like waking up with you, too."

In that quiet, comfortable moment, her stomach grumbled. "Are you hungry?" she asked. "We have time to have breakfast before you go to work."

"Sure," I said. "What do you have?"

"Leftovers…"

I chuckled. "Sounds good."

"I'll go heat it up then."

As she began to pull herself out of my arms, I stopped her. I brushed her mussed hair from her face, tucking it behind her ear. Then I pressed a soft kiss to her mouth.

"Good morning," I said.

She smiled in the dark. "Good morning." She flipped on the light and looked down at me, a giggle bubbling from her lips.

"What?" I asked, grinning at the sound.

"Nothing," she said lightly. But she bit her lips to stop her laughter. "I'm going to get breakfast ready. If you want, I think I have an unopened toothbrush in the cabinet."

After she shut off the unsounded alarm clock, I scooted out of bed behind her. I saw what she'd been laughing at as I stared at my reflection in the bathroom mirror. My hair stood up at angles that I wasn't sure gravity appreciated. I smirked at myself. And in that moment, I saw that I was truly happy.

Wetting my hands, I smoothed my hair into some semblance of order. Then I located the toothbrush Yuti had mentioned and put it to good use.

By the time I'd finished, Yuti was dishing cold leftovers onto a plate. Before I could offer to help, her cellphone chimed from the bedroom.

She tilted her head at the sound. "That's a text message. Could you grab my phone for me please?"

I climbed the stairs to the bedroom and unplugged her phone. The lock screen lit up, and I snorted at the wallpaper. Returning to the kitchen, I pointed to her screen and asked, "Is this why you didn't want me to put my number into your phone that time?" The wallpaper was a picture of me. I was sitting up against a tree in the quad, looking very content amongst the autumn leaves.

Yuti snatched her phone from my hand. "It was reference material, okay? For my art."

"Reference material, huh?" I slipped my arms around her waist and kissed her head. "Well, you just let me know next time you need 'reference material.' I'll be happy to oblige."

She lowered her face, squirming out of my grasp as the microwave beeped. Even without seeing her expression, I could tell she was blushing.

She took the warm plate out and put it on the table with the other one, then she handed me a fork and took a seat. She looked at her phone as I sat across from her.

"Oh, it's from Adrian." She placed her phone on the table.

I flinched. "Yeah? What does he have to say?" I asked, trying to make my tone as light as possible.

"He's coming back this week, wants to get all his books and everything before fall semester starts in a few weeks."

I shoved a forkful of yellow rice into my mouth and chewed slowly, giving my heart time to steady. I swallowed with difficulty. "When is he supposed to arrive?"

"Wednesday night." Her eyes met mine. "You still want to meet him, right?"

I nodded.

"Adrian and I had a tradition our first year. After every exam we would go to that gelato place over on Walnut. Have you ever been?"

I shook my head.

"Well, anyway. My exam is on Wednesday morning. So, if you want, the three of us could meet up for gelato when he gets in."

I finished chewing and took a drink of water before even attempting to answer. "Okay. I work the morning shift that day. You could come into the café after your exam, and we could hang out until he gets here." *I don't want her meeting him first without me there. I don't know what to expect.*

She beamed. "Great. I'm excited for you two to meet. I think you'll really like him."

I took a huge bite so I didn't have to answer.

After breakfast, Yuti got ready and collected her books. She'd decided she would study at the café during my shift. And with Adrian's return looming, I wanted to keep her close.

Walking in the predawn light through campus, I took comfort in her small hand in mine, warming her fingers against the morning chill. The day was finally approaching, and I had far more to lose than when I'd first smelled Adrian's scent.

My worries swirled like so much mountain mist on that morning walk to work, my eyes watching the pavement just ahead of our feet. And when we finally reached the café, I didn't want to let her go.

She picked up on my hesitation even if she didn't know the cause, and smiled up at me. She stood on her toes and kissed me on the cheek.

"I'll set up out here for a bit since you guys aren't open yet." She let go of my hand.

"I'm sure Camille won't mind if you come in."

"It's fine. Even if Camille is great, she's still your boss. I don't want to interfere with your work. Go on. It's not too cold. I've got your jacket after all."

"All right," I conceded. But I didn't move to leave.

"Go on," she laughed.

I pried myself away from Yuti and went inside to start my shift.

53

As always, the café was packed when it first opened, and I tried my best to keep my mind on my work and not watch Yuti study across the room. I'd rate my success at a B minus though I'd give myself extra credit for not breaking anything.

For her part, Yuti was much better at ignoring me. She studied as if she were in a hushed library rather than a bustling café.

With two minutes to go until my shift ended, I sighed as the bell chimed above the door. Nothing was so irritating as a last-minute customer.

But when I looked up to greet the new arrival, the words died in my throat. Konner held the door open for Runa—his glamour firmly in place to cover his fae features—and a female werewolf I didn't recognize.

Runa looked around the café, her gaze finally landing on me as she approached the counter.

"You talked so much about the café in your letters I had to see it for myself." She smiled sheepishly. "And since Lia told us you'd need a ride, I thought we could come pick you up from work."

I didn't know what to say. Lucky for me, my professional impulses kicked in. "Is there anything I can get you guys?"

Runa looked at the chalkboard above my head as Konner stepped up beside her.

"Rowan—" Konner began, his apologetic tone obvious to me, someone who'd known him most of his life.

"It's fine," I said, cutting him off. "Hey, it's good to see you."

Konner sighed in relief and turned to the werewolf behind him. "You two didn't get a chance to meet. This is Andi."

"Lia mentioned you when I talked to her yesterday," I said, my eyes meeting hers.

We didn't exchange the customary greeting between wolves as we were in a human place, but we gave each other a friendly nod.

After taking their orders, I went about filling them.

Camille came out from the back, complaining. "Ugh, Max is late again. That boy… I think I should duct tape a watch to his wrist."

"Do you need me to stay until he gets here?" I asked.

She shook her head. "No, I can handle it but thanks. This for them?" Camille asked, picking up the cold coffee and tilting her head toward Runa, Konner, and Andi.

"For the woman with tawny hair, yeah." I lifted my chin at Andi.

Camille smiled a smile that any wolf would

recognize. And looking at Andi, I could tell that she had not only recognized it but returned it.

"I haven't seen you in here before," Camille said.

"It's my first time," Andi replied.

As I was wondering whether Camille had a type —a werewolf type—Runa hissed at me to get my attention. I handed her the lemon water she'd ordered.

"You're off work now?" she asked.

"Yeah."

"Do you mind if we, you and I, take a walk before we head back?"

I frowned. I knew this conversation had to come eventually. And it was probably better away from the all-too-hearing ears of the pack. "Sure," I said. "Just let me put my apron away and grab my phone."

When I returned, Konner was protesting.

Runa scowled at him. "I won't be long. And for goodness' sake, you've trusted Rowan your whole life. I'm sure he can handle the nothing we're going to encounter."

I didn't blame Konner for worrying. Trusting me with his brother, even with himself, wasn't the same as trusting me with his mate and unborn child. "Don't worry. I'll take care of her."

Runa pouted but didn't so much as grumble when Konner nodded.

As Runa and I walked toward the exit, I met Yuti's gaze from across the room. She raised an eyebrow at me, her eyes flicking significantly toward Runa. I nodded slightly. Yuti's answering frown made me wonder if I'd somehow not made my feelings for her clear. But then she smiled a sad little smile that told me she understood.

Once out in the sunshine, Runa groaned, looking up at the sky. "It's so hot. I thought coming up here would be a relief, but it's only cooler when the sun is down."

"Are you sure you still want to walk?" I asked.

"Just find me a shady place to sit, and I'll be fine."

On the other side of the bridge, I found a bench shaded by a maple tree. Runa squatted, carefully lowering herself onto the seat. I sat beside her and waited quietly for her to speak.

"You were surprised," she said finally.

"I was."

Runa played with the straw in her cup, stirring the ice cubes. She let her breath out in a long sigh. "I wouldn't have come if there had been a better option. Your last letter made it clear that you weren't ready to see me. I'm sorry it turned out this way."

I hated the sorrow in her voice, the sorrow that I'd put there. "I loved you, Runa. I would have done anything for you. I would have left Wilhelm unprotected. I would have died for you."

"I know," she murmured miserably.

"Even when I completed my rite and came here, it was to be closer to you. I knew you didn't love me. But I thought having you in my life, even as a friend, was better than not having you in my life at all."

Runa sniffled beside me.

"I'm not angry with you. I told you once that

you can't help who you love. That's true for you, and that was true for me. And I… I'm so grateful."

She looked over at me, tears rolling down her face. With a small smile, I reached out and squeezed her hand.

"If it wasn't for you, I would never have experienced love. And doubly so now. If I hadn't wanted to be close to you, I never would've met Yuti. So I want to thank you, Runa. Thank you for being true to your heart. And thank you for showing me how to do the same."

54

Runa's answering smile was watery and beautiful. She wiped her tears with the backs of her hands. "I'm so emotional these days," she said with a chuckle.

I waited patiently for her to gather herself. "So when is your due date?"

"I wish I knew," she groaned. "Fae and werewolves have different gestation periods, so it's sort of an individual thing. But it should be soon. The doctor from the Mesa Pack is ready to come at any moment."

I nodded.

"Would you like to feel?" She tilted her head.

"Feel what?"

Runa took my hand and guided it to her belly.

After a tense moment, I felt a sudden bump against my palm, the unmistakable zing of fae magic running up my arm. My eyes widened, and Runa laughed.

"He just kicked you," she said.

"Is he...more fae or werewolf?" I asked.

"We don't know yet," she answered. "There are other half-fae, half-werewolf children out there, but they're all a bit different. Some can shift and use a little fae magic. Some can't shift at all but awaken faster than a faeling. Some can do it all. And some are practically human, with just heightened senses and the ability to detect magic when it's around. We really won't know until he decides he wants to come out."

"Ah."

"So... This Yuti you just mentioned. She was in the café? Wearing the hat, right?" Runa smirked. "Your scent was all over her, and hers on you if you're wondering."

My chest swelled. Even without marking her as my own, other wolves knew she was mine, knew I was hers, at least until we showered and changed clothes.

"Yeah. I stayed at her place last night."

Runa grinned. "Stayed over, huh? Get a little Wolf Moon Festival action?"

My face flushed, and Runa burst out laughing.

"What's with that response? You been hanging out with humans too long or what?" she teased.

"I haven't told her about me yet. So, no, it didn't...feel right." I stared down at my hiking boots; there was a little dirt, dried and dusty, on the left toe. I wondered if I'd gotten a bit muddy when hiking back from the portal. Despite my preoccupation, I could feel Runa's gaze on me.

"You clearly love her. What are you waiting for?"

"It's a big conversation, right? And she has

exams this week. I didn't want to distract her or impact her grades." I'd said it so many times the last few days that it was starting to sound like an excuse. Was it even true? Or had I lost my nerve now that I knew just how much I could lose?

Runa quirked her mouth. "Well, that's very considerate of you, but if you wait too long, it's only going to blow up in your face." Runa saw right to the heart of the matter, saw right through me.

"I know. It'll be done by the end of the week." My chest tightened as the deadline suddenly felt very real.

"All right," she said, clearly unconvinced. "Now, will you help me up? Konner is going to lose his shit if we stay out much longer."

Runa wasn't exaggerating. When we arrived back at the café, Konner was pacing the sidewalk. He rushed to meet us.

"Where's Andi?" Runa asked.

"She's still inside talking with the owner," Konner answered, raking his gaze over Runa.

"I'll get her," I said.

Andi wasn't pleased about being interrupted, but she promised to come back again soon. When I turned around, Yuti's eyes met mine. I jerked my head to the side, gesturing for her to come out with me. She stuffed her books into her bag and met me at the door, which I held open for her.

Andi was already on her way to get the car when Yuti and I stepped outside. Konner and Runa stared at her. Placing my hand on her lower back, I gently guided Yuti toward them.

"Yuti," I said with a smile. "I'd like you to meet my friends Konner and Runa. Guys, this is Yuti."

Yuti offered her hand, and Runa took it.

"It's nice to meet you," Yuti said. "Rowan has spoken of you both."

"Same," Runa answered. "Rowan wrote to us about you a while ago."

I met Runa's gaze sharply. "How did you — ?"

"Everyone knew, Rowan," Runa interrupted.

Konner nodded. "It's true."

Yuti's eyes shifted from them to me, her grin wide as she nudged me in the ribs with her elbow. "You wrote to your friends about me?"

I thought of all the times I'd complained about Yuti in my letters. "Yeah, well, none of it was good."

Yuti burst out laughing. "But you were thinking about me. I'll take that any day."

Just then, Andi pulled the car up.

"Well, I guess I better get on with studying," Yuti said with a sigh. "I'll text you later, okay?"

I smiled down at her. "Okay."

When I went to give her a quick peck on the lips, Yuti stood on her toes, lengthening the kiss until it lingered. My heart jumped, and I wondered if she knew what she'd done. To everyone else, she had just claimed me.

"I'll see you later," she promised with that mischievous smirk of hers.

As she walked away, waving back at us, we watched her go.

"Well, I like her," Runa declared.

I licked my lips, which still tasted of her. *Yeah, me too.*

Once Yuti was out of sight, we climbed into the car, and Andi started to drive us home.

"Ugh, I will be so glad when this baby is out,

and I can drive again," Runa complained from the backseat.

"Why can't you drive?" I asked.

"Because I never know when his magic is going to act up. And with all the electrical components in these cars, I don't want to short it out and be stranded somewhere."

"I don't want to hear it," Konner mumbled. "I never get to play with any of the cool human things. You're only experiencing what I've gone through our entire time here."

"I know. I know," Runa reached out and stroked the tip of Konner's pointed ear, visible now that he'd dropped his glamour.

Andi cleared her throat. "So, Rowan…"

"Yeah?"

"Your boss, she's single, right?"

How is it I keep getting in the middle of these conversations? Do I have a sign on me that says I'm aware of everyone's love life? "She hasn't mentioned a girlfriend to me, and I haven't seen anyone hanging around or anything."

Andi smiled, and I had a feeling she'd be spending a lot of time at the café during the remainder of her stay.

55

Over the next two days, the pack planned for every contingency of my meet-up with Adrian. We went to the outdoor gelato shop and scoped out the surrounding area. Lia decided that she and Ashwin would go with me, one hiding in the woods flanking the shop and the other watching from farther up the street.

Runa, Konner, and Andi were told to stay close to home that day for good measure, and Noire was instructed to stay with them and the pups.

With Adrian's return hanging over me, I didn't like being away from Yuti at all. My skin crawled and itched every moment she wasn't in my sight. Unfortunately, she had an exam to study for, and I had to plan the potential murder of her best friend. So while I saw her when she came into the café, I didn't spend a lot of time with her over the next few days.

But as she walked into the café Wednesday

afternoon, I swore that she wouldn't leave my side that day.

"How did your exam go?" I asked when she came up to the counter.

"I totally aced it. No problem." She beamed.

"Congratulations."

"Yeah, today is a good day." She stretched her arms over her head as if to release any tension left over from studying. "Exams are over. I've got two weeks off, and Adrian is coming back today."

You don't need to remind me. "Wow, I didn't even make the good-day list."

Lifting herself onto the counter, Yuti leaned over. I met her in the middle for a quick kiss.

"Every day is a good day when you're around, Jaaneman."

"You're lucky this place is empty." Camille was watching our exchange from a counter stool.

"I wouldn't have done it otherwise," Yuti replied. "It would only hurt your business if people saw Rowan kissing someone."

Even knowing that humans could be on the fae side of public displays of affection, I didn't quite understand how that would affect the café. "Why's that?"

Yuti laughed. "Do you know how many people come in here just to see that pretty face?"

"I have been told I'm the hottest guy some women have ever seen," I said with a smirk.

"Why do you think I hired you?" Camille remarked. "Did you think it was because you had *so* much experience? You could barely work a coffee pot when you started, and that's not even mentioning the cash register."

I scowled.

"You better take care of that before it costs me business," Camille said to Yuti.

With a grin, Yuti leaned over and kissed me again. "I love you," she whispered.

A smile instantly spread across my face. "I love you, too."

"Then can I get a tiramisu cream soda, barista man?" she asked.

I huffed a laugh through my nose. "You can."

After filling Yuti's order, I placed it on the counter in front of her. She'd pulled out her sketchbook, her eyes flicking between me and the paper.

"Don't mind me," she said.

"How you ever got away with drawing me without me noticing, I'll never know," I commented.

"I got mad skills, stealthy like a cat."

Sneaking around a werewolf, she must be. "Apparently."

Our chitchat came to an end as more exams let out, and the traffic in the café picked up. Thankfully, Yuti stayed on her stool at the counter, no more than ten feet away at any given time. This gave me a little room to concentrate on my work. Yet the nagging buzz under my skin was still there, and it only got worse as our meeting approached.

"So…have you heard anything from Adrian?" I asked Yuti as we left the café once my shift was over.

"Not yet," she said, slipping her hand into mine. "But he said he isn't getting in until tonight. He's got a long drive ahead of him. His mom lives pretty far away."

"Is there…anything you want to do until then?"

She smirked. "Do you think you're good enough to beat me in air hockey yet?"

"You're on. Loser buys dinner."

"Deal."

I was pleased to see I'd gotten better at air hockey over the last few weeks. Yuti put up a fierce battle, but I scored the winning goal. I raised my fists high in the air. "Gooooooal!" I shouted, exaggerating the vowels like a sports commentator.

"All right, all right." Yuti giggled. "No need to be an ungraceful winner."

"This is my first time. Just let me have it." I raised my arms again and declared my goal just as loudly and drawn-out as the first time.

Yuti burst out laughing, the sound more rewarding than my victory.

"Dude, I don't think they heard you in the dorms," Dustin called, smirking from across the atrium.

My smile faltered, and I looked around him to see who was with him. But the lanky male with long hair beside him was definitely not Warren.

Following my eyes, Dustin glanced over his shoulder as they approached. "This is Lloyd, my new roommate. I requested a change after... Well, after Autumn's party."

Yuti smiled up at the tall man. "Nice to meet you, Lloyd. I'm Yuti, and this is Rowan."

An easy smile on his face, Lloyd dipped his head at us. "You two are...together?"

It was the first time anyone had asked us to define our relationship. We glanced at each other. "Yes," we answered at the same time.

"Nice," Lloyd said lightly.

I got the feeling that Lloyd was approachable, easygoing in a warm sort of way. He was certainly more chill than Warren had been, and I was glad Dustin had broken ties with his old friend.

"Are you guys busy? Do you want to get a pizza? Maybe play some pool?" Yuti suggested.

The roommates exchanged a glance, then agreed.

As Yuti pulled out her phone to order the pizza, Dustin racked the pool balls.

56

*D*ustin and Lloyd destroyed Yuti and me in pool. It was no contest at all. Still, I had as much fun playing and eating pizza with them as I could while trying my best to ignore the tension that lurked in the back of my mind. But as Yuti's phone chimed in the melody I recognized as her text-message notification sound, any contentment I was feeling disappeared.

Yuti checked her phone and looked up at the roommates. "Sorry, guys. We don't have time for you to wipe the floor with us again. We're meeting another friend." She turned to me. "You ready?"

I lowered my chin, unable to muster even the hint of a smile. As Yuti pulled on the jacket she'd commandeered from me, I sent a quick text to Lia.

Go.

She and Ashwin had come into town for dinner

and were waiting for my signal. I had every confidence they would be there to back me up.

"I'm kind of nervous," Yuti told me while we walked off campus and toward the gelato shop. "What if you guys don't hit it off? I don't know what I'll do if my best friend and my boyfriend don't like each other."

I had no words of comfort for her. Even the thrill I felt from her calling me her boyfriend for the first time was dampened. I just squeezed her hand and hoped that was enough.

I stared down at our long shadows on the sidewalk. The sun was making its way toward the horizon, but the heat of the day lingered. I felt warm, my nerves on edge. Every bead of sweat that surfaced on my skin sent a shiver through me.

My ears were tuned to every sound, every brush of cloth, every rustle of leaves, every inhale, every exhale. I heard everything to the rhythm of my pounding heart.

I sniffed the air, searching for traces of that not-quite-vampire scent I knew to be Adrian's. Unfortunately, the wind was going in the same direction we were.

"You coming down with a cold?" Yuti asked, concern thick in her tone. "You're sniffling."

"I'm fine." I twitched my mouth into what might have been called a smile.

"All right… Look, there he is." Yuti's face broke into a grin as her eyes lit up.

Adrian was waiting beside a picnic table near the outdoor ice cream shop, shaded by the striped green, white, and red umbrella stuck in the table.

His shoulders stiffened, then his head snapped in our direction.

"Adrian!" Yuti waved her free hand. She made a move to pull out of my reach, but I tightened my grip on her hand.

Adrian was lean but muscular, the sleeves of his white t-shirt filled out with his arms. His brown hair was artfully mussed, and he wore dark-framed, square glasses, which didn't do much to distract from the unusual violet color of his eyes.

When Yuti called his name, he gave her a tight-lipped smile, not showing his teeth. But he only glanced at her for a moment before his eyes fixed on me. His gaze was guarded, not a glare but certainly not friendly.

With a shift in the breeze, I froze, pulling Yuti to a full stop as well. Earth, dark and wet. My nose filled with Adrian's scent. My stomach wrenched, and my limbs started to shake in an effort to maintain human form. This close, I could tell there was still no scent of decay coming from him. But whatever he was, he certainly wasn't human.

"Rowan, are you okay?" Yuti asked. "You're shivering. Are you cold? Do you want your jacket back?"

"I'm fine," I ground out, my skin crawling with every step Adrian took toward us.

"Yuti." Adrian greeted with that tight-lipped smile, his voice far more under control than mine. He opened his arms in a motion that asked for a hug.

She moved to comply with the gesture of mutual attachment, a gesture they had likely shared many times. I stiffened my arm, keeping her beside me.

Adrian frowned, his violet eyes severe with displeasure.

Yuti looked over at me, her eyebrows crinkling. "Rowan, this is Adrian. Adrian, Rowan."

Neither of us made a move to shake hands. We just locked eyes and stared each other down.

"How about I pay for the ice cream for everyone?" My voice was deep but even.

"You don't have to…" Yuti said.

"I want to," I insisted, consciously making my voice lighter, which took quite a bit of effort. "I'll pay for it, but could you go get it?"

Yuti's eyes flicked between us. I could hear the frown in her voice, but I didn't look away from Adrian to see it. "Is this one of those man things where you two measure dicks and don't want me to see?"

I smiled, baring my teeth, by way of an answer and offered her my wallet.

"Okay…" she said, taking my wallet from my hand. "What do you guys want?"

"Strawberry," Adrian answered seriously.

"Whatever you're having," I said.

Yuti headed toward the line to place our order.

"What are you?" Adrian demanded, his voice low.

"I'd like to ask you the same," I countered through clenched teeth. "How long before you fully turn?"

With the weeks that had passed without a change in Adrian's scent, it was a safe bet he was still being fed on or given vampire blood.

Adrian stiffened, sucking in a breath through his nose. "Turn into what?"

I growled, the sound rumbling in my chest. "Don't play with me. Your scent is too stable for you not to know what's going on. It's only a matter of time before you turn into a monster. It's only a matter of time before your thirst for blood puts everyone around you in danger, puts *Yuti* in danger."

"You know nothing," he sneered, his voice dripping with malice. "I've been this way my whole life. I've never once attacked a human. I've never even had human blood."

I pursed my lips, squinting at him. *His whole life? What* is *he?*

"Now it's your turn. What are you? You smell… off. You're *not* human."

His sense of smell is that keen? "You've never met a werewolf before?" I said like it was a threat. I grinned as a little tinge of vinegar mixed in with his salted-earth stench. "I see you've heard of us though, know where we stand compared to the likes of you."

Adrian pulled back his lips, ever so slightly revealing his elongated canines. "I don't know what you're planning, but I don't want you anywhere near Yuti."

I bristled at the challenge, stepping closer to him. His scent—a briny mud puddle—washed over me, filling my nose and likely seeping into my clothes. "You better be careful what you say to me," I warned.

Adrian snorted, his voice defiant despite the fear I smelled on him. "Or what? You're going to wolf out and kill me right here in front of all these people?"

I smiled at the thought. "Maybe. Or maybe I'll just wait until you go home and rip you to pieces when you least expect it."

Doubt crept into Adrian's eyes. He sighed through his nose, and the salt of his anger eased a bit. "Look …" His voice had taken on a tone of reasonability. "I think what we have here is a misunderstanding."

"You think so?" I scoffed.

"I'm not what you think I am. Before you go around murdering college students, don't you think it…prudent to make sure I'm actually a threat?"

"There's no need. I can smell it all over you."

"If you were so sure, you would've killed me long before now. Besides, how do you think people will react when my body is found clearly mauled by wolves? Do you think they'll rest until they've killed all the wolves in the area? And how do you think Yuti will feel when she finds out you killed her *best friend*? Do you think she'll forgive you? She won't."

I growled in frustration. "If you're so harmless, you won't mind explaining yourself to the pack."

He raised an eyebrow. "You want me to surround myself with werewolves who want to kill me? How stupid do you think I am?"

I smirked. "I don't think I'm making myself clear. You don't have much choice in the matter. You want us to hear you out? This is your chance. Come back with us tonight, or you won't see the sunrise."

57

For the next few hours, Yuti tried to find common ground between Adrian and me. She circled around our accomplishments, topics of interest she thought we shared, even the fact that we both teased her about being a vegetarian. But nothing went quite the way she wanted.

"Adrian studies history and folklore." She pushed her small plastic spoon around her long-since-empty gelato cup. "You've been showing an interest in folklore lately, werewolves and stuff. I bet he knows a lot of good sources. Or if you have any questions…"

Adrian's laugh came out as a snort, and the tense silence settled back into place. The longer we didn't cooperate, the more stressed Yuti became. Finally, she stood from the log she was sitting on and snatched the used cups from our hands. The sting of salt dampened her cinnamon and citrus scent.

"I see you're both being obstinate. So I'll make it simple for you. I love you both, and I'm not going to be put in this situation whenever you're around each other. I'm going to throw this trash away. And when I get back, you better have figured this nonsense out." Yuti turned on her heel and stomped toward the trash can.

But a few moments weren't enough for mortal enemies to come to terms for the sake of one small human, no matter how important that human was to us.

Yuti growled a sound that my inner wolf was quite proud of, despite it being directed at him. "Fine," she spat. "Then I'm going home."

"I'll walk you," I said.

"Me too," Adrian seconded.

"So the one thing you can agree on is that I can't take care of myself? Forget it. I'll go alone."

I flinched internally. I didn't like it when Yuti was angry at me, and I certainly didn't like her walking home alone this late at night. But it was far more important to keep Adrian in my sight at the moment. He was the threat that I was most worried about harming her.

Yuti stormed away.

Once she was out of sight, Ashwin and Lia appeared seemingly out of nowhere, flanking Adrian on either side.

"Well, if you insist," Adrian said, his laissez-faire tone undermined by the vinegar mixed into his scent.

Adrian put up no resistance as we escorted him to Lia's car, parked not far away. And he climbed into the back seat with me without complaint. But the farther we drove out of town, the farther from people's prying eyes, the more he reeked of fear. The stench of vinegar-soaked grave dirt made my eyes water.

As Ashwin drove us toward the resort, Lia called Noire on her cellphone.

"Yes?" Noire answered, audible to my wolf ears from this distance.

"We're coming home," Lia informed. "And we've got a visitor. Stay inside."

"All right. Everyone's asleep even the guests. All is quiet."

"Good." Lia hung up.

"Yuti doesn't know about you, does she?" Adrian's voice was deceptively conversational, unperturbed.

I didn't give him the satisfaction of answering, the comfort that breaking the silence—speaking to him directly—would bring. But my skin twitched, the idea of even having a conversation with a vampire—or whatever he was—too surreal.

"Even if you dispose of my body where someone will never find it, even if I just go missing, Yuti will be devastated. And even if you never tell her about your true nature, you'll always know that you're the reason she feels that way."

My stomach dropped.

Lia turned around in her seat. "Do you really think that the feelings of a single human will stop us from erasing you? I'd think carefully about the case you're about to present to us. Because if I deem you a threat to *anyone*, I don't care *who* will mourn you. You will never be heard from again."

Adrian's Adam's apple jumped as he swallowed, the sting of vinegar burning my throat as his terror filled the enclosed space.

Ashwin coughed and rolled down all the windows but the one closest to Adrian.

Finally, after another long stretch of silence, Ashwin pulled into the drive. Adrian took in his surroundings as Lia motioned us toward the back of the house.

Beyond the porch light, I saw Noire moving as she positioned herself on the other side of the glass door.

"Okay." Lia folded her arms. Ashwin and I flanked her. "Speak."

The alpha power she'd injected into her tone made my insides quiver. Standing before us, Adrian glanced at each of us before addressing Lia.

"I'm not what you think I am," he said earnestly.

"You aren't something between a human and a vampire?" Lia asked.

Adrian frowned. "Well, yes... But I'm never going to be any more vampire than I am right now. My mother was fed on while she was pregnant, and it did something to me in the womb. I have fangs, and I'm stronger and faster than the average human, but I don't have the thirst level of a normal vampire. I have a lot more control."

"I heard you tell Rowan you've never fed on a human," Lia said.

Adrian nodded. "I drink pig's blood. And as long as I do every few days, I'm fine. I'm not even tempted by human blood."

Lia stared hard at Adrian, analyzing the veracity of his claims.

"Look," he continued. "I've spent most of my life trying to understand what I am, how I'm different. I've traveled the world looking for answers."

"And what have you discovered?" Lia asked.

Adrian shifted his weight from one foot to the other, and I tensed, prepared to spring should he decide to run.

"Not as much as I would've liked. But I did find some obscure references about the origins of vampires and how they were created by fae."

I froze, my head spinning. "What did you just say about the origins of vampires?"

Adrian's violet eyes met mine, and he tilted his head. "Vampires were created by the fae."

58

I couldn't make sense of what he'd just said. It was as though the words were randomly chosen from a dictionary and strung together.

Adrian's brow crinkled. "I've never met another vampire before. I've never met a werewolf or a fae either. I went searching for these answers for myself, to discover who I am and how I fit in. Are you telling me you didn't know?"

"Explain," Lia ordered.

"Like I said, the references were obscure, the stuff of fairy tales. I'm still trying to piece it all together."

A thick silence confronted him.

My skin twitched and shivered as the night breeze cooled the sweat on my neck and arms. "He's lying," I snarled. "He has to be."

Lia shook her head. "No, I can hear the truth in his words, and he doesn't smell of lies. He believes what he says."

I bit my lip. *Could this be true?*

"Lia… This could change everything," Ashwin muttered.

Lia frowned. "This information needs to be researched, confirmed."

"Well…" Adrian shrugged, holding out his hands. "I mean, I can help you with that, but I can't really do that if I'm dead."

Lia stared at Adrian for a long moment, and his adopted air of ease began to crumble under her steady gaze.

"You have never been tempted by human blood?" Lia asked.

"Not so long as I stay properly fed. Pig's blood really isn't that different from human blood in composition. In any case, I've never fed on a human, never attacked a human. Anytime I get thirsty, I just go to the butcher."

Lia turned to me. "What are your thoughts?"

I forced down Adrian's world-shattering revelation to answer Lia's question. "I don't know anything more than you know, really. Yuti has never indicated that he's anything other than a normal college student. But I've never met anyone like him, never even heard of anyone like him. We don't know what to expect."

"I've never known a vampire to be this…put together," Ashwin added. "And he's not wrong about how the humans will react if he suddenly goes missing. If he's been living a human life, there will be a lot of questions. They don't like it when kids disappear."

"On the other hand, he may suddenly freak out and go on a feeding spree," Lia countered. "As Rowan said, we don't know what to expect."

"I'm right here, you know," Adrian mumbled.

Lia leveled her serious gaze at Adrian, and he stiffened.

"You'll be allowed to live," Lia announced, "for now. But you'll check in with us regularly, and we'll be keeping a very close eye on you. Even a toe out of line, and we'll take the whole leg. Also, I'll be talking with the other alphas about this, so this is only a temporary judgment."

Adrian's cheeks puffed as he blew out a heavy sigh. "Thank you, you won't—" He froze, cutting himself off as his violet eyes widened, his pupils dilating. He breathed deep through his nose, sniffing the air. Then his head whipped to the right.

"Hey, I know it's late, but do you guys have any orange—" Runa halted her approach, her words dropping off.

In a heartbeat, Adrian surged toward her, all of that coherent reason gone from his eyes as his desire for blood took over.

Chaos erupted in bursts of activity and stillness like a series of rapid-fire photographs. Clothes tore as three werewolves shifted to wolf form, Lia shifting mid-stride as she raced to place herself between Adrian and Runa. Runa stepped back and fell with a yelp.

Adrian froze again, flinching to a stop at Runa's cry. His pupils returned to normal. Pain, sorrow, horror, all flashed across his face.

The whole exchange hadn't taken five seconds. Five seconds had only been just enough time for me to shift and take a step toward Runa.

With a ragged release of breath, Adrian dashed into the forest. Ashwin pursued not a second later.

I looked over at Runa, her limbs shaking as she rubbed her belly. Her gray eyes were wide and afraid, and I moved toward her.

Lia growled, jerking her head in a command that told me to forget Runa and help Ashwin.

I obeyed, my wolf's legs pumping to close the distance between us. I could hear them crashing through the brush, and I raced in that direction.

My heart pounded out the rhythm of the hunt.

Up ahead, I heard a yelp as Ashwin cried out in pain. I growled, the sound raw in my throat, and I pushed forward.

I pulled up short, my nose stinging with a scent that overwhelmed my ability to smell. I snuffled and sneezed, but the smell didn't go away. Searching the area by sight, I found Ashwin lying on the ground, whining as he rubbed his eyes and nose with his paws. Beside him was a small, pink tube that I recognized as the pepper spray Yuti had shown me. Adrian was nowhere in sight.

Sniffing around the area, I couldn't pick up Adrian's scent, the smell of pepper spray too strong.

I shifted back to human form. "Fuck," I barked before lifting Ashwin in my arms and carrying him back to the resort.

Noire had joined Lia and Runa in the backyard. Konner and Andi were running up just as I stepped out of the trees. I could see the boys' faces pressed against the glass door from inside.

Lia shifted to human form. "What happened?"

"He got Ashwin with some pepper spray. He must have stolen it from Yuti's purse," I explained.

"And Adrian?"

I shook my head. "He got away. His scent was covered."

A flurry of activity ensued. Noire took Ashwin from my arms, Lia giving orders on how to treat him. Konner and Andi tutted over Runa. But my mind was only vaguely aware of all that.

Adrian was on the loose, and there was one person who remained unprotected, the one person he would likely go to.

I rushed toward the house to put clothes on.

"Rowan, where are you going?" Lia called after me.

"To Yuti's."

59

I didn't care that I didn't have a license to drive. A silly human rule wasn't going to stop me from getting to Yuti. But I was careful to obey the traffic laws because getting pulled over would only delay my arrival.

It was very late when I arrived, and it took a few minutes for Yuti to answer the door after I rang her doorbell. I'd given the area a good sniff on my way up the walk, but I still didn't like her standing out in the open night.

"Rowan — ?"

I rushed into the front hall, pulling her after me by the hand.

"What the hell?" she protested.

But I didn't release her until we were safely in her apartment. I scanned the room, sniffing just in case. Rushing to the other side, I closed the open window and locked it.

Yuti was fuming, her arms crossed over her

chest. "What is your problem? You can't just bust in here whenever you want."

I took a deep breath, trying to steady my racing heart. "Yuti, I have something to tell you."

"And it couldn't have waited until morning?" she snapped.

"No, it couldn't."

She stood glaring at me, but her silence told me she was prepared to listen.

"Yuti… You could be in danger." I tried to keep my voice calm.

"Really?" she said flatly. "And what, pray tell, am I in danger from?"

"Adrian."

She scowled, looking like she would spit. "Come on, Rowan. That's ridiculous. I know you don't like him, but that doesn't give you the right to make shit up about him. I've known him for years. He's my *best friend*."

"Yeah? Well, your best friend is a vampire!" I shouted.

Yuti frowned. "That's not funny."

"Good. Because I'm not joking. Listen, there's way more to this than you even know. I'm…I'm a werewolf. Everyone at the resort is a werewolf. We are a whole pack of werewolves. And when we figured out what Adrian was, we took him out there to question him. And he was fine for a little while. Lia had decided to let him go. But then Runa showed up, and he lunged at her. He would've attacked her, Yuti."

Yuti just stared at me, stone-faced for a good fifteen seconds. "Have you lost your fucking mind? You actually want me to believe that not only is my best friend a vampire, but my boyfriend is a were-wolf? Are you *high*?"

"Do you want me to prove it to you?"

Yuti rolled her eyes. "How are you going to do that? It's not even the full moon."

I bent down and took off my shoes. Then I took off my socks and shirt.

She eyed me suspiciously. "What are you doing?"

"I don't want to rip my clothes when I shift," I said.

She snorted. "Sure. Whatever."

Unbuttoning my pants, I shoved them down my legs and stood in Yuti's apartment in my underwear. Deciding against getting fully naked, I took a deep breath and shifted to wolf form.

Yuti's scream muffled as she clamped her hand over her mouth. Her eyes bulged, and the salt in her cinnamon and citrus scent turned to vinegar. She backed away from me in the small space, bumping into the kitchen counter and knocking a glass off. The shatter as it hit the floor seemed to break some-thing inside me.

Yuti swallowed, the action clearly taking effort. "Y-y-you need to leave." Her voice shook, and she was trembling.

My heart sank, and a howl of sorrow rose in my throat. I swallowed it by grabbing my pants in my mouth. I dragged them down the short hall, my tail low, and shifted back to human form.

After pulling on my pants, I went back for the rest of my clothes. I glanced over at Yuti. She was still rooted in place, her bare feet surrounded by shards of glass.

I collected my shirt, socks, and shoes. "Be careful," I pleaded.

"Leave, Rowan."

I flinched, her tone far stronger the second time. Then I obeyed. As I dressed outside her apartment door, I heard the lock click behind me.

My chest ached as my heart broke. Every breath brought new pain. And when I stepped into the night, even the cool breeze couldn't dry my tears.

I knew I needed to call Lia, needed to update her. But it was a while before I could even form words enough to explain.

As the phone rang, I cleared my throat against the burning lump.

"Anything?" Lia asked.

"He's not here," I replied, my nose stuffed from crying. "How's Ashwin?"

"He's getting better. There won't be any permanent damage, but he won't be comfortable for a while."

"I…" My voice gave out, and it was a moment before I tried again. "I told her everything."

"She didn't take it well?" Lia guessed.

"No."

"Are you coming back?"

"No. Even if she doesn't want me around, she still needs to be protected until we can catch him. I'll stay here."

"Understood. We know where he lives. This is our territory. He won't be able to hide for long."

"How's Runa?" I asked.

"Shaken up but fine. I'll be hearing it from Layton, I'm sure."

"What do you think happened?"

Lia paused. "I think it has to be the baby's fae blood. He said he'd never come into contact with anyone but humans before, and he didn't seem tempted by werewolf blood. It was only Runa showing up that made him lose control."

"He did seem...surprised by his reaction."

Lia hummed in agreement. "Call me with any developments."

"I will," I promised.

As soon as I hung up with Lia, as soon as there wasn't something to distract me, the pain rushed back in. It was an all too familiar feeling, this feeling of rejection, loneliness, despair.

I wondered if love was really worth the risk as I sneaked around to the back of Yuti's building and stationed myself outside her window, staring at the light that was still on.

60

I watched the light in Yuti's window until the dawn made it difficult to tell if it was even on. And still I watched. Eventually, she passed by the window. Then she disappeared from view. Then she passed by the window again. The frequency of this pattern made it apparent that she was pacing the length of her apartment. Her brow was puckered, and she held her elbows. Her eyes stared intently down at the floor. Back and forth she walked, the rhythm mesmerizing.

A breeze carried a scent I knew, and I turned my head toward Noire as she approached me.

"What's going on?" I murmured, my gaze returning to Yuti's window.

"I'm here to relieve you."

I looked at her sharply and opened my mouth to protest.

"You need rest if you're going to effectively protect her. I'll stay here and keep watch until you return."

I frowned, everything in me telling me not to leave.

"Lia's orders," Noire pushed. "Get going."

I grunted, then sighed.

"I'll keep her safe." She squeezed my shoulder.

I nodded and forced my feet to move.

When I arrived back at the resort, I had to admit I was tired. I didn't know what everyone else was doing, but the place was quiet. I just climbed the stairs to my room and crawled into bed. The faster I got to sleep, the sooner I could return to Yuti's. I did manage to text Camille that I wouldn't be coming in that day.

Despite my exhaustion, I didn't sleep more than three hours. And even that little bit of sleep was restless, haunted by images of the previous night. The memory of Yuti's fear was all too fresh in my mind when I opened my eyes. As I shuffled down the stairs, I knew what I needed to do.

I knew the pain I'd felt when Runa had left me was going to pale in comparison to what it would feel like when Yuti looked at me and didn't even know who I was, when I became truly nothing to her.

But protecting the pack, protecting all of were-wolf kind in the realm of origin, was much bigger than me and my feelings. And the hard truth was, Yuti forgetting everything would probably be safer for her as well.

Runa, Konner, and Andi were standing in the living room with Ashwin and Lia when I got downstairs. The boys were making sandwiches in the kitchen, their slow movements saying they were listening to every word.

"Layton has sent word for the Mesa Pack to expect you." Lia spoke to the three of them, but she looked at Runa. "They have more vampire activity than we normally do, but they're by far the biggest pack. So they'll be more than enough to protect you."

Runa nodded.

"We're already packed," Konner said.

"What are you all going to do?" Andi asked, clearly uneasy about leaving us while a vampire ran amok.

"There was no trace of him when I checked his place last night. But the truth is we don't have enough pack members to deal with this type of crisis at the moment. I've called those close enough to come home without delay, and some of the other alphas are sending reinforcements. We'll be fine. One half-vampire isn't a match for us. The trouble is finding him."

Runa sighed. "I guess we better have lunch and get on the road then."

I called out to Konner as he headed toward the kitchen table, motioning for him to step into the front hall with me.

"Could you do something for me before you leave?" I spoke hesitantly as if each word had to be pulled out of me.

"What is it?"

"We need...to erase Yuti's memories, sooner rather than later. Do you know the spell?" Every inch of me hoped he would say he didn't.

Konner's brow puckered. "Are you sure, Rowan? There isn't any coming back from that. Once it's gone, it's gone."

My throat burned as bile rose up from my stomach, but I swallowed it down. I nodded, unable to form even a single word of assent.

"All right. We can do it on our way out of town."

I didn't bother even trying to eat lunch with everyone else. I knew I wouldn't be able to keep anything down. My stomach was in knots, my mind swirling with memories of Yuti. Her smiles, her kisses, her eyes when she saw a wolf in her apartment.

As Andi and Konner packed up the car, I told Lia what I was planning to do.

She pulled me into an embrace, rubbing my back as I trembled against her. "I know," she whispered in a soothing voice. "I know it hurts."

She didn't tell me it would be okay. She didn't say time would heal me. She just acknowledged my pain, and that was all I needed in that moment.

No one spoke while Andi drove us into town, and I was grateful. I don't think I could've held back my tears if they had. The hot sun beat down on my face as I rested my head against the window. I didn't bother to move even as I felt my skin burning.

Too soon, Konner and I stood on Yuti's front porch. I lifted my arm, my index finger an inch from her doorbell, then dropped it.

"Are you sure?" Konner asked again.

Before I could answer, a resident of the building stepped out, and we moved aside to let him leave, stopping the door before it could close.

To me, it seemed like fate was telling me this was the right thing to do. This was the moment. Fate had opened the door and invited me in.

Konner and I shuffled down the hall. By the

time I reached Yuti's door, my fingers were numb and my chest hollow. I raised one heavy fist and knocked.

My heart told me not to look at her as she opened the door. I didn't want to see the fear, the disgust, in her eyes. But I couldn't help it. This was the last time she would look at me with any sort of recognition.

61

Her dark eyes were guarded, and she flicked her gaze between Konner and me. "What are you doing here, Rowan?"

I flinched. *Is that the last time she'll ever say my name?*

"I…" My voice grew thick and gave out. I swallowed and tried again. "Konner is here to make this better for you, safer."

She raised an eyebrow, crossing her arms over her chest. "Better how?"

"Konner is a fae. He has magic. When humans are confronted with this type of information… In order to protect our kind, it's standard procedure to wipe that human's memories."

A splash of vinegar muddled Yuti's scent as alarm entered her gaze. "My memories?"

"Don't worry," I assured. "Only your memories of us will be affected."

Yuti stared at me, then growled. "Are you serious right now?" Her vinegar scent turned briny with salt. "You think I want to forget about you? Rowan, you show up to my house at two in the morning and tell me a whole bunch of stuff that's super crazy. Then you turn *into a wolf* before my eyes! How was I supposed to react? Did you really think I wouldn't need time to process that?"

My heart stopped, and I could hardly collect enough breath to speak. "Y-you *don't* want to forget about me?"

Yuti sighed long and low before her eyes met mine. "Of course I don't want to forget about you, Rowan. I love you."

My mouth was on hers before she could utter another word, all the fear I'd felt since the night before dissipating as she wrapped her arms around my neck.

Konner cleared his throat. "Well…I'm going to just go then. And I'll, uh, tell the others to head home."

I reluctantly broke off our kiss and looked at him. "Thank you," I breathed, knowing that he would tell Noire to abandon her watch in the woods.

He smiled that crooked smile he used to have when Wilhelm and I were being particularly rambunctious. "Anytime. I'll see you around."

I didn't watch him leave but buried myself in Yuti, backing her into her apartment and kicking the door shut behind me.

"Rowan," she gasped, her voice sending tingles across my skin. "Are you sure now is a good time?"

I pulled back, gazing down at her. "Is it not a good time for you?" I asked, reining my wolf in. *I did give her a lot to think about last night. Maybe she wants to digest first.*

She quirked her mouth. "It's not that. I just don't want you to rush into anything because you're relieved we aren't fighting."

I closed my eyes and let out all my breath, willing myself to say what needed to be said calmly. Then I took Yuti's face in my hands and looked into her eyes.

"Yuti, I want you to listen to what I have to say carefully. I have never—not since the first time I realized how I felt toward you—not wanted you. I have controlled myself because it didn't feel right to be with you when you didn't know what I am. It has taken every ounce of patience, strength, and honor I have in me not to claim you in this way. I have not once been uncomfortable or unwilling to make love to you."

Yuti's face took on that warm undertone she had when she flushed. Still, she frowned slightly. "This…claiming… Is that a w-werewolf thing?"

I dipped my head.

"Is it one way, or…can I claim you, too?"

A slow smile spread across my face. "Do you want to claim me?"

"Well, I mean…if we're going to be marking our territory or whatever, then I want to make sure other women know that you're…you know… spoken for… It seems unfair for—"

I cut her off with another kiss, closing my eyes and drowning myself in that maple syrup and caramel scent of hers. My cock was ready, beckoned by the smell of her desire.

She stood on her toes, encouraging me as she

pushed harder against me. Grabbing her by the ass, I lifted her off her feet, shivering as her thighs wrapped around my torso.

The insistent stroking of her fingers in my hair sent a tingle across my skin, and my breath hitched as she slipped her tongue into my mouth. Her kisses were deep, intoxicating, and my head swam. All I knew was that I had to be closer to her—nothing else mattered.

I moved forward, carefully climbing the few stairs to her bedroom. Then I lowered us onto the bed.

My cock jumped, Yuti's weight beneath me pressing against it. She smiled. "Do you want me?" she whispered, grinding her thigh against me for emphasis.

I shuddered. "Yes," I breathed.

Sitting up, Yuti removed her shirt, revealing her breasts. Her dark eyes met mine. "I want you, too."

I removed my shirt as well, smiling as she gazed appreciatively at my bare chest. She was looking at me. She was looking only at me, and she clearly wanted what she saw.

Tentatively, Yuti reached out her hand, her eyes following her fingers as they trailed down my abdomen. My breath came out ragged and heavy at the soft warmth of her hands stroking my skin.

When she reached the waistband of my pants, her eyes flicked back to mine. I held my breath, then gasped, a jolt running through me as she boldly cupped my manhood. Then she smirked that mischievous smile of hers.

"I like that," she told me. "That sound you make. How your eyes glaze over."

"Do you? How about this?"

I kissed her deeply, kissed her until her moan hummed against my lips. Then I trailed my lips down her throat, leaning her onto her back as I did so. The heat from her bare skin against mine made my whole body flush. Kissing down her chest, I popped one pert nipple into my mouth and rolled it gently with my tongue.

She gasped, arching her back as she slid her fingers into my hair. I glanced up at her, caressing her other breast with my hand while I flicked my tongue. Her head was thrown back, her eyes closed, and she let out a moan that made my cock weep.

She trembled beneath me as I trailed my other hand slowly down her body. And when I slipped my fingers into her shorts, she spread her legs wider, a clear invitation. She was already wet, my fingers slick as I ran them up to her clit.

Clutching me to her as she writhed, her voice filled the small bedroom.

"Are you ready?" I pulled back to meet her lust-clouded eyes.

"Yes," she said as though it was a plea. Then she pointed to the bookshelf at the foot of the bed. "There's a condom in that jar."

Following her finger, I went to the shelf and took the lid off a small, round jar. I felt her eyes on me while I removed my pants and rolled the condom on. I returned to her quickly, kissing her deeply.

Her skin was smooth, hot beneath my lips as I trailed kisses down her body. I peeled the rest of her clothes off, reveling in every inch she revealed to me. I was in no rush.

Stroking her thighs, I gently pushed them apart.

Then I buried my face between her legs. She twitched and moaned while I tasted her, and my head spun with the scent of her desire.

"Rowan, please," she begged. "I want you inside me."

Her voice was urgent as if she would cry if I didn't comply immediately. I settled on top of her and caressed her face with my fingertips, staring into her dark eyes. "I love you," I whispered.

"I love you, too."

But when I slid my cock into her, she hissed.

I clenched my teeth at the sound of her pain, analyzing her scrunched face. "Are you okay?"

"Yeah," she breathed. "Just give me a second."

I waited, taking a steadying breath as her tight warmth squeezed my cock.

"Okay," she whispered, relaxing beneath me.

I moved my hips slowly, pulling out slightly, then pushing farther in.

"Keep going," she said when I hesitated.

On my third thrust, her hisses turned to moans.

"Oh, God. Keep going," she begged, her tone entirely different.

Her slick heat, her moans of pleasure, the scent of her lust all around me, it was all starting to be too much. But as jolts and shivers ran though me, I clenched my teeth against the need to give in.

She trembled beneath me and cried out my name. And as her convulsions clenched my manhood, I did the same.

62

"You're beautiful," I whispered as I lay alongside Yuti on the bed.

She smiled contentedly. "So are you."

But as I stroked her hair, her smile faltered.

"Can I ask you about what you said last night?"

"Sure. I bet you have a lot of questions."

Her eyes shifted, looking at one of my eyes then the other, unable to focus on both because of how close our faces were. "All that stuff you've been telling me about since we saw *An American Werewolf in London:* that werewolves don't change on the full moon, that they don't forget what they did while they were wolves, that they don't necessarily have the drive to kill…" Her breath brushed over my face as she spoke, her voice hushed in the tiny room. "Did you tell me all that so I wouldn't be afraid when you told me the truth?"

"Yes." I matched her quiet tone. "There are a lot of things movies get wrong. I didn't want you to think I was a monster…"

She dropped her gaze to my mouth, her finger-tips twitching as they pressed against my chest. "And you... How long have you been a werewolf?"

"Werewolves aren't turned. We're born. I've been a werewolf my whole life."

"But," she countered, "if there are so many of you, why don't more humans know the truth?"

"A long time ago, werewolves lived here, in the human realm, in the realm of origin." With every word of explanation, the anxiety I'd been carrying around—the worry that Yuti wouldn't understand, wouldn't give me a chance to explain—eased. "But we were hunted down by the humans. So we signed a treaty with the fae. They would magic werewolf territory into Faerie if we protected them from the vampires. You see, vampires have a taste for fae blood, but an adult fae's magical abilities make it difficult for a vampire to actually get to them. So they go after faelings, young fae who haven't awakened to their full magic yet. In exchange for giving us a safe place to hide from the humans, the werewolves promised that every werewolf pup would protect a faeling before their awakening. There are some werewolves who still live here, but not nearly as many."

She listened carefully, her eyes unfocused as she internalized my words. "So Faerie...is like another dimension?"

I quirked my mouth, unsurprised that was the part she focused on. "I suppose that's one way to put it."

Her eyes widened, and she popped up to a sitting position. "Holy monkeys, you're an alien."

I huffed out a laugh. "Well, technically were-wolves originated in this realm."

"Then…Konner. You said Konner was a fae. Konner is an alien!"

I chuckled, the motion warm and easy. "I'm not sure how he'd feel about that description, but I guess so."

"Wow." She sighed the word. "Another dimension. This is huge. How do you get back and forth? When you went home to visit your family, is that where you went?"

I nodded. "I went to Faerie to attend my sister's unbinding. That's when a werewolf is released from their oath to protect a faeling because it's time for the faeling to awaken. And there are portals. That's how we get back and forth."

"Portals? Like wormholes?"

I frowned and shrugged. "I guess…I've gone through them, but I don't know their nature."

"Are they in fixed places? Do they move around? Can you only access them at certain times? How do you know where they are?" Her voice grew more and more excited as she peppered me with questions.

"Yes, they're in fixed places. No, they don't move around. You can access them at any time. I have no idea how they're established or how to locate one without already knowing where it is."

She stared at me closely, her eyes alight with curiosity. Then she exhaled, puffing her cheeks out as if to blow her many questions away. "Sorry. This is just really big for me. I can't believe there's a whole other dimension that you can just travel to whenever you want—oh my God," she gasped. "Can humans go there? Could *I* go there?"

I crinkled my eyebrows. "It's pretty unconventional, but I don't think there's any physical reason a human couldn't go to Faerie."

Her dark eyes met mine, begging me. "Will you take me with you, *please*?"

"I'll look into it. I'll ask Lia what she knows."

She grinned, wiggling in excitement. "Ugh, that's so cool."

Reaching out, I placed my hand over Yuti's and stroked it with my thumb. It felt good to tell her everything; this relief, this easy honesty, was what I'd hoped for. "Do you…have anything else you want to ask?"

"Yes. You said all the people at the resort are werewolves too, right?"

I nodded, my hair rustling on the pillow as I did so. "Among the werewolves in the realm of origin, we're known as the Northern Pack. Lia is our alpha."

"So Lia is in charge."

"Right, among other things. Pack dynamics can get pretty complicated."

"Was that a werewolf I saw when I dropped you off the first time then?"

"Yes, that was Braylyn."

"And who was I drawing?"

"Noire."

Her questions seemed limitless. And I tried to answer them as quickly as I could.

"Cool. So if you were born in Faerie, why did you come here? Why did you join Lia's pack?"

I sighed, rolling onto my back and staring up at

the glow-in-the-dark stars stuck to her ceiling. "I sort of told you part of this story already. I was bound with Konner's younger brother, Wilhelm. It was my duty to protect him until his awakening. Runa was bound with Konner. I grew up with their family, but Runa didn't come to the farm until much later. She and Konner fell in love even though it's forbidden for werewolves and fae to mate. I...sort of got caught in the middle. I loved her and asked her to be my mate even though I knew she loved Konner. She accepted. But when Konner was snatched by vampires, she broke our promised bond and went to save him. In the end, they stayed here. And when Wilhelm awakened, I moved here to get away from the expectations of my family, my pack. I'm supposed to find a wolf to mate and have pups so we can bind those pups to faelings and continue the whole cycle."

"You moved here to be near her," Yuti clarified.

"I did," I admitted.

Yuti plopped back down on her side and scooted closer to me. "Well, even if that was your reason, I'm glad you came. And I'm going to have to lodge a formal complaint about this you-finding-a-wolf-mate thing because that's not going to work for me."

My chest glowed at her words, and I couldn't have stopped my smile if I'd wanted to. I turned back on my side to face her again, reaching up and tucking a stray lock of hair behind her ear.

"It's not...forbidden for humans and werewolves to be together, is it?" she asked softly.

"Well, it's pretty unheard of in Faerie, and it's not quite common here. But there aren't any rules against it. As long as the human keeps our existence a secret that is." I gave her a significant look.

"Obviously. I suppose that's why you would've wiped my memories?"

I frowned, stroking her cheek with my thumb.

"How would that have worked though?" she asked. "I mean, you could've taken yourself out of my memories. But I have pictures and sketches of you. I told my family about you."

"It's definitely a task. I would've tried to erase your pictures, taken your sketches, removed any trace of me from your life. As for your family… It can get sort of tricky. But most of the time, the human mind keeps itself in working order—it doesn't like to be uncomfortable. So even if they'd asked about me, you might've wondered what they were talking about for a little while, but you would've moved on pretty quickly."

She reached out and rested her palm on my face, and I leaned into her warmth. "That would've been awful." Her eyes were sad. "I can't imagine what it would be like if *you* suddenly didn't recognize *me*. What would you have done when I came into the café?"

I closed my eyes against the thought, turning my head to press a kiss to her palm. "I don't know," I murmured.

Yuti sighed, her breath caressing my face. "Thinking back, all this explains a lot about your strange behavior and some of the things you didn't know."

I pursed my lips. "I'm not *that* strange."

She raised an eyebrow at me. "You'd never

played air hockey, and you choked Warren at a birthday party, and you'd never—"

"Okay, maybe I'm not always that great at following human rules, but you were under my protection. And when a werewolf sees someone as a potential mate, is courting her in that way… We tend to get a little territorial."

I could feel her looking at me, but I avoided her gaze, focusing instead on the pink stud in her nose.

"I can understand that you have instincts that might not mesh well with what I think of as acceptable male behavior. I certainly wasn't pleased at the time, and I definitely didn't like how pushy you were being the other night when you busted in here."

I flinched at her words.

"But there are bound to be cultural differences. And I'm willing to be patient if you're also willing to give a little."

Looking into her eyes, I said the words that my every heartbeat confirmed. "I'd do anything for you."

Her complexion warmed. "That, uh, level of intensity is going to take some getting used to."

"Sorry."

"Hey." She ran a thumb along my jaw. "You don't have to be sorry. I like it."

And as her dark eyes smiled at me, I swore to myself that, however long I had to wait, this woman would be my mate.

63

*L*ater that evening, as we sat across from each other while eating dinner, Yuti cleared her throat. I looked up from my meatless meal. She pushed dal around her plate, glancing up at me before looking down again.

"Rowan…what…what happened with Adrian?"

With all the many questions she'd asked over the last few hours, she hadn't once mentioned her friend, and I'd wondered when she would get around to it.

I sighed, putting down my spoon and lacing my fingers together. "Adrian is a vampire…sort of."

"How can you 'sort of' be a vampire?"

"When I first smelled his scent, I thought he was still transitioning. But he said he was born this way. Apparently, his mother was attacked while she was pregnant. He said it affected him while he was still in the womb."

Her brow creased. "But I've met his mom. She seems totally fine."

"She probably is. She couldn't have been turned. If she'd been turned, she would have miscarried when her body died. Adrian would never have been born."

She squinted, focusing on some spot over my shoulder as she worked through her thoughts. "But…I mean, I know you said he's a vampire, but…are you sure? I've known him for years. He may be a little odd, but I feel like I would've noticed if he was off snacking on people. He goes out in the sunlight all the time. He eats regular food. You saw him eat gelato."

I frowned. "Even full vampires can go out in the sun. Owls are nocturnal too, but they don't burst into flames in sunlight either. In any case, he's only half-vampire, so he's bound to be a little different, which would account for him eating food. As to him snacking on people, he said he's never had human blood. He said he drinks pig's blood. And we're inclined to believe him. But to answer your question: yes, I'm sure. He even told us about it himself."

"I can't believe it." She dropped her gaze to the plate in front of her.

"You've known him for years. Haven't you ever seen his fangs?"

"He has *fangs*?" she shouted, her eyes snapping to my face. "I never saw them. But he doesn't show his teeth when he smiles, and he always covers his mouth when he laughs. I just thought he had bad teeth and was embarrassed about it or something."

She shook her head, sighing heavily. "I'm just dumbstruck. You said he attacked Runa? Why would he do that? Adrian is the sweetest person I know. I can't even imagine. He even brought me homemade vegetable soup when I was sick for goodness' sake."

"I was there. I saw the whole thing."

"Yeah, but like, what actually happened?"

I held in my distress. Yuti had shown herself to be open-minded and accepting of my werewolf nature, and it seemed that same feeling had been extended to her vampire friend. I tried to explain to her everything she'd missed, tried to tell her just how dangerous he was, as calmly and succinctly as I could. "He was telling us about the research he'd done overseas while studying abroad. Then Lia, Ashwin, and I discussed what we should do. Lia told him that she would be talking to the other alphas, but he was okay to go as long as he checked in with us. Then Runa came up to the house looking for something, and he completely lost his shit. He lunged at her. Runa fell, and then he sort of froze. The next thing we knew, he was running off."

"But why Runa? If he's fine around all the college students, and he didn't act that way around you guys, what would make Runa different? Just because she's pregnant?"

"Lia thinks it's because she's pregnant with a child that's half-fae. Like I said, vampires like fae blood the most. He likely went for her because her baby has fae magic."

"Oh, Adrian…" Yuti whispered. "What happened after that? Where did he go?"

"Ashwin and I pursued him, but he pepper-sprayed Ashwin and slipped away."

"He pepper-sprayed him? So that's where my pepper spray went. Is Ashwin okay?"

I nodded.

Yuti stared down at her plate, her food cold and barely touched. "What happens now?"

"Lia has sent for reinforcements. It won't be long before there are werewolves scouring the area for him."

"And…what will you do when you find him?" Her voice was hardly above a whisper.

"I don't know. It sort of depends on the state we find him in. Will he be back in control? Will his exposure to the scent of fae blood have changed him in some way? We just don't know."

She was silent for a full minute, only moving to breathe. "And if it has changed him, if he's not in control, will you kill him?"

I didn't want to answer that question, and I knew she didn't want to hear my response. But I also didn't want to lie to her anymore. "We'll do… whatever needs to be done."

Yuti's head bobbed ever so slightly.

"You haven't heard from him, have you?"

Her eyes flicked to mine before returning to her plate. "No, I haven't. I sent him a bunch of messages after I told you to leave, but he didn't answer. Why? Do you think he'll reach out to me?"

"I don't know. It's possible. I'd like to stay here with you until we find him. But if you need some time alone, we can just set a guard to watch your place in case he shows up."

She was quiet for a moment, and then her mouth twitched into a sad smile. "Of course you can stay here with me."

Yuti stood up, took her plate to the counter, and returned her uneaten food to the proper containers.

Her movements were slow and smooth as if she didn't need to think about what she was doing.

My stomach clenched, but I picked up my spoon and took another bite.

64

The next few days were some of the most blissful and the most tense of my life. I loved being with Yuti. I loved waking up with her, eating with her, making love to her. But those blissful moments when we were wrapped up in each other were separated by the tension of her still-missing best friend.

Every morning and every night, I would call Lia for updates. And every call ended the same way. They still couldn't find him. By the end of the following week, three of our pack had returned from their summer travels, joined by four from other packs. Andi had even promised to return once Runa and Konner were settled. Despite all those noses to the ground, there was no trace of Adrian.

I managed to keep Yuti occupied both at the café and in her apartment, but I could tell she was getting antsy.

"Hey." I glanced over at her as we sat on the couch late Saturday night. "Are you tired?"

She shook her head, but her eyelids drooped.

"Do you want to watch a movie? We could finish that Bollywood film we started the first time I came here."

"Yeah, okay," she agreed.

"Good. How about I jump into the shower real quick while you make the popcorn? I feel sort of stinky now that the heat of the day is over."

She snorted. "You smell sort of stinky."

"Oh yeah? That silly human nose of yours probably can't even tell."

"Oh, I can tell."

"Really?" Reaching out, I wiggled my fingers on her sides.

She squealed, writhing as I tickled her. "Okay! Okay! I give! Just get in the shower already."

I pressed a kiss to her head, then got up and went to the bathroom. As I removed my clothes and turned on the shower, I heard her puttering around the kitchen: the *plink plink plink* of the popcorn kernels as she poured them into the paper bag, the microwave door as she shut it.

But just when I stepped under the showerhead, I heard a loud clatter. I froze, listening carefully as the warm water ran down my body.

"Yuti?" I called. "Are you all right?"

My only answer was a shuffle on the other side of the bathroom door, then the front door slammed.

"Fuck." I cut the water, my heart jumping into my throat. I pulled on my discarded clothes without bothering to dry off.

Rushing from the bathroom, I scanned the apartment. "Yuti?" I called again.

There was no answer. The apartment was empty.

Grabbing my shoes, I ran out the door, down the hall, and onto the porch. I sniffed deeply while shoving my wet feet into my shoes.

I could smell it, the vinegar marring Yuti's cinnamon and citrus scent. My eyes darted around, trying to locate her, trying to think over the sound of my racing heart, the pounding in my head.

My eyes flicked toward the sputtering of an engine starting, and I dashed in that direction. I threw myself in front of Yuti's car, the tires screeching to a halt when she slammed on the brakes.

Yuti's eyes were wide, tears streaming down her face, as they met mine through the windshield.

My chest tightened, my heart screaming at the pain in her expression. I strode to the driver's side and opened the car door. The stench of her fear poured out, stinging my nose.

"What happened?" I crouched down to her level.

Her hands shook on the steering wheel. "Adrian," she sobbed, her face crumbling.

Her sorrow slammed into me, and I felt nauseated.

"H-he texted me." She held her phone out to me, her hands trembling.

I stared at the message.

> You will always be my dearest friend. I love you, and I'm sorry. You be the pebble, and I'll be the sand.

"What the hell does that mean?" I wondered.

"It means he's going to kill himself." Her voice quivered. "I have to get to him."

"You don't even know where he is."

"Yes, I do. Pebbles and sand. I know exactly where he is."

I took in Yuti's watery eyes, her shaking hands, her ragged breathing. Even if I was okay with her going off to see her vampire friend, she was in no state to drive.

"Move aside. I'll drive."

She froze for only a second, then climbed over the gearshift to the passenger seat.

"Where are we going?" I put the car in drive.

"Out to Willard's Canyon."

Her anxiety, her fear, was so strong I could hardly breathe. "How did you know? What does that mean, pebbles and sand?" I hoped talking would calm her.

She inhaled deeply as though she was gasping in pain. And when she answered, the words rushed out as if she had to say it all in that one breath. "Our first year of college, Adrian and I did a lot of hiking. We both grew up in the city and didn't get out in nature much, so we went out to see the wilderness as much as we could. Adrian's favorite trail was the one that leads up to Willard's Canyon. We used to sit on the edge of the canyon with our feet dangling off and just watch the river rush by at the bottom."

"Okay. What does that have to do with pebbles and sand?"

"One time, we were talking about water, how it's soft, adaptable, but can wear down even the hardest rocks. He said water was like life, always flowing, always carrying you along. And that we're all like pebbles. He said when we die, it was because life had worn us away. When we die, we're just a grain of sand… He's telling me that he plans on dying, but he wants me to live."

65

After I'd pulled into the dark parking lot at the trailhead, I took out my phone. I needed to call Lia. I needed to tell her where we were, where Adrian was. But I'd only managed to see that I didn't have any bars before Yuti jumped out of the car.

She didn't get very far. The waxing gibbous struggled to break through the clouds, not bright enough for her human eyes to see well enough to run.

Taking out her phone, she turned on the flashlight, but even that wasn't very bright. It might've been enough to keep her from falling, but I'd still need to help her.

I led her onto the trail, clasping her hand in mine.

"Can you…smell him?" she asked. "Is he alive?"

I took a deep breath through my nose. "I can't smell him. If he came this way, it was too long ago."

She picked up her pace. "We have to hurry." She

stumbled, yelping as her toe caught an exposed tree root.

I steadied her before she could fall.

"Let me lead. Just hold onto my hand, and pay attention to the ground ahead of you. I'll let you know when I smell him."

She exhaled slowly. "All right."

Yuti and I crept along the dirt path, the natural world closing in around us as if the trees were trying to trap us.

I sniffed the air and pricked up my ears at every sound. Over the pounding of my heart, I could hear Yuti breathing. I could hear the flutter of wings as a bird took flight, the rustle of leaves as an opossum skittered away.

The evening air chilled me, my shirt and pants still damp from my hurried departure from the shower, and goose bumps rose on my skin. I breathed in. I breathed out. Each step took me closer to the unknown, took Yuti closer to danger.

And just as I was thinking of going back to a place where I had cell service, the breeze carried a hint of rich, damp earth to me. I stiffened, breathing deeper.

"You smell something, don't you?" Yuti whispered.

I looked back at her. "I think you should go back to the car." My instincts told me to get her as far away from that scent as possible. "Drive until you get service, and call Lia."

"No fucking way," Yuti growled, snatching her hand from mine. "Adrian!" she shouted, surging up the path.

I quickened my pace, easily keeping stride with

her. "I'm serious, Yuti. We don't know what we're walking into. I don't want you to get hurt."

"Oh, but it's okay if you get hurt? He's a lot more likely to hurt you than he is me," she argued. "Adrian! Can you hear me?"

"Yu-ti…"

The wind that carried the voice sent a shiver up my spine. Something was wrong. Very wrong.

Yuti ran toward the sound.

"Yuti, wait," I urged, pursuing her.

The trail up ahead was steep; stone stairs, cut into the slope, led up to one side of the canyon. Yuti scrambled up the steps, and I followed, trying to get in front of her as the path narrowed.

At the summit, we stood on one side of a canyon, the rushing river flowing far below. Yuti squinted into the night, the beam of her light flashing as it searched the darkness. But my wolf's eyes had no trouble seeing.

"Adrian?" Yuti shuffled forward.

I stepped in front of her, placing myself between her and the vampire, who was lying on the ground.

"*Yuti.*" The warning in my voice was clear. "Not a step farther. He can see you. He can hear you."

"Where is he?"

As I pointed to where he lay, the moon broke through the clouds, illuminating the ground enough for her human eyes.

"Adrian," she gasped, lunging toward him

But I stepped into her path. "Let me handle this." I kept her behind me. "Adrian," I said reasonably, inching toward him. "We've been looking for you. Do you want to tell me what happened at the resort?"

"I...I don't know." His voice broke in the middle. He took a deep breath and froze, his eyes darting toward Yuti. "Keep her away from me."

A shiver ran through me at the warning in his voice.

"I don't...want to hurt her. I don't want to hurt anyone." He sucked in a breath. "It hurts. My throat... It feels like it's on fire."

Yuti's breath caught. "Adrian," she sobbed. "What's wrong?"

"When was the last time you fed, Adrian?" I asked calmly, my limbs shaking at my body's urge to shift.

"When...when I was at my mom's."

"Have you ever gone this long without feeding?" I was getting close to him now, slowly making my way to where he lay on the ground.

"I don't want to feed anymore. I'm a monster," he cried, the agony in his voice squeezing my heart. "I can't believe I tried to attack a pregnant woman. Is...is she okay? Is her baby okay?"

"She's fine," I assured him. "Runa is fine. Her baby is fine."

Every step I took closer to him only made it more clear how unstable he was. His limbs shook, and his pupils had engulfed all the violet in his irises.

"You...won't let me hurt anyone. Will you?" His eyes followed me as I moved toward him. "You'll kill me first, right? Before I can do anything to anyone? That's what you're here for, isn't it?"

"No!" Yuti shouted, rushing forward.

I grabbed her before she could reach him. But

the closer she got, the more he shook with hunger, his limbs convulsing.

His lips curled back, exposing his fangs, but his eyes were fixed on mine. "Kill me. Please. Before I hurt her."

"Rowan, don't!" Yuti cried, sobs shaking her. "He needs blood, right? I'll give it to him. Rowan, you can't kill him. You can't let him die."

My heart shattered at the pain in her voice, at the pleading in his eyes. I swallowed. "I'll…I'll do it. He can feed on me."

Before she could protest, before I could change my mind, I released Yuti and dropped to my knees.

"Hurry." I stared into his black eyes, which glinted like obsidian in the moonlight. "Before you lose control and hurt her."

I leaned my head back and to the side so he would have better access to my jugular. Then I closed my eyes.

The strike was sudden even when I was expecting it. A sharp pain shot through me as his teeth sank into my throat, but that soon subsided as his mouth gently sucked the wound.

At first, I felt warm. But as my head started to get foggy, my hands and feet began to numb.

All I heard was the pumping of my heart and the wet sound of his lips on my throat.

I tried to speak, but I couldn't form the words. My last thought was of Yuti, my hope that she would be safe. Then everything went black.

66

"His hand just moved. Rowan? Rowan, are you awake?" Yuti's voice echoed as if she were speaking from down a long hallway.

I willed my eyelids to open, but it took all my strength. My vision blurred, then came into focus while morning sunlight streamed into the window of my bedroom.

"Hey." Yuti stroked my hair as she smiled from beside my bed. "You okay? Does your head hurt?"

Now that she mentioned it, my head was throbbing, and I swallowed against the pain.

"What happened?" I croaked, glancing around at Noire and the boys, who stood around my bed.

"You gave Adrian your blood," Yuti answered. "You saved him, Rowan."

I lifted my hand to my throat, my fingertips prodding the rough, fabric bandage. "Are you okay? Where is he? "

"I'm fine. I don't have a scratch on me. Adrian is talking with Lia and Ashwin. He's fine, too. He knows to be a lot more careful about how often he drinks. And they're going to try to help him figure out how to deal with his urges if he should ever come across a fae again."

Even though Yuti's tone was upbeat, her eyes filled with tears. Reaching up, I stroked her face.

"Don't cry." My heart wept with her. "I'll be okay, right?" I glanced at Noire for confirmation.

"Well, you're going to stink like vampire for a while, but you'll be okay. He didn't feed you any blood. And even if he had, I've never heard of a werewolf turning into a vampire. We don't even know if his blood is potent enough to turn anyone."

"See?" My eyes met Yuti's. "I'm all right. You don't notice the vampire smell anyway."

Yuti pursed her lips, her nostrils flaring. "Don't you ever do anything like that again."

I certainly didn't plan on feeding any vampires ever again, but I couldn't promise that I'd never be hurt, especially if it was to protect her.

"Come here," I murmured.

She leaned down and placed a soft kiss on my lips.

"I love you," I whispered.

"I love you, too," she said, sniffling.

I glanced over at Noire, who was already urging the boys from the room.

Sitting up, I closed my eyes, clenching my jaw as my head spun.

"Hey, what are you doing?" Yuti protested. "You're not ready to get up."

I breathed deep and let it out slowly. Taking her hand, I pulled her onto my lap. A tingle ran down my spine as she wrapped her arms around my neck, playing with the hair at the base of my head.

"Yuti..."

She trailed feathery kisses along my jaw. "Hmm?"

"Will you be my mate?"

She paused, pulling back slightly to stare me in the eyes. "What is that? Is that like werewolf marriage?"

I quirked my mouth. "Sort of...but it's much deeper than that. There's a bond, a bond not so easily broken."

"Like...when? Now? Because I still have a year of school left..."

"The mate bond can be entered into any time after the promise is made."

"The promise? Like a betrothal?"

I dipped my head. The longer she took to answer, the more vulnerable I felt.

She frowned, and my heart quivered.

"I'll tell you what. When the time comes, I'll go through whatever wolfie mate bond ceremony you want, but ..."

"But what?"

She grinned. "But you have to go through all the traditions that go along with marrying an Indian girl."

"You make it sound like an ordeal."

"Oh, it is," she said seriously though her eyes danced.

"If I'm going to mate a human, then I need to do all the human things, right?"

"Yes, all the human things, especially if you don't want my father and uncles to murder you."

My heart skipped a beat. "You aren't serious…?"

She smirked. "Who can tell?"

I huffed out a laugh, and it sounded a little uncomfortable even in my own ears. "Okay," I agreed.

Her dark eyes shimmered as she gave me a full smile.

"Are you ready then?"

"What do I have to do?"

"You just have to answer my question. Yutika, will you be my mate?"

"I will."

"Now we seal our agreement with a kiss."

When our lips met, warmth spread through me as a little, golden thread tethered my heart to hers. And I knew that all I needed for the rest of my life was her. As long as she was healthy, happy, safe, I could want for nothing.

Pulling back, she sucked her teeth, squinting as she glanced around. "That feels…unusual."

"What does?"

"It's like… How do I put it? It's comforting, like how I felt as a kid when my mom gave me my blanket. No, it's more than that… I don't quite know how to describe it."

I smiled, resting my forehead on hers. "That must be how humans experience the promised bond."

"Huh, well that's interesting."

"What's interesting?" Adrian walked in without bothering to knock. He raised his eyebrows when he saw Yuti in my lap. "I thought I'd taken more blood than that, but perhaps werewolves bounce back fast."

"Adrian," Yuti said with a smile and moved to get up. I tightened my grip around her waist, not quite ready to let go. She didn't fight but relaxed into me. "Did you guys work everything out?"

Adrian nodded. "I think so. We're going to have some growing pains, but I think we've come to terms. They're all very interested in my research into vampire origins."

"What happened to your glasses? Can you see all right?" Yuti asked.

Adrian shrugged. "I never really needed glasses. I just wore them because it gave people a barrier. My gaze…has a certain effect on people sometimes. I must've lost them in the woods. I'll get another pair before the start of term."

"Oh my God, I totally forgot classes start next week. I haven't even gotten my books yet."

"You still have time," Adrian reminded her. "In any case, you said something was interesting when I came in. What's up?"

"That's how Yuti described feeling the promised bond," I told him.

"The promised bond?"

"Yes. Yuti has agreed to be my mate."

Adrian smiled, his fangs flashing in the morning light. "Looks like we're going to be brothers."

EPILOGUE

I smiled as Yuti chased fireflies with Eoin in the Fireleafs' yard. The baby squealed, still a little unsteady on his feet.

Willow handed me a glass of lemonade. "Well, she certainly wasn't what they were expecting, but I think Mom and Dad are pleased you're finally mated."

"Now they'll be coming after you," I muttered.

"Bite your tongue," she growled.

I glanced over at our parents, who were talking with Kat and Ed at the edge of the grove.

The summer evening was only starting to cool down. The day had been long as the best of summer days are. And I couldn't have been more content. My mate, my wife, had finally gotten her wish — to travel to another dimension to meet her alien in-laws.

I was just relieved my parents had been polite when I'd introduced her.

"All right, birthday boy…" Runa scooped her

son into her arms. "It's time for bed. Let's go say goodnight to grandma and grandpa."

The child's cries turned to howls as he shifted into wolf form, trying to escape his mother's arms. His maneuver worked. He slipped to the ground and started running around the yard.

"Damn it," Runa cursed. "Konner! Get your son."

Konner came out of the house, followed by Wilhelm and Arete. Konner spoke his spell, and his son rose from the ground. His little pup legs pumped, but he didn't get anywhere.

Runa picked him up. "Thank you," she said to her mate.

Smiling, Yuti approached my sister and me. "So you ready to come stay with us at the resort?"

Willow nodded. "Yeah, I've about had it with Efren. I try to avoid him as much as possible. You'd think taking classes at a fae university on the other side of Faerie would be a deterrent, but he's very persistent. At least I got to make up with Mom and Dad and say goodbye to Feather and Zeb before I leave."

"Lia will be happy to hear that," I told her.

"I'm just happy to learn from someone who understands I don't actually want to lead a pack," Willow answered.

"Do you think you'll be able to pass yourself off as human?" Yuti asked.

"Are you kidding?" Willow smirked. "Check this out." She cleared her throat and looked at me seriously. "I'll have an iced double-chocolate mocha latte with whipped cream and unicorn sprinkles."

I burst out laughing.

"What are unicorn sprinkles?" Yuti giggled.

"I don't know, but it sounds like a very human thing to ask for."

"Okay. This is just going to be fun to watch," I muttered.

Read on for an excerpt from
D. Lieber's Intended Fates

Intended Enemies

Available now in
ebook, paperback, and hardcover

EXCERPT FROM
INTENDED ENEMIES

This is what it feels like to be in another alpha's territory.

I rolled my shoulders, trying to adjust to the new feeling pressing on my skin—like with a heavy blanket, I couldn't quite decide if it was comforting or oppressive. I'd had only a taste of it when I'd come for that one night last summer, but facing months, possibly years, of it seemed to make the sensation a little heavier.

Staring out at the evergreen forest beyond what was now my bedroom window, I smiled to myself. My window was at the back of the house, where pines and firs, dotted with maples and white oaks, grew in uneven waves on the tumbling foothills. The cheery sight of so many shades of green under the cobalt blue sky of summer blotted out any anxieties over what was to come.

I was finally in the human realm, or "the realm of origin," as the werewolves here called it. I didn't put much stock in the distinction, but it mattered to some.

For an entire year, I'd studied and read everything I could about humans to prepare for this moment. I relaxed into this small accomplishment, letting go of the expectations that had hung over me in Faerie—expectations that I'd never planned on fulfilling but nagged me nonetheless.

I was safe here. And though I hadn't even started my alpha training yet, I was one step closer to my goal.

My brother, Rowan, entered through the already-open bedroom door, a small box wrapped in polka dot paper in his hands.

As I looked at him in the bright summer sunlight filtering through the window, I knew that I needn't have worried about him. Happiness sparkled in the bright tropical waters of his blue eyes. His black hair was thick and windswept from our drive with the windows down. He looked healthy and fit, all well-fed lean muscle. And I knew it was all thanks to his mate. She'd saved him, and I loved her for it.

"Here." He held the box out to me with a smile. "A welcome present."

I glanced up at him. "What is it?" The box was heavier than its size suggested.

He smirked. "Well, it's wrapped in paper so that it's a surprise. Open it."

The thin paper was unexpectedly loud as I tore through it.

"It's a cellphone," Rowan told me while I stared down at the gift.

I scowled. "I know what it is. Jeez... You showed one to me last time I was here, and what do you think I've been doing over the last year?"

He chuckled and held up his hands. "How do I

know how much you know? You could have just been partying the whole time."

I clicked my tongue at his complete lack of faith in me. Then I turned to place the box on the nightstand.

"Thanks," I said. I knew what a cellphone was, but I didn't know how to use one. I hoped there wasn't a big learning curve.

"I want you to keep it with you wherever you go…"

A flash of pink caught my eye outside the window, and Rowan's words filtered into the background as he continued.

I watched the movement making its way through the trees, finally appearing on the small lawn between the tree line and the house. The pink turned out to be Yuti's hat, a baseball cap with her dark ponytail pulled through the back. Yuti looked over at the man accompanying her, her face lighting up as she laughed at something he said. She reached out and gave him a joking push, to no effect.

A tingle ran over my skin, and my heart gave one hard thump as I stared at the man my sister-in-law walked with. He was taller than Yuti—though most people were—with the lithe build of a surfer. His brown hair was warm and sun-kissed as the summer breeze played in it. A dimple peeked out from the side of his mouth as he gave Yuti a tight-lipped smile, all the more striking because of his high cheekbones and sharp chin. I couldn't tell the color of his hooded eyes, but I very much wanted to know.

"Who's that?" I asked my brother, only barely aware that I'd interrupted whatever he was saying.

He moved to stand beside me and looked out the window. "Oh, that's Adrian, Yuti's best friend. Lia will be telling you all about him when she gives you the rundown."

I smiled in appreciation of the beautiful human. *I don't think I'll have any trouble adjusting to this realm after all.* "I'd rather find out about him myself, thanks." And with an excited flutter in my stomach, I made for the bedroom door just as Yuti and Adrian entered the house.

Rowan rushed after me. "Uh, maybe you should wait up here. Lia still has a lot to explain!" he called as I bounded down the stairs.

Right when my bare feet hit the cool wood of the ground floor, I froze. I was still getting used to all the sights and smells in the realm of origin and hadn't yet memorized the scent of each of Lia's pack. But just as I recognized Yuti's unique sweet and spicy, just as I clocked the new hints of hay and bergamot, a much darker scent smothered all the rest.

Earth. Soil, rich and damp.

Vampire.

Every bit of reason—of self—flew from my mind, and I was left with only one word: *protect*. I clenched my jaw, my limbs seizing involuntarily. Fabric tore as my snarl echoed in the front hall. Never before had I shifted on instinct, no thought put into the action...but I did now.

I surged forward, knocking into the hall table beside me. A vase tipped over, water spilling into my fur, followed by a crash as it hit the floor behind me.

Less than a second later, I was in the dining room, the vampire staring at me wide-eyed from the other side of the table. My muscles bunched to spring.

"Adrian, run!" Lia barked.

The vampire took off, heading for the back door.

I lunged to the left, my nails slipping on the floor as I tried to close the distance. But just when I rounded the table, a heavy weight piled onto me.

I twisted and writhed, trying to escape the two sets of arms that grabbed at me.

"Enough!" Lia commanded from across the room, her voice laced with alpha power.

The pressure I'd felt upon first arriving in Lia's territory became heavy and almost unbearable—the crushing weight of an established alpha's command.

Lia walked over to where Ashwin and Rowan held me down. She knelt, her eyes blazing with power as they burned into mine. "I can see we have a lot of work to do."

My lungs fought to expand against the steel in her voice, and my jaws snapped together while I still struggled to pursue my prey.

AFTERWORD

Thank you for reading! I do so hope you enjoyed it. If you have a moment, I would very much appreciate a review on the store where you bought it. Tell other readers what you thought, and help them make a decision on this book.

If you'd like to stay updated on news about my books and events, you can subscribe to my newsletter on my website: www.dlieber.com

On my site, you will also find my blog, where I post all my fun little tidbits.

Thanks again! I hope you will travel through my worlds with me again in the future.

D. Lieber

ABOUT THE AUTHOR

D. Lieber has a wanderlust that would make a butterfly envious. When she isn't planning her next physical adventure, she's recklessly jumping from one fictional world to another. Her love of reading led her to earn a Bachelor's in English from Wright State University.

Beyond her skeptic and slightly pessimistic mind, Lieber wants to believe. She has been many places—from Canada to England, France to Italy, Germany to Russia—believing that a better world comes from putting a face on "other." She is a romantic idealist at heart, always fighting to keep her feet on the ground and her head in the clouds.

Lieber lives in Wisconsin with her husband (John) and cats (Yin and Nox).

Links:
Website: www.dlieber.com
Goodreads: www.goodreads.com/dlieberwriting
BookBub: https://www.bookbub.com/profile/d-lieber